Behind the Veil

DOUG VEEDER

VEEDER MEDIA

Published by:
Veeder Media
PO Box 1862
Apex, NC 27502

Publisher's Note: This novel is a work of fiction. Names, characters, places, businesses, events, and incidents are either products of the author's imagination or used in a fictitious manner. All characters are fictional, and any parallels or similarities to people living or dead is purely coincidental.

ISBN: 978-1-7374597-2-9 (Paperback)
ISBN: 978-1-7374597-3-6 (eBook)

Library of Congress Control Number: 2023900265

Chapter 1

"Help!" Carissa screamed, her cries piercing the darkness. "Help me, Daddy! Help!"

Shooting up out of bed, panic gripped David Zephyr's heart. Running down the darkened hallway felt like a dream. The closer he came to his daughter's door, the farther away it was. His heart was beating hard against his chest as Carissa's blood curdling cries for help kept stabbing at his eardrums.

"I'm coming, baby girl," David yelled, bursting through the door.

Looking around the room in disbelief, David saw his wife, Savannah, kneeling next to the bed, stroking Carissa's forehead, trying to console their eight-year-old daughter who was flailing in her sleep. *What is going on?* David thought to himself. *I swear I heard Carissa yell for help.* Stepping toward Savannah, he saw something that stopped him dead in his tracks. *What is that?*

As he smelled an eerie, foul stench of sulfur, David's eyes burned. Crinkling his nose and turning his head while the sulfuric odor stung his nasal passageway, he asked, "Do you smell that, Savannah?"

Savannah didn't respond. Stepping behind her and placing his hand on her shoulder, David asked again, "Do you smell that?"

"Daddy," Carissa screamed, hiding in the corner of the room.

As he turned in the direction of Carissa's scream, something hit him across the chest. His feet leaving the floor, his body flew backward across the room. Unable to brace himself for the impact, he crashed into the wall and collapsed to the floor in pain.

Grabbing his throbbing ribs, gasping for air, he surveyed the room. Savannah was still on her knees by the bed attending to their sleeping daughter. But in the far corner of the room, he saw Carissa whimpering "Daddy" through her tears.

Dumbfounded, struggling to stand, he felt chills run up and down his spine. The hairs on his arm standing on end, the smell of sulfur grew thicker in the darkness. "What the heck is going on here?"

"Your funeral," a coarse, evil voice cried out in the night.

Feeling something strike the left side of his body, David was airborne again. His body hurtling across the room, he held out his right arm and braced for the impact with the bookshelf. His head collided with the upper shelf before collapsing into a pile of books strewn across the floor. The skin above his right eye ripped open from the shattering shards of glass from a broken picture frame.

"Daddy," Carissa cried out to him, tears streaming down her cheeks.

"Hide, Carissa. I'm okay," David lied. "Just hide."

"Daddy." Carissa was crying as she crawled across the floor toward him.

"I said hide," David yelled, the pain of his bruised ribs radiating throughout his body.

"I'll find her," the coarse, evil voice declared.

Kneeling on the floor, lifting his head, and looking in the direction of the voice, David couldn't see much of anything. He rubbed his eyes, trying to acclimate to the darkness of the room.

"Trying to see me?"

"Don't need to see you…" David declared, seeing its eyes open. They were the darkest shade of red he had ever seen, and he could feel the heat emanating from them. "…when I can smell you."

Attacking, David fought valiantly against the entity, landing punches that had no effect. Whatever he was fighting wasn't human. Infuriated, the creature reached out with its winglike arm, grabbed him by the shoulder, lifted him off the ground, and held him in the air before throwing him like a ragdoll across the room.

Beaten and bruised, he pulled himself up and stared down the creature. Wincing when he drew a deep breath, he prayed for strength and charged at the entity.

Fighting with courage, his assault on the entity had no effect on the creature. David launched into another frenzied assault of blows against his enemy. "You are going to have to go through me before you ever get near my daughter."

"I can grant that wish," the creature hissed.

Throwing another barrage of punches, David was stunned when the creature clutched his fist and started squeezing his hand. David screamed in pain, falling to his knees, feeling the bones in his hand being crushed. Grabbing David's throat, the creature hissed, "Is this what you meant by going through you?"

"Daddy." Carissa was scared, so she started pleading with the entity from across the room. "Please stop, you're hurting my dad. Stop it… Daddy!"

David fought to loosen the hand gripping his throat. "Come hell or high water, I swear you will never touch my daughter."

Shrieking in pain, the creature dropped him. David collapsed on the floor gasping for breath. David tried to scamper away on his hands and knees, but the creature kicked him in the ribs.

Lying on the floor gasping for air, still feeling the pain of the powerful hands that had been wrapped around his neck, David wanted to escape the room, but he couldn't. His daughter's life was in danger. He struggled to stand up. Bracing himself against the wall, taking another painful breath, David wiped away the blood streaming down his face. Stepping toward the creature, he made fists with both hands, stood tall, and puffed out his chest.

The entity stared at David. He winked at the monster, attacked, and dove headlong at the creature. Before he made contact, something crashed into his side, grabbing him and slamming him into the floor. Rolling out of its grasp, David lifted his head off the floor, opened his eyes, and saw he was in an empty office he had never seen before.

"Did you see where it went?" a teenager yelled, kneeling on the floor, scanning the room for evidence of the creature. "Did you see where it went?"

"See what? Where is my daughter?" David raised himself to his knees and looked around the room. "Who the heck are you? Where am I?"

"The beast you were fighting, where did it go?"

"The what?" David was confused. Moments earlier he was in his daughter's bedroom and now he was in an empty office kneeling next to a teenaged, brown-haired kid dressed from head-to-toe in black. The kid clutched a weird looking circular object in his hand, sweat dripping from his forehead, his blue eyes scanning the room for evidence of the creature.

"Did it follow us?"

"Did what follow us?"

"The beast trying to kill you back there."

"Back where?" David became more confused with everything that was happening. Staring at the teenager who was still scanning the room for the beast, he wanted answers. "Where are we? Who are you? Where's my daughter?"

"There isn't time to explain."

"I want answers," David yelled, staring down the teenager.

"Sorry about this."

Before David could respond, the teenager struck him in the chest with the circular metal device. An electrical shock wave pulsed throughout his body.

Chapter 2

David screamed in pain, shooting straight out of bed grasping his chest.

"Daddy," Carissa screamed, her cries piercing the darkness. *Was it all a dream?* His heart raced. "Daddy!"

Jumping out of bed, he felt the pain ripple through his body. He raced into Carissa's room and saw Carissa on her knees crying on the bed, her face buried in Savannah's shoulder. Savannah was stroking her hair, rubbing her back, and trying to convince Carissa she had nothing more than a bad dream.

"No, Mommy… It took Daddy, Mommy… It took Daddy."

"It was just a bad dream, baby girl," David reiterated, sitting down on the bed.

"Daddy…" Carissa jumped into David's arms, squeezing him. "I saw it take you, Daddy. I saw it take you through my wall."

David could feel the pain of his bruised bones and his throbbing head as she squeezed him tighter in her arms. *Was it just a dream? How did she know what happened? Did we have the same dream? Is that even possible?*

"There, there, baby girl," Savannah comforted, wrapping her arms around them both. "Mommy and Daddy are both here. Nothing is going to hurt you."

David wasn't sure about her last statement. His battered body reminding him of what had just happened. *Could it have been more than just a dream? What other explanation could there be?* Fear gripped his heart. *If it had been more than just a horrible nightmare, how could he stop anything from hurting her?*

Nope. David wasn't too sure about anything at the moment, but those were questions he would have to ponder later. The only thing that mattered was making sure Carissa was reassured it had been nothing more than a nightmare. Even if David questioned the veracity of his own claims, he was not going to let his daughter worry about it anymore. His job was to create a world that was safe for her.

David and Savannah spent the better part of the next hour trying to coax Carissa back to sleep. The vivid images of the nightmare left an indelible mark on her. She was inconsolable. She was scared. And unbeknownst to Carissa and Savannah, David was scared, too.

After Carissa fell back to sleep, Savannah and David tucked her into bed and crept out of the room. Slipping back into their room, David went into the bathroom for a drink of water. Following him into the bathroom, Savannah flicked on the light.

"That was a rough one." Savannah rubbed her face while yawning.

"It definitely was." David ran warm water over his sore hands, lowering his head to the sink, and splashing warm water over his face.

"I hope she sleeps through the rest of the night," Savannah said, pulling a hand towel off the rack and handing it to David. "I have a long day at work tomorrow."

"I hope we all sleep through the rest of the night," David added, turning off the water, grabbing the towel, and drying his face.

"What happened to you?" Savannah stared at David's face in the mirror.

"What?"

"Where did you get the cut on your forehead?" She questioned, using her hands to turn his face toward her.

"I must have hit my head on Carissa's door."

"Are you okay?" Savannah ran her finger over the cut, inspecting it.

"I'm fine," David responded, turning his face. "It's nothing."

"Well, as long as you're okay." Savannah let go of his face. "I am going to sleep."

"I'm good. I'll be in in a minute," David replied, taking a long look at himself in the mirror.

"Don't be too long." Savannah kissed him and went back into their bedroom.

David stared at the cut in the mirror. Straightening up, he looked at his reflection. Whether or not the dream was real, David realized for the first time he was truly in his forties. If the reflection wasn't enough to convince him, his aching bones were a physical reminder that he was older.

Staring at the six-foot, brown-haired man he had become, he noticed little flecks of gray hair and the few pounds he had gained over the past twenty years. He turned and gazed at the little gut replacing his once his slim, toned stomach. His adult life had stripped away the tall, strong man he used to be and left an average looking, thicker guy in its place.

David walked out of the bathroom. Standing by his side of the bed, he stared at his beautiful wife who had fallen back to sleep. She was still as beautiful as ever. She was still thin, not as thin as she used to be when they first met, but she had stayed in better shape than he had. Her brown hair fell just off her shoulders and as she slept, David was still entranced by everything about her.

Climbing into bed, he wanted to wake her up and tell her what had happened in his own dream. He wanted to tell her how he somehow ended up in the middle of Carissa's dream. He wanted to tell her about the creature that smelled like sulfur, about the battle that ensued, and about the darkened office where he ended up kneeling next to some strange teenage kid. He wanted to tell Savannah the dream was real or, at least, it had felt real enough.

He couldn't tell her, though, because he couldn't believe any of it had happened. It was a bad dream. That's all it was and all it was ever going to be; just a bad dream. Rolling over to kiss his wife goodnight, his sore ribs and the cut on his forehead told a different story.

Kissing her cheek, David whispered in her ear, "Sweet dreams, sweetheart."

Lying back on his pillow, David stared up at the ceiling. Within moments, he could hear Savannah snoring. He hated how she fell asleep at the drop of a hat, but he loved listening to the soft noise she made in the darkness. It was the perfect, soothing cure for his mind that was now racing.

Chapter 3

"David, get up."

"Huh, what?" David opened his eyes to see the teenager from his dream shaking his shoulders.

"Shh, don't wake your wife." The teenager put his finger to his lips to silence him. "Now get up."

David shot straight out of bed and threw a punch. The teenager stepped out of the way of his wild swing causing David to stumble and catch his balance against the wall.

"Haven't you had enough fighting for one night?" the teenager chuckled.

"I'll tell you when I have had enough," David replied, jumping up, raising his fists, preparing to strike. That was, until he saw himself lying in bed next to Savannah. Dropping his fists and staring at his body. "Am I dead?"

"No," the teenager chuckled, "You're sleeping."

"How?" David was dumbstruck while he stared at himself sleeping in the bed.

"If you were wide awake, David, I wouldn't be here right now."

Bending over the bed, David touched his body and watched himself whisk away his hand. "Trippy."

"Don't do that," the teenager warned. "You do not want to wake yourself up, right?"

"How is any of this possible?" David pinched his arm to see if he was really sleeping. "What is happening to me?"

"I will answer your questions in due time," the teenager remarked, walking toward the door.

"Where are you going?" David asked, following the mysterious teenager.

"We're going downstairs to talk."

"Why?"

"Because if you don't settle down, your wife is going to wake up. And if she wakes you up, poof! I vanish. And with me, go the answers to your questions."

Looking at himself sleeping, David saw he was restless and needed to relax. He wanted answers and whether or not he liked the teenager was irrelevant. He had the answers David needed to make sense of everything that was happening.

"Can you calm down, David?"

"Yes."

"Good. Now follow me."

"Where are we going?"

"Kitchen. Let's get some coffee." The teenager didn't wait for a response before leaving the room.

"Are you even old enough to drink coffee?" David asked, following the teen.

"I'm older than you think, David." The teenager walked to the kitchen while David followed him. David turned on the light and the youngster sat down at the table. David walked over to the cupboard and took out two coffee cups. "What are you doing?"

"I'm making coffee."

The teenager laughed. "Sit down, David."

"Don't you want coffee?"

"The cup of coffee was just a metaphor. I don't want any coffee."

"What?"

"It was a metaphor." The teenager paused for a moment while David stared at him. "It was kind of my way of saying, let's break bread together. People seem to want talk over a cup of coffee. So, I said it as a way of breaking the ice between us."

"But what if I want a cup of coffee?"

"You can have a cup of coffee if you want it, but you don't need the coffee maker."

"Okay, wise guy," David retorted, walking over to the table, holding a coffee cup, and sitting down across from the teen. "Since you seem to know everything, I would like a cup of coffee, how do I go about getting one?"

David stared him down. He was angry. The teenager smiled a smug little snicker of a smile and winked at him. "Look down, David."

"What?"

"It's in front of you." The teenager winked at him again. "Look down."

Looking down, David noticed a hot cup of coffee sitting on the placemat. He was lost in the aroma wafting around his head. He took a sip. Savoring every second of the best cup of coffee he had ever tasted, he took another sip. "How did you do it?"

"Do what?"

"Make the best cup of coffee I've ever had?"

"I didn't make the coffee," the teenager smiled. "You did."

"But how?"

"I am inside your dream."

"What the heck?" David pushed himself back from the table, scared. "How?"

"I know you want to know how, but that will be answered in due time."

"Why are you inside my dream?"

"I'm dream walking."

"Dream walking?"

"Yes."

"Why?"

"Because you were able to dream walk into Carissa's dream, and I don't know whether to be intrigued or concerned," the teenager remarked, rubbing his hands together while staring at David.

"Why the contradiction of feelings?"

"I am intrigued because dream walking is easy to do if you have the ability but, normally, we find dream walkers at a young age."

"Who is 'we'?"

"Another question for another day," the teenager replied, dismissing the question because it wasn't important at the moment.

"Do I have the ability?"

"I don't know. It's rare that it would go undetected into someone's forties."

"Is that why you are concerned? Because I am so old."

"No." The teenager changed his demeanor and looked at David with concern. "The only other way to dream walk is if you are pulled into a dream."

"And this is concerning because…?"

"Because only evil entities would draw you into a dream." The teenager was blunt because he wanted to gauge David's reactions.

"Why?"

"Because they want you dead."

David was stunned, fear running down his spine. "Why?"

"Because you or someone in your family is important to them."

"Important to whom?" David was concerned. He knew about the spiritual warfare happening around people at all times, but if what the teenager just told him was true, the war was much closer than he ever thought.

"The enemy."

"Who is the enemy?"

"Satan."

"I was afraid you were going to say his name," David conceded, his eyes growing wide, his heart skipping a beat as the gravity of the teenager's statement sunk into his consciousness. "What is so important about my family?"

"That's a loaded question, David," the teenager replied, leaning into the table and rubbing his hands together. "Let's just say I know everything that's happened in this house tonight."

"Are you going to enlighten me?"

"In due time." The teenager dismissed his question and David wasn't happy about it.

"You're starting to frustrate me, kid," David warned, becoming agitated with the lack of answers.

"Sebastian."

"Sebastian?"

"My name is Sebastian." The teenager extended his right hand. "Pleased to meet you."

"Stop playing games with me." David ignored his outstretched hand, shooing it away. "How was I able to dream walk?"

"Watch your temper, David," Sebastian advised, sitting back in his chair.

"You know, I am starting to think I need to beat the answers out of you." David pushed his chair away from the table and stood up.

"Sit down, David," Sebastian ordered with authority. "The fact you got pulled into Carissa's dream should be enough to make you sit down, shut up and listen for a few minutes. But if that isn't enough, remember who saved your life earlier."

"Wait?" David paused for a moment. Thinking about the directive, he sat down. "Were you there the whole time?"

"Yes."

"Why did you wait to help me? Didn't you see I was losing?"

"Quite badly, I might add," Sebastian chuckled.

"Then why didn't you do anything to help me?"

"I did help you, David." Sebastian paused for a moment. "I had to let you experience the dream walk."

"Why?"

"If I jumped in at the start of the fight, how could I convince you that this was real?"

"I am so confused." David stared at Sebastian with a perplexed look on his face. "Why were you here in the first place?"

"I was just about to help Carissa again when you burst into the room."

"Again?"

"This isn't the first time, David," Sebastian shared, staring into David's eyes. "Those night terrors she has been having have all been like the one you witnessed tonight."

"So, you let me fight the monster?"

Sebastian lowered his eyes; he was remorseful about his decision. "It was the only way you would understand."

"But why?"

"Because if you have the ability to dream walk, I need to see if you are ready."

"Ready for what?"

"Things you could only imagine in your worst nightmares, but ultimately, they will require you to make some tough choices; to make some sacrifices."

"What kind of sacrifice?"

"All in due time, David, all in due time." Sebastian dismissed his question for the third time while leaning into the table. "This is a lot to take in in one night."

"Enlighten me."

"What I am going to tell you is going to blow your mind, but once I tell you what is happening, you're going to need to decide what to do about it. Alone, without any input from your family."

"You make this sound serious." David was nervous. He had no idea who Sebastian was or why he was talking to him in the middle of his dream. All he knew was that he stepped into something he couldn't defeat on his own and if it was coming after his daughter, he would need help protecting her.

"I'm not going to lie," Sebastian stated, rubbing his hands together again. "It will change your life forever."

"I don't understand."

"I promise to answer your questions soon, but I need you to get out of your family trip this weekend."

"How did you know we're going away?" David furrowed his eyebrows, staring at Sebastian.

"It's my job to know."

"Why do I have to skip the family getaway?"

"If you are going to make the sacrifices required, you are going to need a couple of days to think about what it all means."

"And if I can't make these sacrifices, then what?"

"Then you'll need to forget I ever existed and everything you have seen."

David swallowed hard. *What does he want me to do?* Lifting the cup of coffee, he took another sip. Holding the cup underneath his nose and breathing in the rich aroma, he stared across the table. "Before I consider your options, I have a couple questions."

"Shoot."

"Is my family in danger?"

There was a long silence. Sebastian glared across the table, a deep fear in his eyes. "I believe your family is in grave danger."

"Is there anything I can do to stop them from being in harm's way?"

There was another long silence. Twisting his hands together in frustration, Sebastian continued, "Technically, that's my job, but there are things you can do to help the situation."

David felt the fear and genuine concern Sebastian had for his family. Believing Sebastian was an ally who would protect them, David nodded. "If it means my family will be safe, I will skip the trip."

"Good."

"What else do I need to do?"

"Nothing, David, you have other things to focus on right now."

"Like what?"

"Wake up, David."

"No," Savannah moaned, the music blaring from the radio alarm clock. Rolling over and throwing her arms across David's chest, she pleaded, "Please, tell me it's not time to get up. It's too early."

Lifting his head off the pillow, David looked at the clock. "It's six thirty-one, Sweetheart, time to get up."

Hitting the snooze button, Savannah snuggled up next to David. "Five more minutes."

Staring at the ceiling, David's heart was pounding hard against his chest. *She can snooze, but I have things to figure out.* "I am up, Sweetie. I have a big day ahead of me. I'll shower first so you can sleep."

"Are you okay?" She asked, opening her eyes and looking into his.

"I am fine." David rolled over and kissed Savannah. "I just have a lot of work to do today. I'll hop in the shower. Get some more sleep."

"I love you." Savannah didn't hesitate to take him up on his offer. Rolling over, she went back to sleep.

Chapter 4

David was tired. The lack of sleep made it hard to focus on work. His body ached. He spent most of the day trying to come up with a half decent excuse to avoid going on the weekend trip.

The idea of lying to Savannah bothered him. He had never lied to her before and having to lie to her now pained him. He knew she would find out one day that he had misled her, something he had never done since they met in Sunday school and Savannah decided he would be her boyfriend.

Pulling into the driveway, he remembered that Sunday morning like it was yesterday. Sitting at a table drawing a picture, Savannah sat down next to him and started coloring. When they both reached for the red crayon, they held hands. Looking at each other, Savannah smiled at him. Her big brown eyes and pigtails enchanted him. Then she uttered the first words they had ever spoken to each other, "I like you. You're my boyfriend."

Holding hands for the rest of Sunday school, later that day, she kissed him on the cheek after services. David smiled thinking about that day and the thousands of others that came afterward, the middle school and high school dances, their first real date, first real kiss, and all of the little moments since the day at the crayon table. And now, after all these years, he had to lie to her, the one thing he promised her he would never do.

David walked through the front door just as Savannah and the kids were sitting down to dinner. "I'm home…" David announced, dropping his briefcase at the bottom of the stairs, and walking into the dining room.

"You're late," Savannah barked, putting the last two plates on the table. "Hurry up and wash your hands."

David was quick to wash up and return to the dining room. Kissing his kids on the top of their heads, he sat down at the table and kissed his wife. "Sorry I'm late."

"No worries," she said, turning and looking at her middle school aged son. "Jordan, it's your turn to say grace tonight."

"Yes, ma'am." Jordan waited for them to fold their hands and bow their heads. "Thank you, Lord, for this food, our family, and all the blessings you give us. Give us thankful hearts and help me make the football team at school this year. In Jesus' name, we pray, Amen."

Saying "Amen" in unison, they unfolded their hands, picked up their glasses, and clinked them together as they said, "Bless you" to each other. Then they started eating.

Taking a few bites of his food, David broke the silence. Looking around the table at his family, he announced, "Hey, I've got some news to share."

"Is it good news?" Savannah was skeptical, taking a sip of her drink.

"It depends on how you look at it."

"What is it?" Jordan asked excited.

"Yeah, Daddy, what is it?" Carissa inquired.

"Well, which do you want first? The good news or the bad news?"

"Always start with the bad news. Never give the good news first," Carissa answered, taking another bite of her food.

"I hate when you play this game, David." Savannah was frustrated because whatever he was about to share with the family hadn't been discussed. "The bad news is always bad, and the good news is never any good."

"Trust me, it's not all bad," David pronounced, smiling at her.

"Okay, Dad, let's go with Carissa. What's the bad news?" Jordan asked.

"The bad news is I have to work this weekend. So, I won't be able to go to Grandma and Grandpa's with you."

"No…" Jordan and Carissa whined in unison.

"Now, before you get upset, you haven't heard the good news yet."

"You were going to teach me how to ride a horse this weekend, Dad." Carissa crossed her arms across her chest and pouted after throwing her fork down on her plate.

"And we were supposed to work on football drills to prepare for tryouts this summer," Jordan chimed in, reminding him about their plans for the trip.

"I know we were going to do all of that, and we will, but it will have to wait." David tried to reassure his kids he intended on making up for missing the weekend. "I have a big deadline that got moved up to Monday morning. I have to finish the advertising proposal for a client."

"Maybe we should just cancel the trip and go another time." Savannah was irritated, sitting back in her chair and staring at David.

Seeing the disappointment on his wife's face, he was heartbroken for letting her down. "There's no point in skipping. My parents have been looking forward to this visit. And let's face it, you need a weekend away to relax, too."

"It's not going to be any fun if you aren't there, Dad," Jordan shot back, giving David an icy stare.

"That's not true, Jordan. Your Grandfather Nathan knows football. He'll help you. And we still have time before the summer for you and me to practice before tryouts start."

"He does?" Jordan asked, an inkling of excitement in his voice.

"Who do you think taught me how to play?"

"Okay," Jordan acquiesced, "but it won't be the same."

"I know and I'm sorry."

"What about me?" Carissa continued to pout, using her sad face to tug at his heart strings.

"Grandma Monica rides horses all the time."

"But you were supposed to teach me." Carissa pressed the issue which made David feel worse than he already felt.

"And I will, just not this weekend."

"Are you sure we shouldn't cancel and plan it for another weekend, David?" Savannah asked, crossing her arms and pondering their options.

"I am going to be buried under a mountain of work, Sweetheart. How is staying home going to be any fun for anyone?"

"I don't want to go, Mommy," Carissa declared, puffing out her lower lip.

"Me either, Mom," Jordan agreed with his sister, shaking his head.

"Guys," David reiterated, "I know you're disappointed. I am too. But if this presentation goes well, I am in line for a huge bonus."

"I don't care," Carissa shot back.

"A huge bonus means we would have some money to spend, and I was thinking, we should spend it on a trip to Disney World."

"Yeah…" the kids yelled in excitement.

"David, don't…" Savannah held up her hand to stop him from getting the kids too excited, but it was too late.

"Are you serious, Dad?" Jordan interrupted his mother, brimming with excitement.

"Don't what, Savannah?" David half-smiled at her, knowing he was willing to do what it took to make it up to his family.

"Don't make promises you can't keep," Savannah responded, giving him a side glance of disapproval.

"Don't worry. I'll get this bonus and then we're off to Disney World," David yelled before making plans for their trip with the kids.

Savannah was frustrated, but while watching David and the kids talking, she gave into the dream and joined the rest of the family in making plans for their trip to the Magic Kingdom.

After tucking the kids in for the night, David climbed into bed, grabbed his book off the night table, and started reading. Walking into the room fifteen minutes later, Savannah took off her shirt and threw it in the hamper. "Do you think it's a good idea to promise the kids something you aren't quite sure is going to happen?"

"You're upset about promising to take them to Florida, aren't you?"

"Yes." Savannah threw her bra into the hamper and looked in her drawer for a night shirt. "Money isn't exactly growing on trees these days."

"You know you really are beautiful," David intimated to her while peering over his book and winking at her.

"Really? You're like a hormonal teenager, David." Savannah stared at him for a moment before pulling the shirt over her head. "Can you be serious for a minute? What are you going to do if you don't get the bonus?"

"I'm not worried about it, Savannah," David reassured her, putting his book down. "We've saved up some money over the past few years, what is it going to hurt if we use some of it to go on vacation?"

"That's supposed to be our nest egg, David." Savannah slipped out of her jeans and threw them into the hamper.

"I could get hit by a bus tomorrow. What good is a nest egg then?"

"Don't ever joke like that, David," Savannah scolded, pointing a finger at him. "It's not funny."

"I know, but it's true. No one knows when God might call either one of us home. And yes, I hear you. That money is our nest egg, but is it going to hurt if we dip a little into our savings to create lasting memories for our kids?"

"Do you really have to miss this weekend?" Savannah asked, slipping into bed next to David.

"I wish I didn't have to work, but I don't have a choice."

"But it's our long weekend away."

"I wish I could, but I can't, Sweetheart."

"I know, but we have been planning this weekend getaway for a long time" Savannah snuggled up on his shoulder. "Remember, we were supposed to sneak away to the log cabin… by the lake… a night just for us, as well?"

"I know."

"We were going to snuggle up in front of the fireplace and let the world just melt away."

"I know. I hate it, too," David conceded, the lie starting to eat away at his resolve. "But trust me, Savannah, there will be other weekends. I just have to get through this presentation, and it will be all over. I will be all yours and we will find a night to sneak away together, okay?"

"Fine. I don't like it, but I will make do without you this weekend," Savannah huffed, rolling over and turning out the light on her side of the bed.

"I'm sorry. I wish things could be different. I'll make it up to you. I promise."

Savannah curled up inside her blankets and put her head on the pillow. "Turn off the light, David."

"I have like fifteen pages left in this chapter. Once I finish, I'll go to sleep."

"Who said anything about sleeping, David?" Savannah looked over her shoulder with a seductive grin. "Turn off the lights and come to bed."

"I can read this book later," David responded, flinging the book across the room, turning off the light, and pulling the sheets up over their heads.

Chapter 5

Packing up the car for Savannah and the kids, David had a hard time not changing his mind and joining them. He loved heading out to the farm for long weekends. It was a great retreat that took the family miles away from the hustle and bustle of their everyday lives and gave them a resounding sense of peace. Putting the last few bags into the minivan, he felt a tinge of sadness weigh heavy upon his heart.

"Are we all packed up yet?" Savannah asked, walking out of the house with her purse over her shoulder and a huge cup of coffee in her hand.

"I hate missing this trip." David opened the car door for her. "I'm sorry."

"You have no idea how sorry you are." Savannah smiled at him as she climbed into the driver's seat. "I bought a new slinky negligee. Guess I'll have to return it."

"Savannah, you're killing me."

"You love me," she teased, "and you know it."

"I know," David admitted, closing the door. "God blessed me with an amazing woman."

"And don't you forget it." Savannah yelled back toward the front door of the house, "Carissa, Jordan, let's go."

"I love you."

"I know." Savannah kissed David through the open window. "Now get to work."

Carissa and Jordan came running out of the house arguing with each other about which movie they were going to watch first. David turned toward them and opened his arms wide, "Give your old man a hug."

Looking around the cul-de-sac to make sure none of his friends were playing and could see him, Jordan gave his dad a hug. "Love you, Dad."

"I wish you were coming with us, Daddy," Carissa stated with a heavy heart.

"I know, baby girl. I love you too," David replied, hugging her and kissing the top of her head. "Now you both listen to your mom."

"We will," they replied, climbing into the minivan and putting on their seatbelts.

"And whatever stories your grandparents tell you about me, only one-fourth of them are remotely true," David joked, shutting the back door of the minivan and resting his arms on the driver's side window. Staring at Savannah, he smiled, "I love you."

"I love you, too." Savannah blushed before kissing him again. "Now, really, go get some work done."

"I will." David stepped back from the car as Savannah started the engine and backed out of the driveway. "And don't return the nighty; I am sure we will put it to good use soon."

"We'll see about that, David… love you."

"Love you, Dad," the kids yelled through the open window.

Standing in the front yard waving to them until the car was out of sight, he had a heavy heart. Hating every minute of what he was doing, he walked back into the house and buried himself in work.

He worked throughout the afternoon. Savannah called to let him know they had arrived. He was relieved to know they were safe and his kids were going to have a great weekend at the farm with his parents.

But as the hours ticked away, butterflies fluttered in his stomach. *Who exactly is Sebastian? What did he want with his family? And why were they all in danger?* And those questions were just the tip of the iceberg. Every time David stopped working to take a break, a whole new crop of questions cluttered his mind. He was thankful he had a pile of work to complete so he was able to keep himself pretty well occupied throughout the day.

David felt a hand on his shoulder, shaking him. Opening his eyes, he took a moment to focus on his surroundings. A puddle of drool had collected on the table where he had fallen asleep. Lifting his head and blinking his eyes to adjust to the light in the room, he saw Sebastian standing next to him.

David rubbed his eyes and face with his hands. "What happened?"

"You fell asleep."

"How long was I out?"

"I have no idea," Sebastian responded. "Can I get you something?"

"I would love a glass of water."

Walking over to the cupboard, taking a glass off the shelf, filling it with ice and water from the dispenser in the refrigerator, Sebastian sat down at the table and handed the glass to David.

"Wait a minute, why did you do that?" David was perplexed.

"Do what?"

"Make me a glass of water."

"Because you asked for one," Sebastian responded, contorting his face in confusion.

"I did," David stated, scratching his head and staring at the glass.

"Well, there you go," Sebastian chuckled, pointing at the glass. "A glass of water."

"No, that's not what I mean."

"What do you mean?"

"The other night when I was about to make the coffee, you just…"

"Because you were sleeping," Sebastian interrupted, "you're not sleeping right now."

David stared at the glass of water while he registered the information. "So, you're really here?"

"Yes, David, I am. Now come with me." Sebastian didn't beat around the bush with long explanations. He stood up and walked into the living room.

"This is too weird." David followed Sebastian into the living room. He was startled when he saw three other people sitting on the couch. Dropping his glass of water and watching it shatter on the hardwood floor, he asked, "Who are these people?"

"They're with me."

"I sure hope so," David retorted, bending down to pick up the broken pieces of glass. "Why are they here?"

"David, leave the glass," Sebastian said, kneeling next to David and putting his hand on David's. "We can clean this up later."

Sebastian put his hand on David's shoulder and looked him dead in the eye. There was a long awkward pause and then David dropped the pieces of glass on the floor.

"Okay, Sebastian, let's get started."

"Good."

Standing up and walking over to the fireplace, Sebastian put his elbow on the mantle and waited for David to sit in one of the chairs across from the couch before introducing the three strangers. "On the couch are Peter, Michael, and Zoe. They are the members of my team."

"Why are they important?" David eyed them up and wondered who they were as well as why they were there.

"I'm Peter," Peter said, standing and holding out his hand. David thought he couldn't be more than thirteen years old. He had sandy blonde hair tied back in a ponytail, and he wore the same black attire Sebastian wore. Black shirt, black pants, black shoes and on his hip, a black, circular device like the one Sebastian hit David in the chest with a few days earlier.

"Sit down, kid," David grunted, ignoring Peter's outstretched hand.

"Sorry." Peter sat back down on the couch and raised his eyebrows while rolling his eyes because of the interaction.

"Pardon me for being rude, Sebastian," David grumbled, staring down the apparent leader. "Can you tell me why you're all in my house? And more importantly, what this is all about?"

"If you choose to make the sacrifice and join The Network, we will need their help passing you through the veil for the first time."

"What sacrifice? What veil?" David could feel his anger welling up inside of him at the lack of answers. "What is going on?"

"Those are great questions," Sebastian responded, walking over and sitting down in the empty chair next to David. "But it's going to take a very long time to explain everything."

"Let's start with the obvious, what's the veil?"

"The veil is the thin lining between the world we know as humans and the real world that exists all around us," Zoe interjected, trying to simplify the explanation.

David stared at the young woman who appeared to be about twenty. She wore the same clothing except her brunette hair fell down below her shoulders. Sitting back and running his hands through his hair, David breathed out a deep sigh of exasperation. "What are you talking about?"

"We all are born into this world. We grow, we live, and we exist. We have free will. It's the way God designed life," Zoe smiled before continuing, "but as a Christian, you know there is a spiritual war going on around us every day. The veil is the shield between what we can see and what we know is there, but cannot see. The veil protects us from the spiritual war and the true evil that exists on the other side."

"So why would I want to pass through the veil?"

"To save your family." Sebastian was direct and it startled David.

"And how does this affect me and my family?"

Lowering her eyes, Zoe grew solemn. "I never thought you or your children would be this important, David. It's my fault we are in this mess. It was my job to protect you and I failed. But before I tell you everything, I have to be sure you are ready to hear and see things that are going to change your life."

"Ready for what?" The deafening silence in the room became awkward. No one spoke because they didn't want to answer the question, so the weight of David's question hung in the room. David, sensing they were withholding information, asked the questions again. "Ready for what?"

"Your family is in extreme danger," Zoe blurted out, breaking the silence.

"This is ridiculous," David barked, standing up, walking over to the mantle, and staring at the pictures of his family. Anger coursing through his veins, he turned and stared at them. "Why should I believe you? How do you know what kind of danger my family is in?"

"You're adopted, David," Zoe continued.

"What?" David was caught of guard by her proclamation. He wanted to know how she knew intimate details about him. So, he stared at her for a moment. "How do you know that?"

"We know all about you, David," Peter interjected.

"Why?" David grew more suspicious of their motives and intentions. "Did you go to the hall of records and study my life so you can scam me?"

"David, sit down," Sebastian ordered, pointing at the empty chair. "I know this is hard to believe. It was hard for all of us the first time we heard the truth, but if you want to help your family, I need you to listen."

"Listen? Why?" David roared, turning and pointing at all of them. "I want answers. Who are you?"

"Once Zoe is done telling you what is going on," Sebastian continued, trying to calm David down. "I will do my best to answer any of your remaining questions."

Pausing and staring at them, David's mind was spinning. He took stock of the situation. He was angry, he was perplexed, but most of all, he was scared. A few days ago, he was just a normal guy with a normal life, but as he stood in the middle of his living room, four strangers were telling him about the grave danger his family was in if he didn't do something to stop it.

"Fine." David ground his teeth, walked across the room, and sat down in the armchair.

"I know you were adopted because I was assigned to protect you," Zoe continued. "You had nightmares as a baby, which is rare, and I was assigned to ward off the demons attacking you."

"How? You're just a kid yourself?" David asked, staring at her, feeling an eerie sense of familiarity.

Ignoring the question, Zoe continued, "Then your nightmares stopped altogether. Once you were adopted, I lost track of you because you never had any more night terrors."

"I never had night terrors," David declared, trying to think back to his childhood.

"As a baby, you did."

"Then why did they stop?"

"I don't know why the Zivlian left you alone, but they did…"

"Wait a minute," David interrupted, staring at her with skepticism. "What is a Ziv… you know, what you said… what is it?"

"A Zivlian?"

"Yes. What is it?"

"It's a lower-level demonic entity. It looks like a dog with wings. It's a charred, nasty smelling, vulgar beast used to torment people during their dreams."

"Wait, those things are real?" The hair on David's arms started to stand up. He thought he had been pulled into a dream. He never believed in a million years that what he had come across was real.

"Yes," Zoe responded before continuing, "Like I said, I don't know why the Zivlian left you alone. I think it was by design. I was supposed to protect you and help you pass through the veil years ago, but you disappeared. We didn't have the ability or the advanced technology we have today to find you."

"How gullible do you think I am?" David shook his head in disbelief and balled his hands into fists.

"I know it sounds crazy, David, but it's all true," Zoe added.

"And I was assigned to protect your daughter as her nightmares ramped up over the past year," Sebastian interjected.

"You're not doing a good job of it," David fired back, shooting Sebastian an icy glare.

"I've never seen a child with as much activity. I stumbled upon you by accident when you got pulled into Carissa's dream," Sebastian admitted, rubbing his hands together.

"Do you really expect me to believe all of this?" David was incensed. He started believing this was an elaborate scheme to extort money from him.

"It's the truth," Peter interjected.

"And whether you believe us or not, your family is still in danger," Michael added. "That isn't going to change regardless of what you believe."

"Part of what we are trying to explain to you, David," Sebastian added, "is that you are not going to comprehend all of this in one night. No one could. There is too much to tell you."

"Comprehend?" David laughed in awkward frustration, he had had enough of the charade. "Or believe? This is a joke."

"It doesn't matter what you believe. You still have a choice to make," Peter added.

"A choice to make?" David shot an angry glare at Peter. "Really, and what is that?"

Lowering his voice and rubbing his hands together, Sebastian answered, "You either protect your family with our help, or you can try to protect your family on your own. But mark my words, David, whatever is happening is not going away."

"Yeah?" David asked, becoming smug. "Why not?"

"Because that wasn't a Zivlian in your daughter's dream the other night. It was a Fallen Angel," Sebastian shot back.

"What the heck is a Fallen Angel?"

"They were the angels that followed Satan into battle against God's army," Peter answered. "They lost and were cast out of heaven."

"Somehow you must be pretty high up on the list of the Prince of Darkness if the Fallen Angels are involved," Michael added.

"What does the devil want with me?"

"The devil wants all of us to be deceived and to turn away from the love of God but why he sent a Fallen Angel after you, I don't have the answer yet," Sebastian answered, shrugging his shoulders.

"None of us do," Michael added.

"But we will help you find the answers," Peter interjected, "if you let us."

"Look, David, you don't know us," Zoe said, looking sympathetically at David. "I can only imagine what you are thinking right now."

"I think you're all crazy," David laughed.

"Be that as it may, David, but we are here for you and your family. We are your best chance at dealing with what comes next. The question is simple. Are you willing to accept our help?" Zoe followed Sebastian's earlier lead and was blunt, bringing the conversation back to the reason they were there.

"David, I am not going to lie to you," Sebastian continued, looking David in the eyes. "You can stay here and live your life. You never have to see us again."

"You promise?" David retorted, gritting his teeth.

"If you choose to stay, you're on your own," Sebastian continued, ignoring David's anger. "The attacks won't stop and whatever is happening to your daughter will continue."

"And if I choose to go with you?"

"You will walk through the veil, and we will do everything in our power to help you protect your family."

"Does my family come with us?"

"No," Peter interjected, lowering his voice, "you come alone."

"Why?"

"David, this is a war," Michael interrupted. "You may not survive."

Looking around the room, David felt the weight of their concern. Taking a breath and dropping his face into his hands, he was overwhelmed. *What is happening to me? Why is this happening? What am I going to do to protect my family? Is this even real? God, what do I do?*

David took his time to evaluate the situation and decided to lose his attitude so he could figure out what was happening. He had a million questions for the team, and as much as he wanted to ignore everything he had learned, the fact remained that he had been drawn into his daughter's dream. He had been face-to-face with evil, and he knew he better get answers if he was going to protect his family.

Sebastian, Zoe, Michael, and Peter did their best to answer all of David's questions. It was a long night that provided some clarity, but also left a lot of unanswered questions. Critical information was missing, and David didn't know what to do. He didn't know what the best course of action for his situation was.

At one point, in the middle of the night, the members of The Network knelt next to David's chair, laid their hands on him, and started praying for wisdom in the face of adversity. He felt an overwhelming sense of calm washing over his body giving him the strength he needed to face the challenges ahead. He felt the hand of God on him as he took in the words of their prayers.

When the prayer ended, David sat up in the chair and looked at the four young people who were kneeling next to him. "What do I need to do next?"

Chapter 6

Opening the door, Savannah walked into the house and dropped her bags when she stepped inside. She was tired from a long weekend of activities. Carissa and Jordan followed her through the door and ran past her. "Don't go far, we have a lot of unpacking to do."

"We won't, Mom," they responded in unison before racing up the stairs.

"David, we're home," Savannah yelled, throwing her keys on a side table.

The house was eerily silent.

"David?" She paused for a response and when she didn't get one, she walked into the living room. Heading into the kitchen, she kicked the broken glass on the floor. Bending down to inspect the broken glass, she became concerned.

"David?" She was worried that something was wrong. Standing up, she panicked and started looking for her husband.

"Mom, what's wrong?" Jordan asked, running back down the stairs.

"Is your father upstairs?"

"I didn't see him."

"Go back upstairs and get your father."

"Okay," Jordan responded, running upstairs.

Savannah heard Jordan running from to room looking for his father when she walked into the kitchen and saw David's work sitting in a pile on the table. Picking up the cell phone from the top of the stack of papers, she panicked because she knew he would never leave the house without his phone.

Opening the back door, she walked out on the porch and called out for her husband. Moments later, Jordan came running out onto the porch. "Mom, Dad's not in the house."

"What do you mean? He has to be here." Savannah rushed back into the house.

Racing through every room, fear gripping her heart, Savannah stopped in the middle of the upstairs hallway and tried to think of where David might be. Tears rolling down her face, Savannah walked into her bedroom, sat down on the bed, and dialed the number on her cell phone.

"Nine-one-one, what's your emergency?"

"My name is Savannah Zephyr. My husband is missing…"

Within hours, police swarmed the house looking for clues. Family members shielded the children from the bustling activity while Savannah sat in a catatonic state in the middle of her living room. Detectives grilled her for every piece of information they could, local news crews set up cameras on the front lawn, and neighbors stood in the middle of their sleepy little cul-de-sac wondering what happened.

Her worst nightmare had just come true.

Chapter 7

Special Agent Eric Carmichael was working at his desk. His tie was loosened, the top button of his pressed shirt undone, and the five o'clock shadow was developing on the edges of his chiseled chin. Even though it was late in the day, his short brown hair was combed.

His office was filled with mementos from his career in the military and the Federal Bureau of Investigation. After graduating from high school, Eric enlisted in the United States Army. He was an exemplary soldier who climbed the ranks, and after his service was complete, the Federal Bureau of Investigation recruited him.

Eric's entire life had been a constant pursuit for the truth. He believed there was a difference between right and wrong; there was no room for a gray area in Eric's mind. There were rules in a civilized society, and he believed in following those rules. He was a man of integrity, and his office walls were living proof of his dedication to his belief in the justice system and the oath he took to defend the rights of law-abiding Americans.

So, as Eric sat behind his desk, working late into the day on a difficult case, he raised an inquisitive eyebrow when Deputy Director Walter Johnson walked into his office, dropped a thick file folder on his desk, and sat down.

"Good evening, Deputy Director, what are you doing here this late?"

"I am here because I knew you would be."

"I am flattered, sir, but I highly doubt my working late is any cause for you to be here as well," Eric said, leaning back in his chair and eyeing up his superior officer.

"Well, Eric, you busted me," Deputy Director Johnson laughed. "To be honest, my wife wanted me to go to a neighborhood barbecue with her tonight."

"Avoiding it, sir?" Eric quipped.

"I hate those things, Eric. Everyone is so fake," Deputy Director Johnson confessed, settling into his chair. "So, I told her I had to work late."

Leaning forward and picking the file up from his desk, Eric looked at Deputy Director Johnson with a quizzical look on his face. "Is this the case?"

"That it is."

"All due respect, sir, I am swamped. Isn't there anyone else you can assign this case?" Eric attempted to hand the file back to Deputy Director Johnson.

"Clear your docket, Eric, because this is one of the most complex cases ever to come across my desk. I need my best man on this one."

"Sir, I have other cases."

"This case takes precedent."

"All due respect, sir…"

"Dispose with the 'all due respect' mumbo jumbo Eric and look at the file," Deputy Director Johnson interrupted, pointing at the folder.

Opening the file and leaning back in his chair, Eric started to read through the thick packet of evidence. The more he read, the more confused he became. He was dumbfounded. In a world where the good guy always apprehended his man, what he was reading defied all odds. "This isn't possible, sir."

"What was that?" Deputy Director Johnson raised his hand to his ear. "I couldn't hear you."

"This has got to be some kind of a joke."

"Have you ever known me to have any semblance of a sense of humor, Eric?"

"No, sir, but this case, I don't see how any of this is possible."

"And that is exactly why we need our best man working it."

"A few pages claim there is video evidence to corroborate the written description of the crime scenes."

"There is."

"Do we have the video footage?"

"I have it in the conference room. Would you like to see it?"

"The written account isn't possible, sir, so you know I do."

"Follow me," Deputy Director Johnson instructed, standing up and leading Eric into the hallway. Eric followed him while thumbing through the case file. Walking into an empty conference room, Eric sat down while Deputy Director Johnson went over to a laptop and started the video. "This is the latest video we have from a federal bank in Norfolk. The incident happened a little over a week ago."

"Why is the video so old?" Eric asked, looking up from the file and staring at the screen.

"Because it takes a while before the bank has any knowledge of the intrusion."

"How is that possible?"

"Just watch the video," Deputy Director Johnson advised, leaning back in his chair. "In this case, seeing really is believing."

The video showed a darkened, empty, quiet lobby. The only light in the darkened room came from the exit signs, clocks, and a cubicle light that had been left on at the end of the day.

Out of nowhere, a body flew into the middle of the bank lobby from out of thin air. No doors had been opened, no windows had been broken, and no alarms had been tripped. As far as anyone could tell, nothing in the bank had been disturbed, but in the middle of the lobby floor, clear as day, a man had materialized.

The man was crouched down on all fours. He braced himself against the floor, dressed all in black, he started scanning the bank for something in the room. The man opened his mouth as if he were yelling.

"Do we have audio for this video?" Eric inquired, leaning forward in his chair, intrigued.

"Unfortunately, we don't."

"I can't see what he is looking for, but it definitely looks like he is trying to find something or someone."

"I have watched this film many times, Eric. There isn't anyone else, I have no idea why he is yelling."

The man stood up. Staring off into the distance, he continued talking. Bracing himself in a defensive position, he grabbed a circular object off his belt and swung it across the front of his body. Turning and facing in a new direction, the suspect shouted at something off in the darkness. Stepping forward, he braced himself like he had done before, swung his right hand across his body, and once again, faced the direction in which he had just swung his arm.

"Look… here…" Eric pointed at the screen. "Do you see that?"

"What? Where?" Deputy Director Johnson tried to see what Eric was pointing at on the screen.

"The curtains outside the office door are moving."

"Well, I'll be," Deputy Director Johnson acknowledged, leaning in to inspect the footage. "I hadn't seen that before, but they are definitely moving."

"But how? The suspect hasn't left the center of the room."

"I don't know. I don't see anything. Air conditioning turned on, maybe?"

Stepping in the direction of the office, the suspect spoke again. This time, though, he stood there for a few minutes looking around the room. Breathing hard, he moved his body in an awkward motion and appeared to catch something with his hands before pinning it to the floor underneath him. The suspect appeared to be fighting with something hidden underneath his body in the shadows of the lobby.

"What's underneath him?" Eric jumped up and moved toward the screen for a closer look.

"I don't see anything."

"He's fighting with someone."

"I don't see anything, Eric," Deputy Director Johnson admitted, standing up and walking toward the screen. "It's almost like he is having a psychological break with reality."

"Someone is in the bank with him." Eric pointed at the video on the screen. "But who?"

"That's impossible. We'd be able to see them."

Collapsing to his knees on the floor, breathing hard, the suspect placed his hands on his hips, raised his head, and looked around the lobby.

"I don't know how to explain it," Eric stated, staring at the screen, perplexed, "but I swear I saw someone, or at least something, underneath him."

Wiping the sweat off his forehead, the suspect rolled his head around, picked up the circular device lying on the floor, returned it to his holster, and stood up. The suspect dusted himself off, looked around the lobby once again, and walked toward the bank manager's office. The door closed behind the suspect after he entered the office and the lobby of the Norfolk Federal Bank returned to being a dark, desolate place in the middle of the night.

"Right there. That's the inexplicable part of this case," Deputy Director Johnson pointed at the screen. "When he walks into the office, he never comes back out."

"How does he leave the bank?" Eric asked, walking back to the table and sitting down.

"I don't know. The office is in the middle of the building. There are no windows or doors to the outside world. The only door in the room is the one he just walked through."

"You're telling me he just vanished?"

"I have watched the video repeatedly and I don't know how he leaves the building. And I have six other bank videos where the same thing happens every time."

"Does he take anything?"

"Not one penny."

"Then why does he break into the banks?"

"I don't know."

"He has to take something."

"Nothing," Deputy Director Johnson said, returning to his seat. "He has broken into a bunch of federal banks in the middle of the night, performs the fight scene, picks himself up off the floor, walks into a dark corner of the bank, and vanishes."

"That's not physically possible, sir."

"The videos don't lie, Eric," Deputy Director Johnson responded, shrugging his shoulders. "You saw it for yourself."

"There has to be a trick to it. Nobody just vanishes."

"Evidently, this guy does."

"Is he a magician trying to get a TV special?" Eric chuckled, rifling through the file.

"Not that we're aware of."

"Well, what do we know?"

"On the specifics, we are pretty thin."

"But we have something?"

"Yes," Deputy Director Johnson replied, pausing for a moment. "The suspect's name is David Zephyr. He is married to his childhood sweetheart, has two kids, and he is a senior account executive in a local advertising firm… until six months ago."

"What happened six months ago?"

"He vanished without a trace."

Looking up from the case file, Eric stared at Deputy Director Johnson with a furrowed brow. "What do you mean he vanished?"

"His wife came home from a long weekend with the kids and David Zephyr was nowhere to be found. No one has seen or heard from him since. That is, until he turned up in these federal bank surveillance videos."

"Impossible in this day and age." Eric resumed reviewing the material in the case file. "Nobody disappears. He has to have a digital footprint."

"Not this guy," Deputy Director Johnson responded, leaning into the table. "There is nothing. Not a single digital shred of evidence connected to him except these videos."

"Impossible." Eric slammed the file down on the table. "And I intend to prove it."

"That is why the Area Director and I gave you this case. You always get your man."

Chapter 8

Eric created a task force dedicated to finding and apprehending David Zephyr. After pulling together thousands of pages of documents, analyzing forensic evidence collected at each bank, and reviewing surveillance videos for hours, Eric's investigation turned cold. They had no leads and no idea where David was going to strike next. So, Eric decided to start over. Investigate the disappearance from the beginning and work his way back through each scene until he had a case, and most importantly, a suspect in custody.

It was a beautiful drive into the suburbs. Eric liked working in the field, running down clues, but with the evolution of forensic sciences, his job had become more about reading reports and analyzing data than synthesizing the evidence firsthand.

"Detective Jones?" Eric asked, approaching the desk.

"Can I help you?" Detective Jones looked up from his computer screen, confused.

"Special Agent Eric Carmichael." Eric showed the detective his credentials. "I was wondering if you had some time to talk to me about the David Zephyr case."

"Zephyr, huh?" Detective Jones asked, leaning back in his chair and running his hands through his hair. "How can the Brisbane, North Carolina Police Department help you?"

"I'm not sure yet."

"Please sit," Detective Jones offered, clearing some files off his desk. "Do you have a new lead in the case?"

"I don't know if it is a lead as much as it might be a connection to a case I am working on at the Bureau." Eric nodded his appreciation for the time Detective Jones was giving him and sat down. "I want to flush out some of the details of your investigation to see how they fit together."

"Well, Special Agent, anything I can do to help the Feds," Detective Jones countered with a hint of sarcasm. "What do you need?"

"Great!" Eric took a pen and small notebook out of his blazer pocket. "So where are you on the case?"

"Nowhere."

"Nowhere?" Eric looked at him, confused, writing a note to himself. "Hm."

"It went cold."

"Cold, huh?" Eric stared at the detective before writing in his notebook. "So, you had leads to run down in the beginning of the case?"

"I never had a chance in this case. Calling it a cold case is a massive understatement. This case was a solid sheet of ice the second I walked into the home."

"You had to have had something?" Eric glared at the detective for a moment. He had worked hard cases before, but there was always information found at the scene of the crime. "Missing persons cases always have some clues. Forensic evidence? Something?"

"I had a frantic wife and two distraught kids." Detective Jones started wondering where this line of questioning was going. He didn't like the way Eric was glaring at him. "They came home from a trip and David was just gone."

"David?" Eric parroted, finding the familiarity the detective displayed in talking about the suspect very interesting.

"Yes, David."

"Hm," Eric muttered, writing in his notebook and looking across the desk at the detective.

"The wife said he had a big project due at work. The timeline for the project had been moved up, so he stayed home to work."

"Odd…" Eric paused for a moment before writing in his notebook. "Why didn't she postpone the trip?"

"He insisted they go without him."

"Huh?" Eric muttered, starring the statement in his notebook. "Why did he insist?"

"The wife said he had to work all weekend so there was no point in them staying behind. There was no reason in ruining the trip for the children and the grandparents."

"The grandparents?" Eric added the information to his notes.

"They own a farm a couple of hours west of here. That's where they went for the weekend."

"Could there have been a disagreement between the husband and the wife."

"David and Savannah have a loving family. Though…"The detective's words tapered off as he hesitated to collect his thoughts.

"Yes?" Eric was intrigued by the detective's momentary pause and his familiar connection with the family.

"The grandfather, Nathan," Detective Jones continued, "I think his name is Nathan, he's a real piece of work."

"How so?"

"A big menacing guy with a bad temper," Detective Jones laughed. "Real bad temper. Very protective of the family."

"Interesting…" Eric wrote all of the information down as Detective Jones shared it. He circled Nathan's name a few times. "What did you find at the farm?"

"Never went."

Eric was caught off guard by the response. Furrowing his brow, he stared down the detective. "Why not?"

"I contacted the local sheriff's office and he claimed jurisdiction, said he would have a look around the place."

"Why did he do that?" Eric interjected, writing more notes. "It's your case."

"He knows the family. Confirmed the grandfather was a piece of work and wouldn't take too kindly to outsiders poking around his farm."

"So, you let him investigate for you?" Eric became agitated with the answers to his questions, and it was become harder to hide his frustration.

"Yes."

"What did he find?" Eric put his pen down and stared at the detective while waiting for an answer.

"Nothing."

"And you still didn't feel compelled to go out there and look for yourself?"

"Not really," Detective Jones shot back, leaning forward in his chair. "The sheriff was doing me a favor."

"Interesting." Eric wrote more notes to himself. Then, shifting in the chair, he paused, looked up, and stared at the detective, "And what did the employer say?"

"That David Zephyr was a great employee, worked hard, was a great contributor, was conscientious, kind, helpful, and always punctual."

"No, not about him." Eric dismissed the response and redirected his query. "What did the employer say about the big project due on the Monday in question?"

"I never asked."

"Why not?" Eric barked, staring at the detective with a raised eyebrow. "He stayed home to work on the big project, and you didn't bother to ask about it?"

"David was an upright member of the Brisbane community, an upstanding member of his church, and a great employee at his company. This case read like a kidnapping?"

"Did you ever get a ransom call?" Eric shot back, watching the detective's demeanor.

"No."

"A ransom note?"

"No.

"A ransom email?" Eric asked, shooting Detective Jones a steely eyed glare. "Give me something useful, Detective."

"I can't give you what I don't have, Special Agent," Detective Jones blurted out, leaning forward and putting his hands on his desk.

"It seems like a pretty big leap from missing person to kidnapping, Detective Jones, without any shred of evidence to support your supposition. Why did you jump so quickly to that conclusion?"

"Because all of his work was sitting on the table and his cell phone was left behind."

"Was there forced entry into the home?"

"No." Detective Jones was feeling defensive, like he was the criminal being interrogated as he tried to explain his decisions. "You know as well as I do, there isn't always a break-in."

"Was there a sign of a struggle? Signs of a fight at the scene?"

"No."

"Was there blood in the house?"

"No."

"Then explain to me, Detective," Eric continued, condemnation in his voice, "why did you think this was a kidnapping case?"

"There was a smashed glass in the living room," Detective Jones replied, fidgeting with his hands in front of him. He was growing suspicious of Eric's motives.

"A broken glass? Huh?" Eric added the detail to his notes. "Did you get any fingerprints off the glass?"

"One set."

"Whose?" Eric inquired, expecting to hear the one name he didn't want to hear.

"David Zephyr's."

"Am I missing something here, Detective?" Eric was trying to quell his anger, but the answers he was getting about the investigation made it hard for him to be optimistic about finding anything useful.

"Are you questioning my investigation, Special Agent?" Detective Jones shot back with an icy glare.

"Look at this from my perspective, Detective," Eric replied, trying to smooth over the tension. "There's not a lot going on in this case and you moved a missing person to a kidnapping rather quickly."

"I don't like your tone of voice."

"Frankly, I don't care, Detective," Eric shot back. "Why didn't you ask the employer about the project?"

"What good would it have done, Special Agent?" Anger welling up inside him, Detective Jones tried to remain calm. "A good man is missing; his family is destroyed, and the community is reeling from the loss. So, you tell me, what good would it have done?"

"Maybe David Zephyr was having an affair. Did you think about that?"

"Never happened." Detective dismissed the notion outright while shaking his head.

"Why not?"

Detective Jones took a moment and regained his composure. "I think you're barking up the wrong tree, Special Agent, and I take offense at the line of questioning."

"Do you know the family, Detective?"

"Doesn't matter," Detective Jones replied, brushing off the question.

"Do you know the family?"

"Drop it, Special Agent."

"Do you know the family?" Eric barked, pressing the detective for an answer.

"Yes… I do," Detective Jones yelled, slamming his fist down on the desk. Pausing, he stared down Eric, regained his composure, and gritted his teeth. "Yes, Special Agent, I know David Zephyr and his family. And before you ask, the answer is no. My relationship with the family didn't impact my investigation."

"It might have, Detective." Eric added the revelation to his notes. "Your relationship to the family might have clouded your judgment."

"I was being kind in a difficult situation, but I did my job by the book."

"I applaud your kindness to the family, but that isn't our job. Our job is to find the truth, and I am not so sure you have turned over every possible stone in this case."

"I have."

"Then I wouldn't be here, Detective, would I?"

"That's not fair, Special Agent."

"By not asking the question, you don't know if David Zephyr lied to his wife. And if he did lie to his wife, why? What is he hiding?"

"He's not that kind of man."

"That's not for you to decide, Detective. It's for you to prove with evidence." Eric held up the notebook he had been writing in during their conversation. "You collect and analyze information. You run down leads. You look for clues and you ask every question, even the hard ones."

"What good would it have been to keep turning the knife in the heart of this community?"

"Because you might have found a lead, Detective," Eric declared, shaking his head back and forth. "By leaving this case cold, this community is left to grapple with unanswered questions."

"You don't know what you're talking about." Detective Jones dismissed the accusation that he had failed to conduct a thorough investigation into the disappearance of David Zephyr. "If he knew his attacker, there would be no sign of forced entry, no sign of a struggle, and the broken glass would make sense, especially if he was drugged. He would have passed out, dropping the glass on the floor, and the culprits could have easily carried him out of the house."

"But there was no ransom note, no monetary demand," Eric reminded the detective, looking at his notes. "Maybe he staged the scene and ran off with his mistress."

"But then where is his digital footprint, Special Agent?"

"That's a great point, Detective," Eric said with a hint of resignation. "That's where you've got me, and you blow a hole in my theory."

"No one just vanishes," Detective Jones replied.

"A point I have to remind myself of these days."

"Excuse me?" Detective Jones inquired, wrinkling his nose at the response.

"Nothing," Eric responded, standing up and shaking hands with Detective Jones. "Thank you for your help, Detective. Would you mind if I had a copy of your investigation files?"

"Why? What's the connection to your case?"

"I am not at liberty to fully discuss my investigation." Eric was being evasive on purpose. He didn't want the detective to know he had videos and photographs of David Zephyr. "All I can confirm is that David Zephyr has become a material person of interest in a case I am investigating."

"Really?" Detective Jones was interested in this tidbit of information. "How is that even possible?"

"I am not at liberty to discuss, but your case files could be helpful in piecing together a broader picture of what I am running down."

"If you think they'll be helpful, I'll have copies made for you today."

"Thank you. I will send a member of the task force to collect them tomorrow," Eric responded, walking away before stopping and looking back at Detective Jones. "And if we end up finding David Zephyr, I will make sure the Brisbane Police Department gets credit for being vital members of our team."

Chapter 9

Thumbing through a magazine, Eric sat and waited in the lobby for his appointment. The Zephyr case didn't add up. *How does someone vanish without leaving behind a digital footprint? How did David Zephyr breach those banks? Why didn't he steal anything? Why didn't the local authorities do their due diligence regarding Zephyr's disappearance?*

"Mr. Brooks will see you now," the secretary interrupted, standing up and walking toward him.

"Excuse me?" Eric questioned, having been lost in his thoughts.

"Mr. Brooks is ready for you. Please follow me."

"Thank you, ma'am." Eric returned the magazine to the coffee table, stood up, and followed the secretary down a long corridor. She opened the door and Eric walked into the office.

"Special Agent Carmichael, I presume?" Mr. Brooks stood up, walked around his desk and greeted Eric with a hearty handshake. "Please come in and have a seat."

"Thank you, Mr. Brooks."

"We'll sit over here, if you don't mind." Mr. Brooks escorted Eric to a couple of armchairs situated around a coffee table by the window overlooking the surrounding area.

"Don't mind at all."

"This is Marcus Willoughby, my lawyer," Mr. Brooks added, introducing Eric to the stern looking gentleman sitting in one of the chairs.

"Pleased to meet you," Mr. Willoughby huffed, standing and shaking Eric's hand.

"Likewise." Eric was confused as to why Mr. Willoughby was present. "You know this is just an informal conversation. There really isn't a need for legal representation."

"It's just good company policy to have counsel on hand when discussing an open investigation with law enforcement," Mr. Willoughby replied.

"I hope you understand, Special Agent," Mr. Brooks added, smiling.

"I have no problem with Mr. Willoughby's inclusion in the conversation, I just hope he isn't charging you his full rate."

"Well, good," Mr. Brooks replied, ignoring the statement. "Can I get you some coffee, water, or tea?"

"I'm fine."

"Good, then let's get started." Mr. Brooks sat down. Eric and Mr. Willoughby followed his lead. "How can I help the Federal Bureau of Investigation, Special Agent?"

Taking out his notebook and a pen, Eric opened it to a blank page. "Did David Zephyr work for you?"

"Technically, he still works for me." Mr. Brooks smiled.

"Come again?" Eric stared at Mr. Brooks with a quizzical expression on his face.

"David is family. His job is waiting for him whenever y'all find him and bring him home."

"So, he does work for you?"

"Yes."

"Thank you," Eric replied, making a notation in his notebook. "For how long?"

"Must be about twenty years now. I hired him right out of college. Would you like HR to check on the exact dates for you?"

"No, sir." Eric held up his hand to stop Mr. Brooks from standing up to call human resources. "I think your answer will suffice. Just trying to establish your level of knowledge of the individual in question."

"I would prefer if you referred to the 'individual in question' as David. He is part of our company family, and you make his existence sound so cold and impersonal."

"I apologize. Your request is noted." Eric paused for a moment to collect his thoughts, feeling a bit awkward using a familiar term for the suspect. "Was David a good employee?"

"And if you could, please refer to David in the present tense, I believe he is still alive."

"My apologies again." Eric wrote something in his notebook and forced a smile at yet another arbitrary intrusion into his questioning.

"Thank you," Mr. Brooks said, leaning back in his chair, placing his hands in his lap. "David is an exceptional employee. He has been one of the reasons our company has grown into the best marketing and advertising firm in North Carolina. He is my right-hand man."

"That's great, Mr. Brooks," Eric quipped, writing everything down. "Has David ever been reprimanded for misconduct or for any violation of company policy?"

Mr. Willoughby cleared his throat, leaned over, and whispered into Mr. Brooks' ear. Mr. Brooks nodded and smiled. "On the advice of counsel, without a warrant, personnel records are private, confidential, and protected. Can you please be more specific in the scope of your questioning?"

"Has David ever stolen from the company?"

Mr. Willoughby cleared his throat again, leaned over, and whispered into Mr. Brooks' ear again. Mr. Brooks shook his head to show his apparent disagreement with his lawyer and bit his lip before responding, "On the advice of counsel, personnel records are private, confidential, and protected. Please move on."

Raising an eyebrow at the response, Eric was starting to wonder if David wasn't the exceptional employee Mr. Brooks claimed he was. What other reason would the company attorney have to object to simple questions? "Did David ever lie to you?"

Mr. Willoughby cleared his throat a third time and started to lean in when Mr. Brooks held up his hand to stop him. "Mr. Willoughby is going to tell me that personnel records are private, confidential, and protected. Then you are going to write down I am hiding something in your notebook, which I am not. He wants you to subpoena the records."

"What do you want, Mr. Brooks?" Eric was concerned the disagreement was going to derail their conversation. He wanted to keep his investigation low key and didn't want to have to start asking for warrants.

"I want my friend to come home. So, I want to tell you that personally..."

"Excuse me," Mr. Willoughby interrupted, leaning toward Mr. Brooks.

"Sit back, Marcus," Mr. Brooks ordered, growing visibly angry with his attorney. "I am speaking personally and not to any records that may or may not be in David's personnel file."

"You're starting down a slippery slope," Mr. Willoughby responded.

"Great. It's my private company and I am making an executive decision to defend my friend. If that gets me in hot water with the feds, so be it."

"Proceed then," Mr. Willoughby acquiesced, throwing up his hands in frustration and leaning back in his chair. "But realize you are doing so against the advice of legal counsel."

Facing Eric, Mr. Brooks ignored Mr. Willoughby's declaration. "As I was saying, David has never lied to me, stolen from me or the company. He has been an upstanding member of our firm, our community, and our church. David is an impeccable family man who I wish more people would emulate."

"Thank you, Mr. Brooks." Eric wrote in his notebook. Pausing for a moment, he looked up. "Do you remember the day David disappeared?"

"Yes," Mr. Brooks answered, running his hands through his hair. "I was surprised when I found out David was missing."

"Why was that?" Eric was intrigued.

"He and Savannah had planned on taking the kids on a trip for the long weekend."

"Didn't you have an advertising proposal meeting with a client on the Monday in question?"

"No." Mr. Brooks furrowed his eyebrows, an inquisitive look overtaking his facial expression. "Why do you ask?"

"Are you sure there wasn't a client meeting scheduled?"

"I'm positive."

"Do you want to check your calendar before we proceed?" Eric asked, writing down a few more notes.

"I don't need to."

"Why not?"

"Because if we had a client presentation, I would have panicked if David wasn't in the office by seven. I would have been looking for him."

"Are you positive, Mr. Brooks?" Eric stopped writing and stared at Mr. Brooks. "You cannot be mistaken about this fact. I need you to be completely accurate about the date of the client meeting."

"I am positive," Mr. Brooks expressed, standing up and walking to his desk. He logged into his computer and brought up the company calendar. "There it is on the calendar. David wasn't due to present his advertising proposal for ten days."

Standing up, Eric walked over to Mr. Brooks' desk. "Can I look at that?"

"Sure." Mr. Brooks turned the computer screen toward Eric.

"Huh," Eric muttered, adding the details in his notebook. "Is there any way the calendar is wrong?"

"Highly unlikely."

"But possible?"

"It's impossible." Mr. Brooks was adamant in his declaration. "Our company lives and dies by this calendar. If there was a change to the schedule, it would be logged on the master calendar."

"Can the calendar be accessed remotely by the internet?"

"No."

"So, is it possible that David got a call from the client and the date was changed without being entered into the system?"

"It's possible…" Mr. Brooks thought about the question for a moment.

"But?" Eric pushed for an answer.

"If we are talking about David, not a snowball's chance in hell."

"Why not?"

"There's a whole team of people who work on an advertising proposal. They would've known about any change in the schedule. Storyboards would need to be completed. Copies of the proposal would've been drawn up and prepared. David was meticulous. If he moved a client proposal, his team and I would have known."

"Why would you have known?" Eric raised an eyebrow because this struck Eric as odd.

"This is my company, Special Agent. I attend all client meetings. David would have checked my schedule to make sure it was clear."

"Interesting," Eric muttered, perusing his notes. "One last question."

"Yes?"

"Would you mind sharing the client's phone number with me? I want to corroborate the information with them."

"Not at all." Mr. Brooks pulled up his contact list, wrote the information down on a piece of paper, and handed it to Eric.

"Thank you. This is a big help." Eric looked at the piece of paper and put it in his pocket.

"Anything we can do to help. Please don't hesitate if it will bring David home."

"I'll be in touch," Eric declared, closing his notebook and putting it in his pocket. He thanked Mr. Brooks and Mr. Willoughby for their time and left the office.

Chapter 10

Savannah sat on her back porch with Monica and Nathan Zephyr. Monica was a woman of average height and weight who looked all of her sixty-seven years. Gray hair, crows' feet branched out from her blue eyes, and a narrow-wrinkled face framed her warm, tender smile.

Towering over everyone at six feet eight inches, Nathan looked like a much younger man. His muscles bulging through the sleeves of his shirt were a testament to a lifetime of work on the farm. His black hair and brown eyes accentuated his clear, wrinkle free complexion.

"Mom and Dad," Savannah said, sipping her iced tea. "I can't thank you enough for everything you have done for us. I don't know what we would have done without you."

"Please stop thanking us, Savannah, we're family," Monica smiled, placing a hand on Savannah's.

"Absolutely, my dear," Nathan agreed, lighting the grill. "We love being here and wish we could do more to help."

"Thanks, Nathan. That means so much. We are just glad you could join us for dinner. The kids love spending time with you."

"Grandpa," Carissa yelled from the backyard, "come play with us."

"I will. Right after I grill some hamburgers."

Watching Carissa run into the backyard to play with her brother, a calm resolve settled into Savannah's being. These family moments were the only time she felt normal. Her friends and neighbors had started to talk about David's disappearance in unflattering terms. The whispers and the innuendos were taking their toll and she isolated herself from the community. So, an evening with her family was her chance to feel normal, even if for only a few hours.

Nathan was telling another one of his hysterical, embellished tales when the doorbell rang. Looking at her with a strange expression, he asked, "Are you expecting someone, Savannah?"

"No."

"Probably an annoying reporter," Nathan admonished, standing up. "I'll get rid of them."

Walking into the house, Nathan went straight to the front door. Peering through the windowpanes framing the doorway, he saw a man in a black suit with a briefcase. Opening the door, his massive frame dwarfed Eric's. "Can I help you?"

"Pardon me, sir, I am looking for Mrs. Zephyr. Is she home?"

"She's not interested."

"In what?" Eric asked, a puzzled expression overtaking his face.

"Listen here, buddy." Nathan stepped forward in a menacing manner. "I don't know what you're peddling, but Mrs. Zephyr isn't interested. Good day."

Starting to close the door, Nathan saw Eric holding up his credentials. "I am not a salesman. My name is Special Agent Eric Carmichael. I am with the FBI, and I need to ask Mrs. Zephyr a few questions. Is she at home?"

Catching the door in his hand and opening it a little wider, Nathan inspected Eric's credentials. Sizing up Eric, he stepped onto the front stoop and pulled the door closed. "We're about to have dinner. What is this about?"

"Her husband, David Zephyr."

"David?"

"Yes. I have a few questions for her."

"The local authorities have been looking into his case; why is the FBI getting involved?"

"I am not at liberty to discuss the details with you, sir." Eric pulled out a business card and handed it to Nathan. "If this is not a good time, I can come back. Please have her call me."

Watching Eric turn and walk down the front steps, Nathan called after him, "Special Agent, wait."

"Yes?" Eric stopped and spun around.

"My name is Nathan Zephyr," he said, shaking Eric's hand. "I apologize for being rude. I am very protective of my family. Please come in. Savannah will want to talk to you."

"Are you sure? I wouldn't want to intrude on dinner."

"Special Agent, please," Nathan lamented. "She would hate me if I sent you away, especially if you have any new information about David's disappearance."

"That might be premature; I was just assigned the case."

"Trust me, any news is welcomed. Please come in."

"If you insist."

"I do." Nathan led Eric through the house to the back porch. Monica and Savannah both stared at Nathan for an explanation as the two men emerged from the house. "Savannah, this is Special Agent Carmichael. He is with the FBI."

"Good afternoon, ma'am," Eric said, walking over and shaking her hand.

"It's nice to meet you. This is my mother-in-law, Monica."

"Ma'am." Eric smiled before shaking Monica's hand and nodding his head.

Fidgeting in her chair, Savannah asked, "Do you have some news about David?"

Eric felt like he was intruding upon their family time as he watched the kids play in the yard and the relatives gawked at him. "Ma'am, is there a place a little bit more private where we can talk?"

Savannah was caught off guard by the request. Sitting on her porch, in her backyard, surrounded by her family members, she couldn't think of a more private place to discuss the disappearance of her husband. Then without warning, fear attacked her. *Why was the FBI here? What did he need to tell her that he couldn't say in front of the rest of the family? Did she need to follow him to the morgue to identify a body?*

Feeling intense pangs of sadness and pain, she started to fear the worst about David. Had six months of hoping, praying, and wishing for a positive resolution to David's disappearance come down to this moment that would strip her of everything she had prayed for?

Tears were welling up inside Savannah's eyes. *If the FBI had come to tell her David was dead, they better be able to provide answers to some of her questions like; 'Why? How? And who did it?'* But for now, Savannah was frozen with fear, tears rolling down her cheeks. She didn't want to go some place private. If she was about to find out the man she loved had died, she wanted to be surrounded by her family.

"Excuse me, ma'am? Are you okay?" Eric interjected, breaking the silence.

Wiping away the tears, Savannah half-smiled, "If you have bad news, I would rather be surrounded by my family."

"Savannah," Monica gasped, moving closer and putting her arm on Savannah's shoulder, "You can't think like that."

"Ma'am, I'm not here to give you bad news."

"Oh, thank God," Savannah uttered, relief washing over her body.

"Ma'am, I was just assigned the case. I have some questions about your husband. I just thought there might be a quieter place where we could talk."

"I am surrounded by my family… David's family. If there is something you would like to ask, you can ask it in front of them."

"Okay, ma'am." Eric sat down at the table and opened his briefcase. "I apologize if I upset you."

"I'm fine."

"I'm hoping you can clear up some confusion for me."

Taking a deep breath, Savannah could breathe more easily knowing David was not waiting for her in the morgue. He was still out there. She didn't know where he was, but, for the moment, she knew he was still out there and that gave her hope.

"Mrs. Zephyr, when was the last time you saw your husband?"

"What?" Savannah was taken aback by the question and felt attacked.

"When was the last time you saw your husband?" Eric repeated the question, raising his eyebrows and looking at her sideways.

"Special Agent, I don't know what kind of sick game you're playing, but I haven't seen my husband for six months."

"Why did he send you to your relatives?"

"Excuse me?" Savannah remarked, frustration welling up inside of her at the line of questioning because she felt like a suspect.

"Why would you go on a family trip to visit relatives without your husband?" Eric rephrased the question before pausing to reflect for a moment. "Seems kind of odd, doesn't it?"

"David had a project due at work. He had to stay home to work on his proposal."

"Are you sure about that, Ma'am?"

"These questions were asked months ago; did you even bother to read the police reports?" Savannah shot Eric an icy, angry glare.

"I spoke with the police, Mrs. Zephyr, but unlike the local police, I followed up with David's boss." Eric paused, pulling his notebook out of his briefcase, and looked over his notes. "He claimed David didn't have a client meeting for another ten days. So why the discrepancy between your story and the truth?"

"David told me he had a deadline," Savannah replied, looking at Monica and Nathan with confusion. They could see she was worried about the direction of the questioning. "I had no reason not to believe my husband. Maybe the meeting got moved up and someone forgot to change it on the calendar."

"I thought of that too, so I checked with the client," Eric stated, looking at his notebook. "They corroborated the date David's boss gave me."

"What is going on here? Am I a suspect, Agent Carmichael?" Savannah sat up in her chair and stared at Eric in disbelief.

"Can you explain any of these discrepancies to me, Mrs. Zephyr?"

"I don't like your tone of voice. So, unless there is something else you would like to talk about, I'd prefer to end this conversation."

"There is something I would like to know, Mrs. Zephyr."

"What?" Savannah asked, slamming her hand down on the table. "Please get to the point."

"Are you sure that the Friday morning in April is the last time you saw your husband?"

"Who do you think you are?" Savannah asked, anger filling the very core of her being.

"Are you sure?"

"Special Agent, my children and I have cried ourselves to sleep every night for the past six months. So, yes. I am positive I haven't seen my husband," Savannah barked, pushing her chair back from the table and standing up. "How do you have the audacity to walk into my house and question me like this? Who do you think you are?"

"This is ridiculous, Special Agent," Nathan interjected, taking a couple of menacing steps toward the table. "My daughter-in-law has answered your questions. Get to the point quickly or I am going to escort you from the house for being rude. Do I make myself clear?"

"I understand your frustration, Mr. Zephyr." Eric held up his hand in Nathan's direction. "But I think you need to see something before you get too angry."

Reaching into his briefcase, Eric took out a manila folder. Laying the manila folder on the table in front of Savannah, he took out six photographs of David and placed them on the table. Savannah leaned forward to inspect each of the photographs and sat down, hope swelling in her heart because she knew David was still alive.

"These photographs, Mrs. Zephyr, were taken in six separate federal banks over the past few months."

"That can't be," Monica uttered, picking up one of the photographs and staring at it before handing it to Nathan.

"Mrs. Zephyr, can you identify the man in each of these pictures?"

"It's David," she confirmed, tears of joy trickling down her face. "That's my husband."

"With this new information, Mrs. Zephyr," Eric pressed, noting all of the changes to Savannah's demeanor. "I have to ask, once again, have you had any contact with David?"

"I don't like your tone of voice," Nathan intervened, staring at Eric.

"All due respect, Mr. Zephyr," Eric declared, standing up to address Nathan's imposing body posture. "Federal crimes have been committed and it appears David might be involved."

"David's not a criminal," Savannah uttered under her breath. "There is no way David would be involved in this. There has to be another explanation."

"You've got the wrong person," Monica added, looking through the photographs.

"I'm sorry, Mrs. Zephyr, I have to treat this like a criminal investigation and your husband is my prime suspect. Have any of you spoken to David in the past few months?"

"I have had enough of this," Nathan interjected, walking up to Eric and towering over him. "I would like you to kindly leave."

Realizing how massive and muscular Nathan was, Eric tilted his head back and looked up into Nathan's face. Eric was nervous.

"I asked you to leave," Nathan demanded, staring down at Eric. "Any other questions you have, Special Agent, should be referred to my lawyer."

Locked in a staring battle, Eric knew it was time to leave. He had accomplished his goal. He had ascertained the information he needed. All he could do now was to wait to see if they would take the bait and contact David. "You're right, Mr. Zephyr; I should go."

Placing the photographs back into the manila folder, Eric packed up his briefcase and turned to leave the house. Nathan escorted him to the front door and slammed the door behind him as soon as his feet hit the landing.

Chapter 11

Walking into her room, Savannah sat down on the bed. The impact of the meeting with Special Agent Carmichael was still weighing upon her heart. She was relieved to know David was still alive, but she was confused about his involvement in a criminal investigation.

Her heart ached. Savannah wanted this nightmare to end. Whether David was a criminal or not didn't matter, she just wanted David home. They could face whatever challenges that awaited them together.

Looking out the window, she took a deep breath, knelt on the floor, folded her hands, and prayed, "Father God, thank you for this day. Thank you for your grace. You have blessed us with an abundance of more than we can ever thank you for."

A tear rolling down her face, she continued, "I trust in you, Lord. I know whatever you have planned for David and me, it will be done to promote your greatness and glory. Please protect David as he fulfills your will. Please continue to protect our children during this ordeal."

Staring out into the quietness of the night, Savannah paused for a moment and let the Holy Spirit wash over her with a sense of calm. Engaging in fifteen minutes of silent prayer and reflection, she then continued to pray, "Thank you, Father God, for your love, grace, peace, and wisdom. May we continue to praise your name through your son, Jesus Christ, through whom all our blessings come, Amen."

Staring out into the night for a few more minutes, Savannah climbed into bed, turned off the light, and went to sleep.

A few hours later, David crept up the stairs in the darkened house. Knowing every inch of the floor plan, he could walk through the house with his eyes closed. Reaching the top of the stairs, he felt the floor creek underneath his foot. *Same old house* he thought to himself, stepping over the top step.

Creeping down the hallway, he stopped at the doorway to his bedroom. He peered inside and saw Savannah sleeping. He had witnessed the conversation between Savannah and Special Agent Carmichael earlier in the day, and he was angered at the insinuation he was a criminal. His only crime was defending the world against the evil that existed within it.

Walking over to the bed and standing over Savannah, David's heart ached. He wished he could tell her the truth, where he was and what he was doing, but he couldn't. He knew the truth would put her and their children in danger.

He wanted Savannah to understand that no matter how much it hurt both of them, it was better this way. He prayed Savannah knew how hard the decision was to leave, but when people are faced with a difficult decision, they have to make hard choices. When God asks you to follow Him, there isn't much of a choice but to follow.

Vanishing without a trace was the sacrifice David had to make in order to protect his family. He couldn't leave a note, a message, or a call to explain what he was doing. He just had to walk out the door, step through the veil, and disappear. It was his job to take on the battle so his wife and children would be safe from the evil lurking just beyond their reach.

Standing next to his bed, a part of him wished he could go back and choose to stay home. There were days where he wished he had told Sebastian, Zoe, Peter, and Michael to leave him and his family alone. After everything he had seen and fought against for the past six months, he knew the only choice he could have ever made was to leave his old life behind.

Walking to his side of the bed, David sat down on the mattress. He was tired, but most of all, he was homesick. He laid down and felt the mattress comfort him. Closing his eyes for a moment, he thought to himself; *maybe when I open my eyes, it will all be a dream.*

Opening his eyes, nothing changed. Rolling over and moving closer to Savannah, he wrapped his arms around her, closed his eyes, and reveled in holding his wife in his arms.

"One day, Savannah, one day you will understand everything," David whispered into Savannah's ear.

"Understand what, David?" Savannah asked, whispering back while she slept.

David was startled. He hadn't spoken to Savannah in months and his heart melted when he heard her talking to him. He wanted to pour his heart and soul out to her, to tell her about everything, but as he watched her sleep, he knew he couldn't. His was a story for another day. All he wanted to do now was lie next to his wife and embrace the tenderness of her touch.

"Please know how much I love you, Savannah."

"I know, David, I love you, too. Please come home."

"I wish I could."

"What's stopping you?"

"That's a very long story, Savannah, revolving around those three simple words; I love you."

"I love you, too, David."

"Promise me you will never believe what they say about me. I'm not a crook."

"I never thought you were."

Squeezing her in his arms and giving Savannah a sweet, soft kiss on her cheek, he whispered, "I need to go now, Sweetie. I love you."

"Please, David, don't go. Stay a little longer with me."

David gave her another kiss on the cheek. "It's time for me to go. I have work to do."

Rolling over and climbing out of the bed, David stopped and took another second to watch Savannah sleep. In the farthest reaches of his heart, he hoped the words he had shared with Savannah would sink into her conscious mind and comfort her.

David placed his hand on the circular device seated on the right side of his belt, pushed the buttons, and stepped back through the veil.

Chapter 12

David isolated the whimpering in the darkened room. Noticing a wife trying to nudge her sleeping husband, David crept to the far corner of the room and stood in the shadows, pressing himself against the wall. David, dressed in black, blended into the shadows and was hidden.

David tried to keep his mind focused on other things while he watched the husband's dream become more violent. He thought about the days and nights he had missed with his family. The meals, the sports practices, the jokes, and the hugs he had missed over the past six months. It gave him solace in the darkness since he knew what was about to happen.

David saw the young man dart across the room while his wife tried to console him as his dream became more violent. David saw the Zivlian crawl out from underneath the bed and approach the man who was panicking against the far wall. The doglike creature was jet black with red eyes and long snarling, sharp teeth protruding from its mouth. Standing in the middle of the room, the Zivlian growled and unfurled its wings.

Intervening as the Zivlian was reaching out to grab the man who was cowering in fear, the creature never saw David coming. Slamming the circular Hellfire Device into its side, electricity burning into the creature's body, he launched the monster into the wall across the room.

"Why don't you pick on someone your own size?" David yelled, glaring at the monster trying to regain its footing. The demon stood on its hind feet growling at David, staring at him, before dipping its head and charging.

David stepped aside to avoid the charging entity, grabbed the beast by the arm and swung the Zivlian across the room into the wall. "Is that all you've got for me? Come on! Fight like a demon!"

Scampering to its feet a second time, the beast looked more menacing and angrier than it had been the first time David launched it across the room. David thought the monster was about to take flight when he watched it snarl its teeth and open its wings.

"It looks like I finally have your attention, Rover. Want to play?"

Lowering its head, the beast charged at David. He sidestepped the Zivlian, but the evil entity grabbed David's arm and threw him to the floor. The demon crawled on top of David as he put an elbow into the chest of the monster and tried to escape its clutches. The Zivlian forced David back on the ground, pinned him down, brought its sharp claw to David's face. It dragged its claw along his cheek, cutting open the skin.

Wincing in severe pain, David refused to scream. Blood flowing from the gash in his cheek, he fought back underneath the beast. Breaking free with one arm and searing another electrical blast in the devilish monster, he tried to crawl away. Screeching the most heinous sound, the Zivlian growled, picked David up, and threw him across the room.

Crashing into the wall and falling to the floor, David landed with a solid thud. Dazed and confused for a moment, he scuttled to his knees. It had been a while since a Zivlian had put up a decent fight and manhandled David; he readied himself for the next attack.

"That's right, little puppy, come puppy, come on, come on, come get me." David steadied himself against the wall, blood streaming down his face. "Come on puppy, come and get me."

Staring down the Zivlian, waiting for the beast to attack, David put his hands on his side. Running straight at David, the hound from hell was close when David lifted the Hellfire Device and rammed it into the Zivlian's chest. Grabbing the beast with his free hand, he pulled the beast through the wall onto the floor of the Wilmington Federal Bank.

Crashing to the floor, David rolled over while the Zivlian scurried at lightning speed into the darkest corners of the bank. Bracing himself on the bank floor, David caught his breath. Breathing hard with blood dripping on the floor, David was reminded that these battles were never easy. Each one took a toll on his body.

Laboring to his feet and looking around the bank, he located the beast and continued to taunt it. "Now that the playing field has been leveled, let's see what you've got now… Come on you vile beast, come and get me."

Spreading its wings, the monster tried to intimidate David. Bracing his feet and gripping the circular device with his right hand, he stared down his opponent. The demon charged. David threw a punch into the jaw of the winged beast and discharged a massive electrical pulse causing the beast to retreat to the far corner of the bank, weakened.

"Is that what you're bringing to the fight tonight? Come on, boy, give me something more than that. Challenge me. Make me sweat. Come draw some more blood."

David knew the next attack was imminent. The creature stared at David with fire in its eyes, the angry growls became fiercer with teeth protruding from its jaws like sharpened spears, anger emanated from every pore of its body.

Charging at David, the beast leapt at him when it was close. David threw a punch into the underbelly of the beast and discharged another electrical blast as he stepped out from underneath the lunging demon. The beast crashed in distress on the floor and darted to a dark corner of the bank.

"That's right, you can feel it now, can't you?" David taunted the monster as it struggled to its feet. The Zivlian was faltering. Taking a couple of steps toward the beast, David mocked, "It won't be long now. You'll go home and be subjected to the torment you deserve. And when you get there, I hope your master punishes you severely."

Struggling to stand, the Zivlian readied itself for another assault. David's insulting comments angered the creature. Seething with pure hatred, the entity wobbled against the wall and growled.

Waiting for the next charge, David knew it was weak and couldn't survive another electrical blast. With all of its remaining might and fury, the Zivlian rushed him with its wings open wide.

Grabbing the beast's arm and holding it with all his might, David leapt and brought his right hand down on the monster. He delivered a constant barrage of electrical surges as the vile creature crashed to the floor underneath him. David moved the circular device to the chest of the demon and pressed it into the beast's body. "In the name of my Lord and Savior Jesus Christ, I send you back to the depths of hell."

The Zivlian let out the vilest screech and disappeared in a fiery blast. Collapsing on the floor exhausted, David knelt for a moment until the remnants of the foul stench of the Zivlian burned his nasal passages.

Standing up and looking around the bank, David placed the Hellfire Device back on his belt. Running his hand across his face, he noticed blood was starting to clot. Taking a deep breath and peering into the darkness, David squinted until he saw the red light of the surveillance camera on the wall.

Walking over, he looked up into the lens. Making some hand gestures, David spoke into the camera. He stared at the camera for a brief moment before walking into a dark corner of the bank and vanishing.

"Stop the tape right there," Eric ordered, staring wide-eyed at the video. "Roll that footage back."

Everyone stopped working and stared at the video being replayed. Surrounded by a slew of federal agents, Eric asked, "Can anybody make out what he is saying?"

In the back of the room, a young Asian man sitting at a computer spoke up, "I think he said, 'I see you.'"

Looking at the agent, Eric asked, "What was that?"

"He said, 'I see you.'"

"And you are?"

"Agent Quyen, sir. I was assigned to this case from the counterterrorism unit. Special Agent Donovan sent me. I break codes, read lips, and translate fifteen different languages."

"And you think he said, 'I see you'?"

"Yes, sir, I do." Quyen walked toward the screen as the video played in a loop. "It's a classic bravado hand gesture he is making."

"Show me, Agent Quyen."

As the loop of David walking toward the camera started over, Agent Quyen pointed at the screen. "Right here, he is walking up to the camera in a bold move. It's almost like a dog marking his territory. He wants to make sure he has someone's attention.

"When he makes the 'V' with his fingers." Quyen imitated the gesture playing out on the screen for Eric. "That is a classic, nonverbal cue to grab your attention. If you look closely, he is being demonstrative about the message. He wants someone to clearly understand him."

"What is the message, Agent Quyen?" Eric inquired, growing impatient with the agent.

Reading David's lips as the video looped again, Agent Quyen repeated the words, "I see you. Leave my family alone."

"Leave my family alone?" Eric paused for a moment. He was stunned by the revelation, but wanted to make sure that is what Quyen had deciphered from the video. "Are you sure that's what he said?"

"Yes, sir," Quyen responded. "Did you do something to his family, Special Agent Carmichael?"

Ignoring the question, Eric stared at the video screen and mumbled under his breath, "She lied."

"What was that, sir?" Agent Quyen asked.

"She lied to me..." Eric addressed the room of agents. "Savannah Zephyr lied to me. How would David know I visited his family unless she told him? Now get back to work, so we can nail this guy."

Walking over to a window overlooking the city while the agents went back to their work, Eric stared out into the night. "Where are you, David Zephyr? Where are you?"

Chapter 13

Savannah took the kids to the mall. It was a rare day when they didn't have any activities scheduled, and she wanted to pick up a few items the kids needed. She decided to make a day of it. She let the kids eat at the food court, play in the arcade, and roam through the toy stores. She loved watching them be kids again.

"Why am I following the family?" Quyen asked, following Savannah and the kids through the mall at a safe distance.

"I know she met with him. I just don't know how or when," Eric responded through Quyen's earpiece, watching the lower level of the mall from his vantage point on the second tier. "The video from the last bank confirmed it."

"So, you're going to sit in the food court drinking coffee, while we surveil the suspect?" Quyen smiled while fist bumping his partner who was walking next to him.

"She knows what I look like," Eric answered, smiling to himself. "What was the fist bump for, Agent Quyen?"

"You saw that?" Quyen spun around and looked for Eric. "And just so I am up to speed, men in suits with wires running to their ears won't tip her off? We don't exactly look like shoppers."

"We have a job to do, men." Eric took a sip of his coffee and looked at his watch. "And if you look up, Agent Quyen, you'll see I'm on the upper level watching everything."

Looking up and behind him, Quyen spotted Eric. "Touché."

Eric was destined to find David. He knew the family had to have made contact, so he assigned teams of agents to follow Savannah twenty-four hours a day. When he learned about the shopping trip to the mall, Eric blanketed the mall with several teams of agents because a public space with multiple exits would be the perfect place to meet.

Savannah had been at the mall for hours and the team was growing restless. David was nowhere to be seen. The search was becoming futile. *Maybe he made one of the agents in the mall and left*, Eric thought to himself. *Maybe she saw one of us and tipped him off. But how? We have tracked her phone calls, texts, and social media accounts. If she had alerted him, we would have known it. How are they doing this?*

"Agent Carmichael, I think the package has arrived at the west entrance," a voice chimed in over the earpiece.

"Can you confirm it's David Zephyr?"

"Negative," the voice responded, "he's wearing a baseball cap and sunglasses. If we try to confirm the package, we'll tip him off."

"Stay behind him. Follow at a distance and don't let him double back to the entrance," David barked, walking across the second-floor platform to get a better look at the west entrance. "Units two and three, secure your entrances. If it's David Zephyr, we're not letting him out of the building."

Both teams affirmed the order as Eric moved into position next to the escalators and started to scan the crowd. He needed confirmation before turning the mall into an armed confrontation with the perpetrator. Not seeing anything in the west corridor, he barked another order, "Quyen, secure your primary objective. Do not let them evade you. If they try to meet up with David, take them into custody."

"Got it boss." Quyen closed the distance between his team and Savannah to make sure they could take her or David into custody.

"Teams five, six and seven, converge on my location at the center escalators on the second level," Eric ordered, trying to look down the corridor below to see if he could confirm David was in the building.

All agents affirmed the orders and moved to their locations. Arriving at the escalators, the six agents from teams five, six and seven helped Eric scan the mall for David. His heart beating against his chest, adrenalin pumping, Eric knew he was close to solving the case.

"When I see him, unit six, go to the south escalators and unit five, go to the north," Eric ordered, surveilling the mall. "Unit seven, you're with me. I want to keep him pinned down on the first floor, so he can't reach the parking decks on the upper levels."

"Yes, sir," they responded.

Waiting for what seemed like an eternity, Eric started to fidget. He knew he was close to apprehending David, but he wanted to be sure they didn't create a panic in the mall. "Team one, do you still have the package in your sights?"

"Yes, sir," the voice responded through the earpiece. "Suspect has meandered into stores and is now sitting on a bench outside of the coffee shop. He's maybe thirty to forty feet from your vantage point."

"What is he doing on the bench?" Eric inquired, wondering why he stopped moving deeper into the mall.

"Nothing, sir. Just sitting there."

"All teams move into position," Eric ordered, turning to the three teams with him. "Go secure those escalators. And you two, get ready to move on my order."

"Yes, sir," they said, moving to their positions.

"Unit two, secure the south exit," Eric ordered, "We are going to re-route him in your direction."

"Yes, sir," came the response

"Unit three, move toward the escalators, he must have made unit one and is pondering his options. I want him to see you blocking the east exit when he makes a run for it."

"On our way."

"Quyen, abort your primary objective. Converge on the center escalators," Eric ordered, making sure the agents were in place before engaging the suspect. "When he makes a run for it, I want him to think the only way he can get out of the mall is through the south exit."

"On our way."

"Unit one," Eric continued, moving to the top of the escalator. "Is he still on the bench?"

"Affirmative," the agent confirmed, "the package has not moved."

"Unit seven and I are going to make ourselves known and flush him out. Here we come." Eric, followed by the other two agents, stepped onto the escalator and descended to the first floor. "Show time."

Sitting on the bench and looking around, David saw Eric coming down the escalator. He had agents behind him blocking his exit, so he stood up and walked toward the escalator. Seeing agents moving up the hall from the east and the north corridors of the mall, David ran toward the escalator and when he entered the central artery connecting all of the mall's hallways, he headed toward the south exit.

"Stop!" Eric ran down the escalator, pulled out his service weapon, and chased David through the mall.

Joining in the chase, the rest of the agents followed Eric down the hallway. David was in a full sprint, bumping into people and pushing them out of the way. He saw the team of agents at the top of the south escalator and knew there must be a team of agents waiting for him at the south exit. They had him surrounded. He was pinned in, and he didn't have much time to think. He didn't know all of the rules The Network had, but he knew the most important one, avoid public displays at all costs.

Noticing a hallway to his right up ahead, David turned the corner, ran full speed into a shopper, and they both fell on the ground. Scampering to his feet, he said, "I am so sorry. So sorry."

Running a few more feet down the hallway, he heard Eric pull the corner and yell, "Freeze! Or I'll shoot…"

Stopping, David spun around and started backing up down the hall while Eric and his agents trained their weapons on him and inched their way toward him. Still backing up, David said, "It doesn't have to be this way, Special Agent."

"How so?" Eric trained his weapon on David and moved slowly toward him in case David pulled a weapon.

"Leave my family alone," David stated, backing up. "This doesn't involve them."

"Let's go to headquarters. We can discuss it," Eric countered, "Then they won't have to be involved in any of this."

"I can't do that," David laughed, walking backwards.

"Why not? Spare them this nightmare."

"You really have no idea what you've gotten yourself into, Agent. You really you should let this case go."

"Why's that?" Eric asked, inching toward him. "Enlighten me."

"Let it go, Agent." David backed up into the wall behind him. "If you know what's good for you, you'll let it go."

"Looks like you have nowhere to go," Eric stated, smiling and inching closer to the suspect. "Time's up."

"Not so much." David turned and ran down an adjoining hallway.

Eric and the rest of the agents ran after David and when they turned the corner, they saw him run into the bathroom. Running up to the door, the agents flanked both sides of the bathroom entrance. Opening the door just a little bit, Eric yelled, "Federal agents, come out with your hands up or we're coming in."

Hearing some rustling on the other side of the door, the agents prepared to pounce. The door opened a little, and a frightened voice said, "Don't shoot. It's just me and my son."

Opening the door, Eric ushered the man and his son to safety. "Who else is in there?"

"Just a man dressed in black," the man responded, shaking in fear. "He told us to leave before you came in shooting up the place."

"Is there anyone else in there?"

"No, sir," the man responded, trembling. "We were the only ones."

"Thank you," Eric said. "Get out of here."

Running down the hallway with his son, the man disappeared around the corner while Eric opened the door. "You're cornered, David. There's nowhere to run. Come out with your hands up."

Not hearing anything, Eric waited for a few seconds. Hoping David would surrender on his own, it became apparent they were going to have to go in and arrest him. Turning to his team, he ordered, "You'll follow me inside. Do not shoot unless absolutely necessary. I want him alive. Is that understood?"

"Yes, sir," they responded.

"Let's go get him." Eric and the agents stormed the bathroom with their guns drawn. Kicking open stall doors, David was nowhere to be found. Angry, Eric kicked the last stall door three times in frustration "How? We had him cornered. How did he escape?"

Chapter 14

Trudging along the city streets, David embraced the cool wind blowing against his face. He had already fought and sent back three demons. He was tired, and his was body beaten. The toll of battling beasts was settling into his psyche and every step reminded him of the battles he had fought.

The beauty of the moon sinking on the western horizon was in stark contrast to the barren, run down, abandoned part of Raleigh he now called home. Boarded up and burnt-out houses lined the street. Drug dealers and the homeless slithered in and out of the shadows for protection from a world that had forgotten them. Feeling a tinge of sadness at the sights around him, David arrived at the steps of his rundown home.

The hideaway was in the center of the block of vacant row houses. Once the epicenter of social gatherings and the city's elite, the house was old and run down. Time and neglect destroyed this part of the city. The history it claimed became nothing more than a footnote in the annals of the memory banks of those who cared to remember.

Limping up the front steps, David slipped inside the door. The house had been overrun by cobwebs and years of dust, old pictures hung on cracked, damaged walls. Walking up the stairwell, he dragged himself down the hallway into the makeshift living room and flopped face down on the couch. Sinking into the cushions, he welcomed their soft embrace.

"You were awesome tonight," Peter said, looking out from behind the computer screens lining a long dining room table.

"How do you know?"

"It's a very rare occurrence lately," Peter answered, returning to the computer screen, munching on a granola bar, "but on quiet nights when I am not pulled into a battle, I get to monitor all the action as it gets recorded."

"The computer system records us?"

"This system is one of the most technologically advanced pieces of equipment I have ever seen. It monitors everything on both sides of the veil, recording billions of pieces of data around the world simultaneously."

"Interesting."

"It's not the same rush as going out and battling demons, but it's a lot safer."

"I imagine it is." David rolled over and sat up on the couch. Watching Peter stare at the computer screens, curiosity got the best of him. "I know this is kind of rude to ask considering I've been here for a while, but how did you end up here?"

"What?" Peter asked, looking up from the computers.

"We haven't had a lot of time to just hang out. How does a kid your age, with his whole life in front of him, end up in the middle of this mess?"

"The question isn't why or how I ended up here? The real question is why wouldn't I want to be here?"

Laughing at Peter's response, David could feel his aching bones, reminding him of the miles that had grown farther and farther between him and his family. "All due respect, Peter, but I will never understand why somebody would choose this life of solitude and loneliness over actually living their lives."

"But I am living my life."

"Be serious, Peter."

"I am." Peter turned and faced David. "I had two choices. Listen to the spirit of God or continue to commit every computer crime imaginable. This was the most logical choice."

"Logical choice? How could this be the logical choice?"

Peter took a deep breath and folded his hands in front of him. "You have to understand where I come from. I was privileged. My parents have money, and I had every opportunity you could imagine."

"Sounds nice."

"Not really. My parents weren't involved in my life. They were too busy for me. So, I became infatuated with computers, mesmerized by how they worked, what they could accomplish, and what could be done with them. I was so enthralled with them; I built my own by the time I was seven years old."

"You built your own computer by the time you were seven?"

"Yes," Peter continued. "And by the time I was nine and a half, I hacked a government database, because it was the only challenging thing left to do."

"You hacked a government database?" David questioned in disbelief.

"If I gave you a list of the computer crimes I committed, it would make your head spin."

"That's crazy."

"It is."

"So, how did you end up here? You should be running a mega corporation, changing the world."

"That or jail," Peter laughed, running his hand through his hair. "Had my eighth or ninth nanny not taken me to church with her, who knows where I would be right now?"

"But it still doesn't explain how you ended up in The Network."

"I started going to church and reading my Bible. After I was baptized, I realized my life was a cry for help. The more I grew in my faith, the more ashamed I became of how I had been acting. Then, one night, Sebastian showed up…"

"I know what that's like," David interrupted, rolling his eyes.

"You cannot imagine how it was for me to meet Sebastian."

"He puts you between a rock and a hard place with the choices you have to make."

"Not for me." Peter stood up and walked over to a chair next to the couch. "Sebastian gave me a chance to change my life, an opportunity to do something extraordinary. And in my heart, I could hear a voice saying, 'Go. Do this.' and I did."

Staring wide-eyed at Peter, a lump developed in the back of David's throat. "You ever miss it?"

"Miss what?"

"Your family? Your youth? The years you have missed out on?"

"How can you miss something you never had?" Peter asked, looking at David with a confused look on his face.

"You had a family, Peter."

"My family was a revolving door of nannies."

"I am sure your parents love and miss you."

"My parents were off spending money on their lavish lifestyle; they never noticed or even bothered with me."

"What about your friends? There has to be someone in your life who misses you… Isn't there?"

"I wish there was."

"No one?"

"My friends are here. You are the first people who have cared about me."

"I'm really sorry, Peter. I wish I had known you back then, I could have helped. You deserved so much more," David lamented, feeling sorry for the kid.

"I have more. What we're doing here is so much bigger than ourselves."

"Yeah, right," David responded, rolling his eyes.

"I know it doesn't seem like it," Peter responded, holding out his arms and looking around the room. "Heck, the world doesn't know we exist. But every time we fend off a demon, we are fighting a battle for God that protects people from the enemy."

"We just chase the demons off; we don't help people see the light."

"People have free will. Our job is to protect the weak. It is their job to find the path."

"But how many do you think find the path?"

"Some do," Peter answered, pausing for a moment to reflect. "Probably more than we know, a lot less than we hope or pray for."

"How can you be so sure?"

"Faith," Peter responded, shrugging his shoulders. "I hope they pick up their Bibles, find salvation through God, and make a difference for somebody else."

"And when they don't?"

"We continue to pray for them."

David was awestruck listening to Peter. For the first time since joining The Network, he felt compassion for the kid. He saw Peter as a faithful warrior of God, fighting the good fight and believing he was doing his part to save the world.

Amazed at how Peter could dedicate his life to something bigger than himself, David said, "I am blown away by you, Peter. Where does someone so young find the conviction to believe this is his purpose in life?"

"We all have it, David. We're all here for the same reasons."

"I wish I could say the same."

"You will." Peter stood up and returned to monitoring the computer screens. "It's why you're here. I won't pretend to know how hard it was to leave your family behind, but I think deep down in your heart, you have these same convictions."

"Thanks, I'm glad one of us believes that," David muttered because he had nothing else to say.

David was ashamed of himself. He complained about his own sacrifice without realizing everyone in The Network had to make similar sacrifices. They all had followed different paths to arrive at this point in their lives, but in the end, their faith in God took precedence. Laying down their lives and giving up everything, they chose to make a difference in the world.

Standing up and walking into the kitchen, Peter grabbed two ice cold colas from the refrigerator. Popping the tops off the bottles and walking back into the living room, Peter handed David one of the sodas, "You deserve one of these after the night you've had."

"Thanks, Peter."

"A toast." Peter raised his soda bottle. "Thanks be to God who gives us everything we need. Amen."

"Amen." David tapped his bottle of cola against Peter's and took a long swig of the caramel flavored beverage. Laying back down on the couch and closing his eyes, David held the bottle next to his hip.

Twenty minutes later, Michael and Zoe returned from an epic night of battles. Exuberant, they sat down on one of the other couches, laughing and joking about their exploits.

"Can you be a little quieter?" David interjected. "People are trying to sleep over here."

"What's wrong, old man?" Zoe teased, mocking him. "Another tough night at the mill?"

"Every night seems to be a tough night lately," David responded, lifting his head off the couch, toasting both of them with a tip of his soda bottle, and taking a sip.

"We're teasing, David," Michael said.

"I know, but I'm still tired," David responded, placing his head on the cushion and closing his eyes.

"You can be such a jerk sometimes." Michael was frustrated with David's attitude. "Learn to lighten up."

"Come again?" David challenged, lifting his head and staring at Michael.

"You're letting everything get you down lately," Zoe interjected with a calm resolve. "Maybe if you looked at things with a new perspective, it might not bring you down."

"Okay. Enlighten me," David encouraged, sitting up and feeling the anger welling up inside of him. "How should I be looking at things, Zoe?"

"Man," Michael interjected, "you're a real buzz kill."

"Really?" David questioned. "Because things are so awesome?"

"You're missing the point."

"What point?" David pressed.

"Dude," Michael answered, smiling, "relax. We get to protect people from the things that scare the living daylights out of them. We get to kick their gnarly, ugly looking butts all the way back to Hell. How cool is that? This gig rocks.'"

"Maybe, Michael, I am old enough to see the world from a different perspective."

"You're not old," Zoe said, chuckling at the insinuation. "You just like to think you're old; it makes you feel better about yourself."

"How does thinking I am old make me feel better about myself?"

"I don't know," Zoe agreed, standing up and walking over to the windows "I am still trying to figure that out. But every night, you come back tired while the rest of us come back rejuvenated for doing something amazing with our lives."

"Because I'm battered and bruised," David stated, looking at her. "I'm worn out."

"So are we." Zoe threw her arms up in exasperation and faced David. "But take a moment and thank God you're still alive and be done with it. Geesh."

"Will you two stop picking on David?" Peter interjected, looking up from the computer screens.

"Why?" Zoe inquired. "It's fun."

"Whatever," Peter uttered in disdain. Changing topics, he continued, "Michael, we need you to make another grocery run tomorrow."

"Again?"

"You keep buying food for four people, there's five of us now," Peter responded.

"How come Michael is the only one who gets to go shopping?" David challenged, looking at Peter for an answer.

"Because I am the only one who doesn't have someone looking for him," Michael admitted.

"I don't follow," David said, looking perplexed.

"Well," Zoe interjected, "Peter joined The Network five years ago. He has a rich father who is looking for him. How many times has your face been on the back of a milk box, Petey?"

"I lost count," Peter chuckled.

"They still put faces of kids on the back of milk boxes?" David questioned.

"When your dad has as much money as mine does, your face ends up on everything."

"Must be rough to have someone care so much," David added with sarcasm.

"Care? Ha," Peter snickered. "No, not my dad. For him, it's all about appearances. Having a child run away in his social realm is bad for his status among his peers."

"I see," David acknowledged, "but it doesn't explain why Zoe and Sebastian don't go shopping?"

"Vanity," said Peter.

"Vanity?"

"Yes," Zoe added, looking up with a sheepish smiled. "When you slip back through the veil, the Hell Fire Device can only keep our desired appearance for a certain amount of time. Sadly, when it wears off, you see yourself at the chronological age you truly are."

"Plus," Peter added, "it freaks people out when you rapidly age in front of them."

"There's that too," Zoe laughed, smiling with a slight head bob and a wink. "So that's why I don't spend a lot of time on the other side of the veil."

"Sorry, I didn't know," David conceded.

"No apologies necessary. There is so much about this life you still need to learn." Zoe stood up and left the room.

"I hope I didn't upset her," David stated after she left.

"She's not upset," Michael smirked. "She's busting your chops."

"Yeah," Peter added, "vanity is her excuse. Zoe doesn't like to slip back through the veil because most of the people she knew have either passed or are living a meager existence. It's a different world than the one she grew up in. It makes her nostalgic for the good old days."

"I can relate to that," David agreed.

"I bet you can, old man," Michael joked.

Bursting into the room, Sebastian yelled, "What are you doing to me, David? Are you trying to make our lives difficult?"

"Whoa, wait a minute," Michael interjected, while David jumped up and stared down Sebastian. "What's going on Sebastian?"

"Do you want to tell them, David?" Sebastian admonished.

"I don't know what you're talking about, Sebastian."

"No?" Sebastian was irate as Zoe stepped back into the room to see what was going on. "Are you going to stand there and tell me you haven't been trying to communicate with the agent investigating your disappearance?"

"He had no right," David shot back.

"To do his job?" Sebastian challenged, raising his hands in front of him.

"My family is off limits," David yelled, pointing a finger at Sebastian.

"He's doing his job, David," Sebastian retorted, shrugging his shoulders. "What did you expect? You bring demons back to federal banks and put your face on video. How could you think he wouldn't harass her?"

"Hubris, David," Michael said, shaking his head. "Hubris."

"And what about the stunt at the mall? You didn't think I'd find about your little field trip?" Sebastian asked, annoyed with the conversation. "You can't do that, David. You put us all in danger."

"I'll do whatever it takes when it comes to my family," David bellowed, throwing his hands up in frustration. "That is non-negotiable."

"David, we are trying to help you make the transition…" Sebastian added.

"Just stop, Sebastian," David interjected, cutting him off.

"We told you not to take demons to places with video cameras," Sebastian added. "This is what happens when we don't follow the rules."

"Rules?" David guffawed. "All you told me was my family was in danger. You told me I had to protect them."

"All true," Sebastian concurred.

"I spend most of my time fighting monsters in dreams of other people I don't even know. How is that helping my family?"

"You're doing your part," Sebastian assured him.

"My part. Funny… And if that wasn't funny enough, we don't even get to fight with real weapons. Guns? No. … Swords? No. … Nothing. Nada. Zip. We get to hit them with the Hell Fire Device." David slammed the circular device down on the table. "We are told to take them back to a safe place, wear them down, and send them back."

"That's right, David, a safe place," Michael concurred.

"Well, the safest place I can think of is a bank," David shouted, staring down Sebastian.

"Think of another place then," Sebastian suggested.

"In the heat of battle when I am trying not to die, I don't really have a lot of time to stop and think of another place."

"This is why we don't bring adults into The Network, Sebastian," Peter inserted into the conversation.

"Really, Peter, that's all you have to say for yourself?" David challenged.

"It's not what I meant," Peter backtracked.

"Well, I am sorry I messed up your plans," David conceded, looking at Peter. "The last I checked, running around playing Dungeons and Dragons wasn't part of my plan either, but voila, I'm here."

"What he means by that," interjected Zoe, trying to deescalate the situation.

"I know what he meant," David responded.

"Do you?" Zoe asked.

"What's that supposed to mean, Zoe?" David questioned, frustrated with the group.

"We tiptoe around you, so we don't upset you," Zoe advised David. "We get it. We didn't have any relationships or strong bonds to keep us grounded on the other side. It was easy for us. You have a family which makes it hard for you to make a clean break from the world."

"And those relationships are dangerous," Peter interposed. "If you're not careful, those relationships are going to get you killed."

"Remember what we said to you on the very first night, David," added Sebastian, calming himself down. "If they kill you on this side of the veil, you die for real."

Staring across the room at Sebastian, David broke the gaze as it dawned on him. The only four people who he could have regular contact with were all standing in the room. He was in the world, but he was no longer a part of the world. It was one thing to want to save his family from what was threatening them, but he was going to need The Network in order to protect them. He was going to have to begin trusting them, even if that trust was difficult to come by.

"You're right. I have to be more cognizant of my choices," David conceded. "It's just hard not to protect my wife and kids."

"We know it's not easy for you," Zoe declared. "We have your back. Trust us."

"I do," David responded, pausing before heading for the door.

"Where are you going?" Sebastian asked, not done with the conversation.

"I need some time to think," David replied, walking out of the room, down the stairs and out the front door.

Standing on the front step, David looked around the city and shrugged at the level of cluelessness the rest of the world lived in. *Ignorance is bliss* he thought to himself, recalling the events of the night and the three Zivlians he defeated.

David walked along the city streets and everywhere he looked, he saw people without a care in the world, reveling in the promise of a new day. Some were followed by bright white spiritual entities protecting them, while others were clouded in the dark aura of the evil entities who had come to steal them away for the Prince of Darkness.

David had seen so much since he passed through the veil. Watching the free will of mankind give the dark aura a foothold in the world bothered him. *Deception, distraction, science and mysticism are the weapons of choice for the Enemy,* he thought to himself, strolling through the city streets, watching people passing him by, never knowing he was there. *But as long as the world has God, Jesus, His angels and to a much smaller degree, the members of The Network to fight the battle, any attempts to conquer and destroy this world with evil would be futile.*

Chapter 15

Five a.m. was early for a trip to the grocery store, but Savannah was less likely to see neighbors and friends. Hearing the whispers and rumors about how David had run off with another woman, she was tired of the phony people she encountered. She was tired of being subjected to their pity and judgment.

"Mom," Jordan asked upon entering the store, "can I go look at the magazines?"

"Yes, but stay there. I will check on you in a few minutes," she responded, grabbing a shopping cart and holding Carissa's hand.

Jordan perused the magazine rack looking for the latest issues of sports publications. Finding one, he took it off the shelf and started thumbing through the pages. Leaning against the shelves, he was enraptured with the latest exploits of his favorite athletes.

Walking down the aisle and pulling a magazine off the shelf, Eric started reading. "Any good articles this month?"

Startled, Jordan looked up from the page. "Nah, not really. They don't have comic books here, so I make do"

"I hear you, Jordan," Eric said, smiling at him. "I am a comics book guy myself."

"How do you know my name?" Jordan was nervous while looking around for an escape route like David had taught him.

Pulling out his badge and showing it to Jordan, Eric introduced himself, "My name is Special Agent Carmichael, Jordan. I am with the FBI. I am working with the local police to find your father."

Staring at the badge, Jordan inquired, "What are you doing here? Shouldn't you be out looking for my dad?"

"You're a smart kid, Jordan," Eric responded, putting his credentials away. "I am here because I was hoping you could help me."

"Me?" Jordan stared at Eric with an awkward expression. "How can I help?"

"You'd be amazed at the number of ways you could help."

Jordan shrugged his shoulders. "Well, if you think I can help."

"You see, Jordan, your dad has been gone for a long time." Eric continued thumbing through the magazine while engaging Jordan in conversation. "Sometimes, as investigators, we have to go back to the beginning of the case and turn over every stone to find a clue."

"Find anything?"

"I did." Eric stopped reading, rolled up the magazine and leaned against the shelves. "As I read the notes, I noticed no one from the police spoke to you about his disappearance."

"They asked me a couple of questions, but not about anything important."

"I was thinking exactly the same thing."

"You were?"

"I was," Eric agreed, pointing the rolled-up periodical at Jordan. "So, I figured I would ask you those important questions. Do you mind answering some questions for me?"

"I could try, sir, but I don't know if anything I have to say would be of any help."

"You let me be the judge of that, okay, Jordan?"

"Yes, sir."

"Good boy," Eric smiled, patting Jordan on the shoulder. "Now, Jordan, your dad's been gone a long time and my team is extremely baffled. You see, we turn a missing person's life inside out and you know what we have discovered about your dad?"

"What?"

"Nothing."

"Oh," Jordan replied, feeling deflated.

"Your dad hasn't used a credit card, an ATM machine, his cell phone, or his email. All of those things are part of what we call a digital footprint, and your dad doesn't have one."

"Is that bad?"

"In this day and age, son, it is impossible for a person to just up and disappear." Eric paused for a moment to study the boy's reaction and to collect his thoughts. "Are you following me, Jordan?"

"My sister thinks my dad is dead."

"Your dad is very alive, Jordan. I have seen pictures of him."

"You have?" Jordan probed, hope welling up inside him.

"I have."

"Wait 'til I tell Carissa."

"And because I know he is alive," Eric continued, knowing he was crossing many ethical lines by continuing his line of questioning, "I am trying to bring your father home, but for me to be able to do that, I really need you to be honest with me, okay?"

"Yes, sir."

Eric collected his thoughts. "Jordan, how often does your mom or grandfather see your dad?"

"What?" Jordan questioned, tilting his head and staring at Eric.

"How often does your mom or your grandfather see your father?"

"They haven't seen my dad."

"How do you know?"

"I just know."

"How?" Eric pressed, raising his voice a little.

"Because they couldn't keep that kind of a secret from me."

"Did they tell you about the pictures of your dad I showed them a while ago?"

Jordan was confused. "You showed them pictures of my dad?"

"I did," Eric affirmed, watching Jordan's reactions. "And if they didn't tell you about the pictures I showed them, how can you be so sure they haven't seen him?"

"You're lying."

"Am I lying?" Eric pulled out a picture of David and handed it to Jordan. "This is a picture taken last month."

"And my mom saw this picture?" Jordan demanded, growing visibly upset.

"That's enough, Special Agent Carmichael," Savannah yelled, standing at the end of the aisle with Carissa in disbelief.

"Mom?" Jordan questioned, looking at her with the picture of David in his hand, tears welling up in his eyes.

"Mrs. Zephyr," Eric responded, whirling around to face Savannah. "I'm only trying to find your husband. We should be working together, not against each other."

"You should've called me instead of ambushing my son in the middle of the grocery store." Savannah stormed over to stand between Jordan and Eric. "You should be ashamed of yourself."

"Ma'am," Eric countered, smiling at her, holding his hands wide, and looking around. "I'm in a public place having a chat with a young man reading magazines. I haven't violated any laws."

"Don't try to excuse yourself, Special Agent. There is nothing you can say to excuse your behavior."

"Mom?" Jordan questioned, continuing to stare at the photograph.

"I will explain this later, Jordan." Savannah took his hand in hers. "Come on, we're going home."

"Mrs. Zephyr, let's hash this out."

Rushing past Eric and heading for the front door, Savannah stopped and said, "You, sir, are a horrible person. If you have something to say to me, come say it to me. Don't ambush my kids. Do you have any idea what they have been through? Do you?"

"No, ma'am, I don't," Eric conceded, taking a couple of steps toward her.

"That's right, you don't," Savannah yelled, staring him down and shaking her hand at him. "Don't come near my kids again, Special Agent Carmichael, or I will have your job."

"Mrs. Zephyr…"

"Stop. Not another word," Savannah yelled, pointing her finger at Eric. "What just happened here is wrong. Just plain wrong. May God have mercy on your soul."

Grabbing her children's hands and heading toward the front door of the store, Eric yelled after her, "Mrs. Zephyr, I am going to find your husband with or without your help. And when I do, you all have a lot of explaining to do."

Chapter 16

Sitting on a park bench, watching the sun rise, David rehashed the argument he had with Sebastian. Thinking about the struggles Peter faced, he thought about his own kids and the struggles they must be facing. Reminiscing about his family, happy memories flooded his thoughts and tugged at his heart. He was homesick.

The world had changed for David over the past few hours. Invisible to those passing him by him in the park, he watched them going about their day without a care in the world. Some of the people were being protected by angels, while many others were clouded by the dark entities using their free will against them.

"David?" Zoe questioned, approaching the bench from behind.

"Yes," David responded, seeing Zoe approaching him. "What are you doing here?"

"Do you mind if I join you?"

"Not at all," David answered, making room on the bench. "How did you find me?"

"By accident," Zoe replied, chuckling as she sat next to him. "I started looking for you about an hour after you left the house."

Looking at her with a perplexed look on his face, David asked, "So how is this by accident?"

"I had given up. I was going back to get some sleep. You just happen to be in the park I was walking through to get back to the house."

"Why didn't you ask Peter? I am sure he could have found me."

"It's a little harder to trace you when you leave your Hell Fire device behind." Zoe held out the circular device for David.

Taking it from Zoe, David attached it to his belt. "Thank you."

"So, what are you doing out here?"

"I was walking around the city, trying to blow off steam. Part of me wanted to pass through the veil, go home, and pretend none of this had happened."

"But?" Zoe inquired with a questioning expression.

"Well, first of all, I can't cross the veil without this," David smirked, tapping the Hell Fire device attached to his belt.

Laughing, Zoe agreed, "True."

"But when I calmed down, I realized Sebastian was right. You all are."

"It's not about being right, David."

"I've been behaving poorly. So, I came to the park to pray."

"How did that work out?"

"I had a nice, good long talk with God this morning."

"Sometimes, it's all we can do."

"After that, I just sat here watching people pass by me, blindly starting their day," he pronounced, pointing at them. "I wanted to run up and tell them about the spiritual war going on. I wanted to wake them up to the reality that escapes them daily."

"Why didn't you?"

"For starters, I am on the wrong side of the veil." David laughed and paused to collect his thoughts. "But even if I wasn't, they would think I was crazy."

"Not all of them."

"Funny," David smirked, shaking his head while looking down.

"But you're right, a lot of them would think you're crazy. It's the price we pay for free will."

"It's weird to me."

"What is?"

"Savannah and I gave ourselves to Christ when we were young. We've always been around the church. It's second nature to us."

"Not everyone knows God, or the church, or even about the Word. They have to find faith somewhere along their own personal journey."

"But that's the thing," David declared, looking at Zoe. "I see the people who are asleep to the truth, I see the struggles they go through, and I just want to help them."

"And you're doing that," Zoe empathized, placing a hand on his shoulder. "You are helping."

"It doesn't feel like it."

"The Network is about doing our part. It seems crazy at times and sometimes, it doesn't make sense, but God has a plan. We fight against the forces of evil, that's our plan."

"How did we get here?"

"That's simple. We made the sacrifice and walked through the veil."

"No, Zoe, how did this happen?" David sat back and stared at the people walking in the park. "Who discovered all of this? Who was the first to walk behind the veil? How did they know it existed?"

"You really want to know?" Zoe queried, giving David an opportunity to decline.

"After all I've been through, I think I'm entitled to know."

"It started back in the sixties," Zoe started explaining. "There was a young man hired to work on a top-secret government project. They were developing the ARPANET systems…"

"The what?" David interrupted, wondering what she was talking about.

"The ARPANET Systems, in a nutshell, were the earliest developments in computer technology linking computers together. Simply put, it's what was developed before the widespread use of the internet."

"Oh, I didn't know that."

"But they were also experimenting with mind control, out of body experiences, and invisibility. Clandestine technologies," Zoe continued. "One night, this young scientist was working in the lab. It was late and he stumbled upon a discovery he believed would change the world. In his zealous approach, he tested the discovery on himself instead of waiting until morning and using the military personnel who had volunteered. And lo and behold, he slid behind the veil.

"What he saw over the next few hours horrified him. When he crossed back into the world, he destroyed the device and the video footage he had taken, and the next morning, he resigned his commission with the government. He spent the next two years hiding out in a monastery studying the Bible.

"A short time later, he started a successful technology company. He also created a secret project called 'The Network' in order to combat Satan and the forces of evil. He funnels millions of dollars into The Network annually."

"Wow!" David exclaimed, wondering aloud, "I wonder what he saw."

"He saw what we see, David. Angels, demons, the spiritual battle; all of it."

"What did he create back in the lab?"

"The original Hell Fire device," Zoe stated, taking the circular device from her hip and holding it in her hand. "It didn't do half of what it does now, but it was the catalyst for his crusade against the Enemy."

Staring at the device Zoe held in her hand, David questioned, "Is that how we all ended up here?"

"Yup."

"Progress," David expressed, shaking his head in disgust.

"You could call it that." Zoe put the device back on her belt.

David was quiet. Had he not crossed through the veil, he might find it hard to accept the level of spiritual warfare in the world. "Can I ask you a personal question?"

"Shoot."

"When we first met in my house, you told me I was assigned to you as a baby. How is that possible, Zoe? You're so young."

"Sebastian hasn't told you why we broke the rules and pulled you into The Network?"

"Zoe, to be honest, I'm not sure I know all of the rules yet. So, I'm not sure which ones have been broken and which ones haven't."

"Yeah, you probably don't," Zoe laughed, putting her hands on her knees and drawing a deep breath. "Sebastian should really explain this."

"Zoe," David pleaded, placing his hand on hers, "please, I need to know."

"Okay," Zoe agreed, taking another deep breath. "We don't usually bring people older than twenty into The Network. They have too many connections to the world. It makes the transition difficult."

"You don't have to tell me twice."

"Two years before you were born, I was brought into The Network. That year was crazy. We were fighting multiple attacks every night."

"Kind of like it is now?"

"Exactly like it is now, David," Zoe exclaimed, agreeing with him. "When I was recruited, it was a very turbulent time. We actually thwarted a huge event."

"Really?" David probed, intrigued at the revelation. "How so?"

"Someone tried to open the veil permanently so evil entities could cross into the world."

"Who?" David was shocked. "How?"

"A demonic cult. They believed they could circumvent the apocalypse and change the world order. Luckily, with God's help, we stopped it from happening."

"I don't follow," David confessed, staring at her, confused. "What does that have to do with me?"

"You are one of the only kids we have ever known to have these nightmares occur as a newborn," Zoe admitted, pausing, looking away, and settling her emotions. "Then your nightmares stopped. You were given up for adoption and never had another nightmare. I lost track of you."

"But what about the technology?"

"Wasn't a thousandth of the ability we have now. Those dreams were how we tracked you."

"You said 'one of,' there were others?"

"Yes," Zoe conceded, nervous about the line of questioning, "one other."

"Who?"

Zoe looked into David's eyes. "Carissa."

"What?"

"I convinced Sebastian to bring you into The Network because I think it is happening again," Zoe admitted, amping up her nerves. "I can't prove it, David, but I think someone is trying to unleash the forces of evil, and I believe your daughter is at the center of it all."

Chapter 17

Frustrated with the progress of the investigation, Eric vowed to turn over every stone. He was going to follow every single shred of evidence, regardless of where it led him. After reading thousands of documents, inspecting photos, watching surveillance videos, conducting countless interviews, almost apprehending David in the mall, and assigning teams of agents to follow Savannah, Eric went back to the basics. He decided to visit each bank David had broken into to see if he could uncover new evidence that might help him catch David Zephyr.

Driving from bank to bank to investigate was wearing out Eric's patience. He traveled to the banks in the order David had broken into them. Having traveled to Tennessee, Kentucky, Ohio, Pennsylvania, and Virginia, Eric was glad he had company for the long trip. Eric had taken Agent Quyen on the road with him. Not only did Agent Quyen help with the investigation, but his presence on the trip also helped Eric pass the time on the road between cities.

Standing inside the Wilmington Federal Bank after having returned to North Carolina, Eric took out his notebook. Looking around the lobby of the bank, Eric consulted his detailed notes of the surveillance tapes. Moving throughout the bank, notebook in hand, Eric added additional notes and crossed out previous observations or thoughts as he investigated. Taking a lot of pictures with his digital camera, he cross referenced his observations with notes from the previous banks he had visited.

"There it is," Eric exclaimed, pointing and taking several pictures.

"What?" Quyen inquired, puzzled.

"It's subtle, but it's there." Eric walked over to the wall and pointed at something. "Look there and tell me what you see."

Inspecting the wall, Quyen didn't find anything. Looking at the floor and feeling dumb, he turned and faced Eric. "I don't see anything."

"This," Eric indicated, running his fingers across the wall, enthusiasm welling up inside of him at the discovery. "Do you see that?"

"The chipped paint, sir?"

"Yes."

"I don't follow. It's just chipped paint."

"It looks like chipped paint but look closer. Look," Eric encouraged, pointing at the wall.

Kneeling down and inspecting the wall, Quyen examined the chipped paint from every angle. He didn't see anything and was reluctant to share his observations knowing that Eric wasn't going to like his answer. "It looks like someone scratched the wall when they moved a desk or filing cabinet."

"Come here and look…" Eric walked over to one of the counters in the lobby while Quyen followed behind. Eric showed Quyen the display screen on his digital camera and enlarged the photo. "Now what do you see?"

Examining the photograph, Quyen mumbled, "It still looks like a scratch."

"It is," Eric celebrated, bubbling over with excitement. "Look at the definition of the scratch, look at the curvature of the indentation and look at the depth."

Leaning over and inspecting the mark in the photograph, Quyen was dumbfounded. "I still don't know what I am looking at, sir."

"This wasn't caused by a desk or a bookshelf."

"It wasn't?"

"No," Eric theorized, staring at the picture. "A desk would have made a blunt impact. This has definition and texture, like something was bracing itself against the wall and pushing off."

"What caused the marks?"

"I don't know, but there is another one over here." Eric walked across the lobby and showed Agent Quyen a second set of scratches. "There is a set of scratches on the tile here… and here."

"What?" Quyen was confused as to how the tile floor was scratched. "How, sir?"

"I don't know," Eric mused, walking across the lobby with Quyen close behind. "Still think it's a desk or a filing cabinet?"

"I don't know. Maybe."

"Then look here."

"There are more?"

"There is another set of marks on the wall here." Eric stopped, pointing at the wall and the floor, "And there on the floor."

"This is crazy, sir. Have you seen anything like this before?"

"I have pictures of similar markings on the walls and floors of every bank we have visited. There's no way it's a coincidence."

"Are you saying…?"

"I am," Eric confided, staring at the young investigator. "Someone was in the banks with David Zephyr."

"Or something, sir," Quyen pondered, "those marks don't look human."

"Footwear." Eric dismissed the suggestion of some kind of entity or animal. There would be no logical explanation to support the claim. "Technology has changed. Could be a spiked shoe of some sort."

"So, what does this all mean, sir?"

"We now know someone else was in the banks with David Zephyr."

"We don't have video proof to corroborate that, sir."

"If you look closely at the surveillance tapes, really closely, I think we do."

"Let's assume for a minute you're right," Quyen stated, doubting the veracity of Eric's claim. "Then who is it?"

"I don't know." Eric was stumped. He had new information supporting his theory, but he didn't have any actual proof to support his supposition. Like everything else in this investigation, the evidence didn't seem to add up to a solid conclusion. "I don't know."

Chapter 18

The Network banded together better than they ever had. David found a strengthened respect for the members of the team. He spent more time exploring his faith with Zoe, while learning about the technology from Peter. He had to trust and believe in them if he was going to survive. More importantly, he had to give himself over to being more open to what they were trying to achieve if he wanted to protect his family.

"The greatest play I have ever seen? Huh?" Peter thought about the question for a moment. He wasn't the most sports-oriented member of the Network, but he had watched a few games. "Okay, I got it. The championship game in 2012 when Etteman hit D'Nell Johnson for the winning touchdown. His toes barely touched the ground on the dive."

"Come on man," Michael laughed, throwing his hands toward Peter in disagreement. "Johnson was out of bounds."

"Replay said he was in." Peter shot back.

"Ugh. Replay." Michael rolled his eyes.

"Okay, tough guy," Zoe interjected. "What's the best play you have ever seen, Michael?"

"Easy," Michael exclaimed, "The B-1 Bomber himself, Bobby Baxter, in his first professional game after being the number one pick in the draft. He threw for six touchdowns in his first game but the first one was a thing of beauty…"

"Come on, Michael, really?" Zoe interrupted, laughing at him. "Are you really going with B-1 Bomber?"

"It was a thing of beauty," Michael continued, "he dropped back, avoided three sacks, was running for his life, and on a dead run, threaded the needle between two defenders, forty-five yards downfield for a sideline touchdown."

"Still not the greatest play ever," Zoe laughed.

"Then what is, Zoe?" Michael stared at her while she taunted him from across the room.

"The Immaculate Reception, baby. Boom! Drop the mic." Zoe celebrated by mimicking a mic drop and raising her hands above her head to indicate a touchdown while doing a little endzone dance.

"You're so old, Zoe," Peter laughed, mocking her dance moves.

"What about you, David?" Michael asked, "What's the greatest play you've ever seen?"

David smiled. "I don't know if it's the greatest play in history, but it is to me."

"Oh, this is going to be good," Zoe quipped, sitting on the couch. "What is it?"

"I took Savannah to her first college football game ever in 1996. I am a huge fan of Chapel Hill University, and we were playing Tigerville on opening weekend. Brockman was knocked out of the game, Spiers threw more interceptions than completions, and by halftime, we were losing big."

"Is there a play in here somewhere?" Peter asked.

"I am setting the stage, Peter. You see, Savannah wasn't a huge fan of football, and the first half wasn't helping my cause. CHU was getting destroyed."

"So, what happened?"

"Veeder McLean happened," David smiled, recalling the events of the day. "Savannah wanted to leave, but I convinced her to stay, and I am so glad I did."

"Why?" Zoe inquired, rolling her eyes and looking around at the other guys in the room. "Your team was getting blown out."

"The coaches put McLean, a freshman, in the game to start the second half and he led the Cobras to an unforeseen comeback. With six seconds left, it was fourth and goal on the four yard line. The ball was snapped, everyone was covered and as Mclean rolled right the middle linebacker hit him hard and knocked him sideways. Looking like the game was over, he braced his body with his left hand, he was parallel to the turf when he fired an under his body pass into the corner of the endzone just as more defenders buried him in the turf."

"What happened?" Peter asked, on the edge of his seat.

"War Memorial Stadium erupted in pandemonium," David recalled, smiling as he told the rest of his story. "He had somehow seen a receiver break free and when the ball was caught for a touchdown, the place went crazy. Savannah jumped into my arms to celebrate and became a lifelong football fan right there in that stadium."

"Wow," Michael exclaimed, "I never heard about it."

"The video is on the internet. It is one of the most amazing games I have ever seen and what made it more special is I was there with Savannah. I don't know if I watched her or the game more in the second half. It is a day I'll never forget."

"Still not the greatest play ever," Zoe interjected. "Great personal story, but not the best football play of all time."

Walking into the room, passing by the couch, and tapping David on the shoulder, Sebastian said, "Come on. Let's go. We've work to do."

"Where are we going?"

"We have a mission to run."

Looking out the window at the sun shining into the room, David was baffled. All his battles had taken place at night. "Since when do demons attack during the day?"

"You are on a need-to-know basis." Sebastian was frustrated with game of twenty questions. "And right now, all you need to know is we have a couple of things to get done."

"Like?" David stood up and opened his hands wide.

"You'll find out when we get there. We're leaving in a few minutes."

Sebastian walked out of the room. David was frustrated. "What's up with him?"

"I have no idea," Zoe responded, sitting back on the couch. "He's been agitated all morning."

"Is it possible the Zivlians have started attacking during the day?"

"It's rare," Michael replied, picking up his Bible and moving to the rocking chair. "They could attack during the day, but it draws too much attention from angels"

"Angels?"

"Yes," Michael chuckled, looking up from his Bible. "And for that reason alone, we wouldn't be involved either."

"Then what is Sebastian up to?"

"I have no idea," Michael answered, shaking his head. "We all seem to be on a need-to-know basis right now."

Walking back into the room, Sebastian asked, "Ready to go?"

"Yeah, I guess."

"Good. Let's get out of here."

Following Sebastian down the long, cobweb filled hallway, David was nervous as they made their way to the top of the steps. They sprinted down the stairs to the front door. David was skipping two steps at a time just to keep up with Sebastian.

Walking out the front door and stopping on the front stoop, Sebastian took a deep breath, closed his eyes for a second, and remembered what it was like to embrace the promise of a new day. Exhaling, Sebastian opened his eyes, sprinted down the front steps and up the street.

David was winded, but did his best to keep pace with Sebastian. He could feel the twenty-year difference between him and his in-shape younger counterpart. David caught up when Sebastian slowed down to a brisk walk. "So where are we going?"

"Trust me, David. You're better off not knowing."

David had come to trust Sebastian with his life. It bothered him when he didn't know the plan, but he didn't question Sebastian any further. Sebastian was methodical. There was a reason for every action, every mission, and every decision.

Turning and walking up the front steps of an abandoned warehouse, Sebastian opened the door, "After you, David."

Peering through the open door, David shrugged his shoulders and walked past Sebastian. It was dark and David could barely see. Sebastian grabbed David's elbow, activated the Hellfire Device and, in an instant, David and Sebastian were standing in the entryway of a building filled with blinding sunlight.

"I know this place." David squinted his eyes and looked around the familiar hallway.

"I hope so," Sebastian quipped, walking down the hall.

"This is Jordan's school. What are we doing here? Is Jordan in danger?"

"Patience, David. Patience."

Following Sebastian down the hallway, David was nervous. They walked with a sense of purpose as Sebastian made his way through the corridors. He had memorized every inch of the blueprints and knew exactly where he was taking David.

David's heart became heavy as they walked further into the school because he feared Jordan might be in imminent danger. Sebastian led David into the cafeteria which was full of loud middle school students.

"What are we doing here?"

Stopping and pointing at Jordan, he ordered, "Talk to Jordan. You're not a criminal. He needs to hear it from you."

"Why didn't you tell me we were coming here?"

"Because you wouldn't have come."

"You're right, I wouldn't have," David snapped, frustration evident in his words.

"I understand your frustration, David, but I have asked you to sacrifice a lot to join The Network," Sebastian countered in a moment of compassion. "I can't have your son thinking you're a criminal. It's not fair to either of you."

"And you think my showing up is going to change that?"

"He's confused, David. He needs a few moments with his dad."

"I don't even know what to say to him."

"You're his father, David, tell him you love him," Sebastian said, putting his right hand on David's shoulder. "Tell him as much of the truth as you can think he can handle. Just seeing you for a few minutes will change everything for him… and you."

"I can't just walk over, sit down across the table from him and say, 'Hey, I'm here.'"

"You're wrong," Sebastian said, smiling. "You can just walk over and talk to your son."

"What are you talking about?"

"Remember the first night you and I spoke?"

"Yeah, you came to me in my dream. What does that have to do with anything?"

"Normally, David, we are unable to speak with adults. You were an exception to the rule," Sebastian admitted, looking over at Jordan and pointing, "but you can speak with kids. Their minds are open to the boundless possibilities in the world. It's why they believe in fairy tales and magic. To make a long story short, go talk to your son."

"Are you telling me I could've seen and spent time with my kids over the past year? I could've explained everything that has been happening?"

"You could have, David, but the second you walk over there and talk to Jordan, you put his life in more danger than it already is."

"How does my talking to my son put his life in danger?"

"I don't have time to get into all of it right now, David," Sebastian answered, looking at his watch and at the door with a heightened sense of uneasiness. "Go talk to your son. He needs you."

"How do I appear to him?"

"Your son is already asleep. He's been falling asleep every day at lunch." Sebastian tapped on the circular device attached to his hip. "Dream walk. When you are ready to talk to him, activate the device. With your other hand, touch his arm or shoulder like I did when we were in the warehouse a few minutes ago."

"That's it?"

"It really is that simple, David."

Collecting his thoughts, David walked across the cafeteria toward Jordan. Jordan was sitting alone, his chin was resting on the palm of his right hand, his right arm braced against the table, propping his head up while he slept. Sitting down across from Jordan, David stared into his son's face. He missed talking to Jordan, playing football in the backyard, and playing pranks on Savannah.

Reaching across the table, David touched Jordan on the arm. As Jordan opened his eyes and looked at David, David smiled at him. "Hey kiddo, what's up?"

"Dad!" Jordan yelled, jumping up out of his seat, running around the table, and throwing his arms around his dad. David held his son in a strong embrace. It was the first time in almost a year he had been able to hug Jordan and he never wanted to let go.

"Where have you been, Dad?" Jordan pulled away from David's hug and stared at him.

"You wouldn't believe me if I told you."

"I met a man from the FBI, Dad. He told me you're a bank robber."

"I've never stolen anything in my life, Jordan. I'm not a thief."

"He had pictures of you, Dad."

"Jordan, I'm going to tell you something you're not going to believe. Somehow you are going to have to find it in your heart to trust me."

"I want to trust you, Dad. I really do, but you left us. Why would you do that?"

Swallowing hard against the lump developing in his throat, David fought back the tears and mustered up the strength for a smile. "I know, Jordan, you're right. You have every right to hate me for what has happened, but please believe me, I am doing all of this for our family."

"You're right," Jordan huffed, crossing his arms, "why should I believe you?"

"Have I ever lied to you?"

"No."

"Then why would I start now?'"

"If you're not a thief, Dad, where have you been?"

"That's a very long and complicated answer Jordan."

"I'm listening."

"I wish I had enough time to answer your question. What I can tell you is I have never been far away. I have been watching over you guys. I'm so proud of you and one day, I promise, this will all make sense."

"What will make sense, Dad?"

"Jordan, I joined a team of people who fight evil in the spiritual realm on the other side of something called the veil," David blurted out. Jordan stared at David. Taking a deep breath, realizing how crazy everything he had just said sounded to his son, he continued, "I know what I'm telling you isn't going to make any sense, I need you to believe me… to trust me."

"I don't believe you," Jordan pouted, pulling away from David.

"I am sitting in the middle of your lunchroom, and nobody has called the police," David declared, looking around the room. "I have been missing for almost a year and no one is concerned about me sitting here talking to you. Why do you think that is?"

Jordan froze. He looked around the cafeteria and noticed the lunchroom monitors were going about their business, the kids were behaving the same way they always had, and out of the corner of his eye, he could see the principal just walking around.

David could see the confusion developing on his son's face, "Jordan?"

"Yes, Dad?" The slow deliberate response startled David.

"Are you okay?"

"I don't know," Jordan admitted, trying to pinch himself.

"They can't see me, Jordan."

"How?"

"I have a device allowing me to make myself visible when you're asleep."

"I'm not sleeping, Dad, I am at school."

"Jordan," David stated, pausing for a moment, "look where you were sitting."

Turning around, Jordan saw he was still sitting in his chair, propped up by the palm of his hand, sleeping. "Dad, what's happening to me?"

"Nothing, Jordan," David chuckled, giving his son a big hug. "Absolutely nothing. You're sleeping."

"So, you're not a bank robber?"

"Never have been, never will be. I can promise you that."

"When are you coming home?"

"I don't know, Jordan," David replied, fighting back the tears. "I wish I did, but I don't. I love you guys. Everything I am doing; I am doing for our family."

Walking up behind David and putting his hands on David's shoulders, Sebastian ordered, "David, we've got to go. Now."

"What's up, Sebastian?" David asked, looking at Sebastian.

Looking around the lunchroom, Sebastian appeared scared. Sebastian's face was as white as a ghost. David had never seen Sebastian scared of anything and it made him uneasy.

"Dad, who's that?" Jordan questioned, pointing at Sebastian.

"My name is Sebastian, Jordan." Sebastian reached out and patted Jordan on the top of his head. "It's nice to meet you kid, but your dad and I have to go right now."

"It's nice to meet you, sir."

"David, listen to me," Sebastian instructed, looking straight into David's eyes, nervous. "I am leaving now. You've got about ten seconds to be right behind me or things are going to get pretty hectic. Do you understand what I am telling you, David? Ten seconds."

"What's going on, Sebastian?"

"No time, David. Ten seconds." Sebastian raced across the cafeteria for the door at the other end of the room.

"I've got to go, Jordan."

"I don't want you to, Dad," Jordan muttered, wrapping his arms around David.

"I know, Jordan, I don't want to go either, but I have to. Tell your mom and sister I love them. Can you do that for me?"

"I will, Dad, I will."

"I'm sorry, Jordan, time to go back to class."

Reaching across the table, David pushed the arm Jordan was using to prop up his chin. Watching Jordan's head slide off his hand, fall against the table, and wake him up, David's heart sank when Jordan looked around screamed, "Dad? Where are you, Dad?"

Standing up and staring at his son, he wished he had never bumped Jordan's arm. He wished he could have left Jordan asleep so he could have spent more time with him. He wished everything could go back to the way it used to be as he watched the tears streaming down Jordan's face as he searched the cafeteria for David.

"David," Sebastian screamed across the room, "Run!"

David ran across the cafeteria in Sebastian's direction. The doors behind him crashed open and something bound through the door and was chasing him. Running through the door Sebastian was holding open, David looked to catch a brief glimpse of the large black, evil figure chasing them.

Sebastian ran past David looking for a place to hide, "Follow me."

"What is that?" David asked, following Sebastian.

"A Fallen Angel and it knows we're here," Sebastian responded, turning the corner and running down the hall. "Whatever you do, stay close behind, and don't let it catch up to you."

They heard the cafeteria doors fly open with another large crash. Sebastian kept trying to find a safe place for the two of them to hide. As they turned down another hallway, David pointed at the double doors ahead of them, "Gymnasium."

Sebastian felt a little relief when he ran through the double doors into the gymnasium because they were one step closer to safety. He panicked when he realized he was the only one running into the gymnasium and David wasn't behind him.

David knew he made a mistake by activating the Hellfire Device when he ran into the gymnasium and ended up in the science lab. *Wait. What? What happened?* He thought to himself. He hadn't moved through the veil to safety like he thought he would and now he had to find a way out of the building before the entity chasing him was able to capture him.

Breathing hard, he walked toward the door on the other side of the room. He tried to remember the layout of the school when he heard the Fallen Angel crash through the door behind him. David sprinted for the door across the room when the evil entity picked up a table and threw it at him.

He dodged the table, pressed the buttons of the Hellfire Device again, and found himself in the library. He was perplexed, so he ducked into an aisle of books to catch his breath. Taking deep, slow breaths, he couldn't understand why he wasn't able to escape the school.

David heard the Fallen Angel crash through the large metal doors of the library, and he could smell the eerie scent of sulfur. Without hesitation, David raced to the end of the row and high-tailed it for the door at the far end of the library. The Fallen Angel saw David running and knocked over the first bookshelf. Within seconds, row after row of bookshelves were falling like dominoes toward David as he raced toward the exit door.

Books started landing at David's feet as he raced toward the exit door. It was now or never. He leapt and pushed the buttons on his Hellfire Device. He looked back, covered his head, and screamed as the last bookshelf started falling on top of him.

David opened his eyes. He was lying on the gymnasium floor. He didn't have time to waste. He jumped to his feet and raced across the gymnasium hoping the two large exterior doors would provide an exit from the building.

David's eyes grew wide when he looked down and saw the doors had been chained together and padlocked. *Darn!* He thought to himself. *I'm in trouble. The Hellfire Device isn't working. I can't escape. It's only a matter of time before that thing finds me.*

David looked for another way out of the gymnasium. He spotted another set of doors and was about to make his way to them when the Fallen Angel crashed into the darkened room through those very doors.

David crawled on to the stage, hid behind the curtain, and looked for a safe place to hide. He saw a pile of gymnastics equipment in the back corner, scurried across the stage, and buried himself under the pile of padded mats that was surrounded by playground equipment. He laid there motionless and tried to control his breathing after his all-out sprint through the building.

David heard the Fallen Angel coming closer to the stage. He slowed his breathing and prayed for help as the sulfuric smell permeated the room and burned his eyes. Huddled under the mats, he listened for the Fallen Angel. Sweat rolled down his face and dripped onto the floor, his heart pounded against his chest cavity while he waited for the Fallen Angel to leave, and fear gripped his entire being.

Seconds seemed like hours; David lost track of time. He couldn't hear the creature walking around the gymnasium anymore. He didn't know whether or not the Fallen Angel had left, so he remained huddled up in the corner of the stage, praying to God, hoping he would live to fight another day.

His muscles cramped up and started contorting in awkward positions as he hid. It hurt. When the pain became almost unbearable, he decided to ease the pain. His heart continued to pound against his chest when he crept out of his hiding spot. Before he could comprehend what was happening, the Fallen Angel swung its arm across its body and smacked the entire pile of playground equipment David was hiding in as hard as it could. The strength of the Fallen Angel was enough to launch David and all of the equipment across the stage.

David winced in severe pain when his body hit the wall and crumpled into a pile of equipment on the floor. David raced to his feet and gained his bearings when he noticed the dark figure was slumped over in the middle of the stage. Then it stood up and the Fallen Angel grew to about eighteen feet tall. It had four wings stretching about eight feet in width as the gargantuan beast stared down at him. Its eyes burned like fire in their sockets. Its face was pure evil and scared David to the very core of his soul.

David was frozen in his tracks because he had never seen anything so terrifying. He tried to take a couple of steps to his left, but the creature mimicked his movement. He stood motionless for a moment, staring down the beast in front of him. He knew he couldn't outrun the Fallen Angel, so he had to find a way to defeat the entity.

He took a couple steps to the right, paused, and then took a couple steps back to the left in order to size the creature up and find a weakness. He prepared himself for battle as the creature towered over him in the middle of the stage, just staring at him. *This thing has at least twelve feet on me. His arms are longer than I am. There is no way I can get close enough to do any damage before it kills me.*

David made peace with the inevitable realization that he wasn't making it out of the gymnasium alive. Waiting for the beast to make a move, he looked up and stared into the fiery eyes of the Fallen Angel. If the creature were to make a move toward him, he believed he could slide underneath the monster and use the Hellfire Device to stun the entity long enough for him to escape. It was either that or death.

David was waiting for the Fallen Angel to attack when the creature bent over and cried out a loud, heinous, evil shriek.

"David," Sebastian screamed from the other side of the stage, "run!"

David didn't think twice about the directive and ran toward the doors to the hallway. Sebastian raced past him, and declared, "Follow me, I found a way out of here."

Running through the doors and sprinting down the hallway, they busted through another set of double doors. As they stood on the loading dock, they heard the Fallen Angel crash into the hallway. Sebastian opened the dumpster and pushed David into the garbage before he jumped in and pulled the lid shut above them.

"Roll around in the rotten food. It'll cover our scent," Sebastian ordered, ripping open a watery, white milky bag and pouring the garbage all over himself. "And be quiet."

Chapter 19

"Ow!" David squirmed in pain as Zoe tended to his cuts while he sat on the kitchen counter.

"Stop flinching or this is going to take a lot longer to clean."

"It stings," David whined, moving his head every time she touched a cut with the alcohol preps.

"If you want my help, you need to stop flinching." Zoe grabbed his chin with one hand and held his face steady while she continued to clean the cuts on his face. "I don't understand why you guys didn't run."

"We did run," Sebastian answered, walking into the kitchen, and sitting at the table while drying his hair with a towel.

"Then how did David get all messed up?" Peter questioned, grabbing a couple of colas from the refrigerator and handing one to Sebastian as he sat down at the table.

"Thanks." Sebastian opened the bottle and took a sip. "We got separated."

"That was my fault, Sebastian," David interjected. "Sorry about that. I thought I could escape the building."

"Fallen Angels are powerful. We don't know how they do it, but they are able to keep us confined to the building we are in when we are locked in a battle with them."

"That explains why I couldn't move freely through the veil."

"For all the technology we have," Sebastian stated, taking another sip, "they are more powerful and can shut it all down."

"I didn't know," David responded, shaking his head before Zoe grabbed his chin again.

"We didn't think we'd ever have to tell you," Michael interjected. "The only way to leave a building when encountering a Fallen Angel is by escaping, taking it with you, or in rare instances, if it lets you go."

"Don't worry about it," Sebastian said. "You had no idea that Fallen Angels can follow our vapor trails when we move from place to place behind the veil."

"But how?" David asked.

"Speaking from a technical point of view," Peter interjected, "you have to look at everything like a computer program."

"Come again?" David raised his eyebrows, baffled by Peter's response.

"Think of it like an Easter Egg in a video game," Peter continued. "We were created in one realm with a set of rules. The angels were created with a completely different set of rules. And let's face it, technically, when we are behind the veil, we are in their realm. The Easter Egg is the ability to pass through the veil, but we are still human, and this side of the veil is their turf."

"That's a good way of looking at it, Peter," Sebastian nodded, smiling at him for the explanation. "The best bit of advice I can give you is this; whenever you encounter a Fallen Angel, run or hide."

"How did you get discovered by a Fallen Angel in the first place?" Zoe questioned, leaning against the kitchen counter. "The whole reason we wear black is so we can move around more easily behind the veil."

"We were in a place where we were easily discoverable," Sebastian responded.

"I was using the Hellfire Device for an extended period of time," David added, looking at Sebastian. "Is that why?"

"Don't worry about it, David. We took a calculated risk and got caught," Sebastian nodded with a hint of understanding. "The important thing is we all came back alive, and you got a few minutes to clear up some things for your son."

"Wait. You took him to a school. You know better than that." Michael was irritated to learn they had gone to a place where they would easily be detectable by the Fallen Angels.

"He did it for me," David responded. "Carmichael messed with Jordan's head."

"Doesn't matter, David," Michael shot back, staring down Sebastian. "There are rules we all have to follow.

"Sometimes rules have to be broken." Sebastian returned an icy glare.

"Don't you think you should have discussed it with the entire team?"

"No, Michael, I don't," Sebastian retorted, growing agitated with the line of questioning. "I am the team leader, and I made an executive decision. Sometimes I get to do that."

"Not when it puts all of us in danger," Michael yelled, slamming his hand down on the table.

"Yes, Michael, even when it puts all of us in danger," Sebastian fired back. "Like it or not, it's done. I made the decision. End of story. Now does anyone else have an opinion they would like to share?"

"It's not what he meant, Sebastian," Zoe interjected, trying to cut through the tension.

"I know exactly what he meant, Zoe," Sebastian gave her an icy glare. "There's nothing more to discuss. It's done. We went. We can't change it. Instead of arguing about rules, we should be processing the fact I got close enough to a Fallen Angel to hit it with the Hellfire Device."

The other four were quiet for a moment. He was right. There was no sense in rehashing something they couldn't change. The debate would only frustrate them.

Michael, on the other hand, was angry because he wasn't consulted about the plan. But as Sebastian stood in the middle of the room, ready to take on anyone who dissented, Michael acquiesced. He looked down and let out a long, slow breath of frustration. Now was not the time or the place to disagree. What was done was done.

"Hitting it is good, but you didn't send it back," Peter interjected, fishing for information, "so that doesn't help us much."

"But I knocked it down. That has to account for something. It's knowledge."

"A reminder that whenever a Fallen Angel discovers us, we should run," Zoe chuckled.

Sebastian stared at Zoe for a minute. The battle with the Fallen Angel was a turning point in his mind. It was an essential piece of information in their ongoing war with the forces of evil proving the Fallen Angels weren't invincible. If the Hellfire Device could stun one, he wondered how they might be able to capitalize on the knowledge in the future so they could defeat one. Sebastian shook his head in disbelief and walked out of the room.

"I'm going to take a shower," David said, jumping down from the countertop.

"Please do, you really do stink," Zoe teased, holding her nose and leaving the kitchen. David noticed Michael staring at him in frustration before standing up and leaving the room.

"You want to see something?" Peter asked, sitting at the table while sipping from his bottle of soda.

"Can it wait? I really need a long, hot shower."

"Come on." Peter ignored David and walked out of the kitchen. "It'll only take a minute."

David wanted to take a shower, but curiosity convinced him to follow Peter down the long, cobweb filled hallway. Stopping at the end of the hallway, Peter looked around to make sure no one was around.

"Follow me." Peter opened a door to the attic stairwell. Slipping inside the stairwell, Peter turned on a small handheld flashlight and put his pointer finger to his lips telling David to *be quiet*. Peter crept up the stairs while David followed him.

At the top of the stairs, Peter opened another door, held it open for David, and closed it behind them. Peter turned on a light. David saw a long table in the middle of the room. On the table, there was something covered by a white sheet. "What is all of this?"

"It's a secret project I have been working on for the past couple of years," Peter replied, walking to the side of the table as David followed.

"If it's a secret project, why are you showing it to me?"

"Because no one else has faced a Fallen Angel and lived to talk about it."

"I wouldn't say I 'faced a Fallen Angel,' Peter. Had Sebastian not come back for me, I might not be standing here."

"But you saw the Fallen Angel in its full stature," Peter declared, pulling back the white sheet, and revealing a long, javelin lying in the middle of the table.

David was intrigued and moved around the table to inspect it. "What is this?"

"It's a spear."

"A spear?"

"Not just any kind of spear. It's fourteen feet long with a large point at one end, hand grips throughout the fourteen-foot shaft and a power surge amp to create the energy needed to send a Fallen Angel back to the depths of underworld.

"It's designed to deal with the fact the Fallen Angels are big. The length of the spear allows the user to stand clear off the wingspan of the creature while plunging it into the Fallen Angel's body when the user has a clear shot. If it works, it will change the entire landscape of what we can and can't do in our battle against the Enemy and his underlings."

As Peter described the device, David inspected it. "How do you power it?"

"Hellfire Devices."

"How many?"

"Two." Peter opened the amplifier and showed David where the Hellfire Devices would be placed.

"I like what I see, Peter," David confessed, continuing to inspect the device. "But I don't know if two will be enough. Sebastian hit it with one device, and it only stunned the beast."

"It needs more power?"

"I don't know." David leaned over the table and picked up the spear. He bounced it in his arms, judging the weight and mobility of the weapon. "When I saw it fall, I ran. I know one wasn't enough. If I had to make an educated guess, I would say you need a lot more power."

"I can work on it."

"It's heavy," David acknowledged, swinging the spear around the room.

"It's a prototype," Peter responded, puffing out his chest. "When it's ready, I hope Sebastian will take me to the benefactor and he'll make it out of lighter materials."

"This thing is amazing." David smiled while continuing to swing the spear around the room as though he were in a battle with a Fallen Angel. He liked how it felt in his hands. Even if it was heavy, he felt more powerful holding it.

"You think so?"

"I do," David declared, putting the spear down on the table. "If you can get this to work with enough electricity to fry a Fallen Angel, it will change the landscape of this war forever."

Chapter 20

The sound of the kids running around upstairs was starting to irritate Savannah. It was almost nine o'clock, the kitchen was still a mess, and she could imagine the battles the kids were going to wage when it came to bedtime. Turning off the water and leaving the dirty dishes in the sink, she walked through the house and started up the stairs.

"I hope the two of you have brushed your teeth and are in your pajamas."

"We did," Jordan and Carissa responded in unison, running to their rooms.

"We'll see about that." When she reached the top of the stairs, she popped her head inside Jordan's door. "You brushed your teeth?"

"Yes, Mom." Jordan smiled at her and looked up from the book he was pretending to read.

"Good book?"

"Awesome book."

"Next time, make sure the book isn't upside down before answering. Now read."

Jordan flipped the book over and started reading. When he heard Savannah go into Carissa's room, Jordan put down the book, shimmied across the bed, opened the curtains, and stared at the moon.

The meeting he had with his dad in the school cafeteria had thrown him for a loop. He spent most of the day wondering whether he had dreamt the entire encounter, but it felt too real to have been a dream. His dad felt real in his arms, the joy in his heart felt real, the tap against his arm when his dad knocked his head off his chin felt real, and the pain he felt in his chest when he woke up to find his dad wasn't standing in the cafeteria was real.

Jordan continued to stare at the moon. He longed to see a shooting star so he could wish for his father to return. He prayed, asking God to bring his dad home. All the while, taking sneak peaks at the sidewalk just hoping his dad would come walking down the street.

Lost in thought, he didn't hear Savannah walk down the hallway. She had been standing in the doorway watching Jordan for about ten minutes just wondering what he was doing. "Wishing upon a star?"

"Not really," Jordan resigned, sadness engrossing him.

"Hey, buddy." Savannah was concerned above the tone of his voice, so she sat on the end of the bed next to him. "What's up?"

"I miss Dad."

"I know, Jordan," Savannah empathized, putting an arm around his shoulders. "We all miss your dad, but he'll come home when he can."

"I don't know if he will, Mom," he replied, tears rolling down his cheek.

"Jordan, what's going on?" Savannah implored, wiping away his tears. "You know he is going to come home."

"What about the FBI?"

"We'll cross that bridge when we get to it. We're a family, Jordan; there isn't anything we can't handle."

"Mom, can I tell you something?"

"You know you can tell me anything."

Jordan looked at Savannah. Staring into her face, he saw her optimism as well as the concern she had for him. Feeling her reassurance, a small, insecure smile crossed his face. "Never mind, Mom, it's no big deal."

"Jordan Adam Zephyr, you know you can tell me anything."

"You'll think I'm crazy."

"Sweetie," Savannah reassured, giving him a big hug. "No matter what you tell me, there is no way I would ever think you are crazy."

Jordan rested his head on his mother's shoulder. In that moment of tranquility, his worries and fears started melting away. He felt safe in his mother's arms. No matter how crazy his world had become, he could tell her anything. He took a deep breath. "I saw Dad today."

"What?" Savannah questioned, pulling back, holding Jordan by his shoulders, and staring straight into his eyes. "What do you mean you saw your father today? How? Where?"

"I saw him at school."

Savannah closed her eyes and pulled Jordan back to her shoulder for another big hug as she fought back her own tears. "Oh, Sweetie, I know you probably think you saw your dad, but if your father came to school, they would've called me."

"They didn't see him, Mom."

"Oh, Jordan," Savannah whispered, holding him in her arms while tears rolled down her face. "I know how much you want your dad to come home. We all do. And one day he will but what you saw today, you were daydreaming, Sweetie."

"I wasn't daydreaming," Jordan argued, pulling away from Savannah. "I knew you wouldn't believe me, Mom, but I saw him. He was there."

"Okay, Jordan, did he say anything?"

"He's not a crook."

"But you knew he wasn't a thief," Savannah responded, forcing a smile, and wiping away her tears. "Did he say anything else?"

"That everything would make sense one day."

"What would make sense?"

"I don't know."

"Did he say anything else?"

"No," he recalled, wiping away a tear. "He had to go, but I couldn't go with him. But he said all of this would make sense one day. What was he talking about, Mom? How is all of this going to make sense? How?"

"I don't know, Jordan, I don't know," Savannah whispered, wrapping Jordan up in another big hug and cradling him in her arms. She held him in a strong embrace and stroked his hair while staring out the window at the moon.

Chapter 21

Eric drove along the old country road. On each side of the dirt pathway was a stone wall about four feet high separating the road from the dense thicket of trees hovering over the narrow passageway. The volume on his truck's radio was turned up as he sang along with the latest country hits. Paying close attention to his surroundings, he made his way along the narrow winding road.

Driving out of his way for more than ninety minutes, he decided to follow the investigation to the one place he hadn't visited. Traveling along the country road, he felt like he had left western civilization and entered a time warp smack dab into the middle of nowhere.

The disappearance of David Zephyr had taken on new significance. This was the first time in Eric's decorated career he had not been able to ascertain a firm hold of the facts and build a path to a solid conclusion. The Zephyr case didn't make sense on the surface and as he peeled back layer after layer of the story, he ran into one stone wall after another. Nothing made sense. The more questions he asked, the fewer answers he found. The more evidence he uncovered, the more baffling the answers became. No matter what the facts of the case told him, the narrative of the investigation never matched the perception of who David Zephyr was as a person.

Eric had exhausted every lead. He had spoken to everyone who had ever come in contact with David Zephyr. They all told him the same thing. David was a dedicated, hard-working, Christian man who had a strong community presence as a volunteer and who championed efforts to improve his neighborhood. David was a man who put God and family above everything in his life. David didn't fit the profile of a thief or any other type of criminal. Eric had been chasing bad, and in many cases, evil men, all of his life and nothing in David's past would indicate a predilection for criminal activity.

No one could believe a good man had gone bad overnight. They all believed the justice system had come to the wrong conclusion, and they began to sympathize with David. They could understand why he was on the run. In their minds, the government was on a witch hunt to target a pillar of the community, which made Eric's job even more difficult. The more he asked questions, the more indignant they became toward him. He started to feel like he had become the criminal for intruding in the life of a good man.

He was out to prove to himself and all of the acrimonious people who had come to loathe his investigation that sometimes people aren't always who they appear to be to the rest of the world. He believed David was a good man who turned evil. He believed with every fiber of his being that David was a criminal and although David hadn't stolen anything yet, there was only one reason why David would be involved in so many break-ins. David was the mastermind of a future bank job of epic proportions; multiple banks at the same time for a total take that could extend into the hundreds of millions. The only problem with Eric's theory was he couldn't prove it.

Thinking about the case that had consumed his days and nights, Eric followed the old dirt road for the better part of another half an hour. When he came to a fork in the road, he veered to the right and followed the pathway for another two hundred feet. He tacked right again and drove another quarter mile up the long, desolate driveway until he came to a stop in front of the farmhouse.

"Well, I'll be." Eric shifted his truck into park and shut down the engine. "The Zephyr farm really is in the middle of nowhere."

He left the keys in the ignition of the truck, hopped out of the truck, and released the top of his holster just in case he needed to grab his weapon. He hadn't taken more than ten steps toward the farmhouse when Nathan jogged across the property from one of the barns.

"That is far enough, Agent Carmichael," Nathan yelled, closing the gap between him and Eric. "I don't know why you have decided to come out to my farm, but I wouldn't take another step. You're not welcome here."

"Nathan, I have come out here to ask you a few more questions about your son's disappearance," Eric responded, walking toward Nathan with his right hand extended. "I could really use your help finding David."

"That's Mr. Zephyr to you, you're not one of my friends," Nathan grunted, ignoring the outstretched hand and staring down the agent he towered over.

Placing both hands on his hips and looking around at the scenery, Eric commented, "You sure do have a beautiful place here, Mr. Zephyr."

"You're in the wrong place, Agent. You're barking up the wrong tree."

"Mr. Zephyr, I can understand the level of disdain you have for me. I really can…"

"You have no idea how much I hate you, Agent," Nathan barked, towering over Eric with a scowl on his face and puffing out his chest.

"I completely understand your hatred for me, Mr. Zephyr, but I still have a job to do. I was hoping we could bury the hatchet and start over again."

With eyes burning in anger, Nathan stared into Eric's face, "You have spent the last few months trying to convince my daughter-in-law, my wife, and my grandchildren that my son is a criminal. You expect me to believe you have come out to my farm to bury the hatchet and work together? How stupid do you think I am, Agent Carmichael?"

"I don't think you're stupid at all." Eric glared back at Nathan. He could feel the tension between the two of them. Nervous, he moved his hand just above his weapon in his holster. "I figured we only find the truth when we find David. Since we haven't done that separately, I figured we might have a better chance if we worked together."

"You're not interested in the truth. You're interested in putting my son behind bars. I refuse to be the one who helps you put the nails in his coffin." Nathan was seething under his skin and Eric was doing everything in his power to get Nathan to let his guard down.

"You have it all wrong, Mr. Zephyr. I do want the truth. I want to know why your son disappeared. I want to find him and bring him home to his family. But if David is planning to pull off a crime in a few days or a few months, well, you're right, I want to know that, too."

"You want to put my son behind bars."

"There are some unanswered questions, Mr. Zephyr. I am not going to lie to you. I do have a job to do and only truthful answers to those questions will dictate what happens next."

"And somehow, you thought you could come out to my farm and sweet talk me into becoming your partner?" Nathan scoffed, laughing in an eerie manner at the insinuation.

"No, sir, I didn't." Eric was caught off guard by the menacing laugh. It sent shivers down his spine and made him wonder about Nathan's sanity. "I drove out here today so you could prove me wrong."

"What?" Nathan asked, furrowing a brow, caught off guard.

"You see, Mr. Zephyr, I don't think your son ever disappeared."

"You don't, do you?"

"No, I don't." Eric walked around in a small circle with his arms outstretched while he looked around at the surroundings. "If I wanted to disappear and never use my credit card, an ATM, or a cell phone, I would need a really good place to hide out."

"Get to the point quickly, Agent."

"See, Mr. Zephyr, your son has done all of those things. I bet he is somewhere on this farm because if I were David, this is exactly where I would hide out."

"Excuse me, Special Agent?" Nathan asked, taking a menacing step toward Eric. "Are you accusing me of something?"

Eric held his ground, staring Nathan down while wrapping his hand on the grip of his handgun. "Mr. Zephyr, I am an officer of the law. You need to stand down and step back. Do I make myself clear?"

Nathan clenched his fists, he wanted to pound Eric within an inch of his life, but he didn't want to deal with the legal complications. The vein in his forehead pulsing, Nathan clenched his jaw and acknowledged the order. "Yes, Officer."

Nathan waited a moment and took two steps backward. Mission accomplished! Eric made the old man angry and that was the same as strapping a lie detector to him. Locked in an icy glare with the gargantuan farmer, Eric decided to push a little farther. "To answer your question, I haven't accused you of anything yet, Mr. Zephyr."

"Then you should leave," Nathan huffed, clenching his whole body to contain his fury.

"But if you're telling me David isn't on this farm, then you wouldn't mind if I looked around for myself? Would you?"

"You're not looking anywhere," Nathan yelled, his fury emanating from every pore.

"Why not?" Eric needled, knowing he was pushing Nathan to lose his self-control. "Prove me wrong."

"Special Agent Carmichael," Nathan regained his composure, "do you have a warrant to search my property?"

"Do I need one?"

"You've got nothing," Nathan laughed, rubbing his hands together. "You're bluffing. You played your cards so I would let you look around without a warrant and guess what? You lost."

"Is that what you think I am doing, Nathan?"

"Unless you have a piece of paper in your back pocket allowing you to search my property, you made a very long trip out here for nothing."

"What are you hiding, Mr. Zephyr?"

"Nothing."

"Then show me around the farm," Eric persisted, raising his eyebrows and using his facial expressions to taunt Nathan. "If David isn't here, I'll leave you alone."

"Special Agent Carmichael," Nathan retorted, grinning a wide-eyed, a smug little smile. "To put it nicely, I don't like you. And after the stupid stunt you pulled with my grandson, I have nothing to prove to you."

"I was doing my job."

"Doing your job?" Nathan was filled with contempt. "Unless you have a warrant in your back pocket, I hope you enjoy the two-hour drive back to the city."

"This is your last chance, Mr. Zephyr," Eric insisted, imploring Nathan to reconsider. "If you make me come back here with a warrant, I am bringing an army of agents to rifle through every inch of this farm?"

"I'd like you to leave now," Nathan responded, pointing down the driveway.

"Are you sure you want to do that, Mr. Zephyr?" Eric pressed, staring down Nathan.

"I don't think I'm allowed to tell you what I'd prefer to do to you. So in lieu of my options, I'd like you to get the hell off my property."

"Is that a threat?"

"Leave!"

Eric stared down Nathan. He knew he didn't have enough evidence to charge Nathan with threatening a Federal Agent. And even though no one would question the word of a decorated agent against the word of farmer, he wasn't a dirty cop. The rules are clear. A threat is a threat. The rules did not leave room for his own interpretation of what he thought might constitute a threat. As much as he wanted to slap the cuffs on Nathan and make the next twenty-four hours of Nathan's life miserable, he knew better.

"Good day, Mr. Zephyr," Eric smiled, walking back to his truck, and climbing into the driver's seat. Starting the engine, he rolled down the window. "I really wish you had done this the easy way."

"Get off my property before I have you arrested for trespassing," Nathan scoffed, pointing down the driveway.

Eric put his truck in gear and drove away. He watched Nathan head back into the main house in the rear-view mirror. When he was out of sight, he picked up his cell phone and dialed a number. While the phone rang, the blue tooth played the call through the speakers.

"Hello?" said the voice on the other end of the line.

"Is everyone in position?"

"Yes, sir."

"How many helicopters do we have?"

"Three. They are waiting in a field about a half a mile away."

"Good. Wait for my orders."

Nearing the end of the driveway, Eric hung up the phone. The solitary dirt road he had driven in on earlier was now full of a caravan of black federal vehicles. And in front of his car was a white police cruiser from the county sheriff's office.

Stopping his truck at the end of the driveway, he put it in park and exited the vehicle. He approached the middle-aged officer and shook his hand. "Are you Sheriff Wilkins?"

"I am, sir. Are you Special Agent Eric Carmichael?"

"I am. Did my team go over the operations plan with you?"

"Yes, sir, they did." Sheriff Wilkins placed his hands on his hips. "I am surprised that Nathan Zephyr would be involved in something like this. I have known Nathan for almost thirty years. He is a good man."

"Hopefully, you are right, Sheriff," Eric responded. "Please remember you are here as an observer. We invited you because of your relationship with Mr. Zephyr and because we wanted to make sure your office was aware of our actions today."

"I understand," Sheriff Wilkins confirmed.

"The team is in position, Boss," Quyen said, walking up to Eric.

"Then, let's get to it. Sheriff Wilkins will follow me. Everyone else follow him. And as we start up the driveway, I want the helicopters in the air, and I want sirens blaring. I want Nathan and David to know we are coming."

Quyen turned and headed back to his car, barking orders into a radio for the rest of the team to prepare. Sheriff Wilkins climbed into his car and started it up while Eric jumped into his truck, whipped it around, and raced up Nathan's driveway with sirens blaring as a convoy of federal vehicles followed behind him. Rushing out of his house, Nathan heard the sirens racing toward his farm. He stopped at the driveway when he saw Eric and a cavalry of vehicles come roaring around the corner.

Slamming on his brakes, Eric's truck came to a screeching stop across the gravel driveway about ten feet in front of Nathan. Hopping out of the truck and pulling a piece of paper out of his back pocket, Eric announced, "I almost forgot, Mr. Zephyr."

"You're going to pay for this, Carmichael."

Eric held the warrant above his head. "I have this search warrant allowing my agents and those helicopters you hear to pull this place apart."

"You have no right," Eric yelled, balling his hands into fists.

"I have every right," Eric barked, handing him a copy of the warrant.

"I'm sorry, Nathan," Sheriff Wilkins added, walking up behind Eric. "That is an official warrant from a Federal Magistrate. You have to let them search your property."

"Okay, boys, go to work," Eric yelled, gloating while Nathan seethed with anger.

Sixty federal agents broke into teams and headed off to every corner of the farm. Nathan watched as the federal agents descended upon his farm like a swarm of locusts.

"You're making a huge mistake, Special Agent Carmichael," Nathan huffed, anger coursing through his veins.

"No, Nathan. You made the mistake. I gave you a chance to do this quietly. You chose not to work together, and I told you this is what would happen."

"You're not going to find David here."

"We'll see about that," Eric responded, walking off to search the farm. He stopped and faced the sheriff, "Sheriff Wilkins."

"Yes, sir?"

"Keep a close eye on Mr. Zephyr," Eric paused before smiling to himself. "If he tries anything, anything at all, shoot him!"

Chapter 22

David and Michael spent the morning working out in the abandoned plant Michael had found a few years back. Over the years, he had turned the dilapidated factory into his own personal gymnasium with various types of physical endurance drills. It had taken him a while to create the space, but he spent at least two to three hours every day working out. Fighting demons was life or death work. He had to be in the best physical shape in order to remain effective.

He created a free weight system from metal bars and varying metal pieces that had been left behind at the plant. His favorite work out was the think fast program, a spinning metal pole with well-placed metal bars requiring him to react by leaping over, ducking under, or dropping flat on the ground as the centrifuge spun faster. In the field behind the old plant, he built a running track.

David had long given up on working out. With the birth of his children, he didn't have time to dedicate to personal fitness. Work, church, and his family took precedence in his life. As the years went on, he added a good twenty pounds to his frame, but after the encounter with the Fallen Angel, David knew he had to strengthen his muscles or his next encounter with one of those colossal beasts might be his last.

David and Michael were running on the track. As they came around the last corner by the back of the building, David starting sprinting. He overtook and passed Michael, who had a ten to fifteen-yard lead. Michael chuckled and ran faster.

"Come on, old man, beat me to the end of the straight away."

"You're on," David challenged, running as fast as he could while gasping for oxygen.

Racing hard down the final hundred yards of the track, David trailed Michael by at least five steps. Crossing the finish line, Michael slowed to a walk, putting his hands on top of his head, and breathing in through his nose. David, on the other hand, ran to a grassy patch and fell to the ground gasping for air. He lay there, staring at the sky, his chest heaving up and down as he sucked in as much oxygen as he could.

Michael walked over to a cooler, took out two cold bottles of water, walked over to David, and offered one to him. "Here, drink this."

"Thanks." David sat up, opened the bottle, took a big swig, and then poured some on top of his head to cool off.

"Good work out, Old Man."

"I'm trying," David responded through his deep breaths.

"You'll get there. Rome wasn't built in a day."

"But it burned in one."

"That it did. That. It. Did."

"Okay, tough guy," David declared, taking another swig of water. "I have to ask. What's your story?"

"My story?"

"You said no one was looking for you," David stated, reminding him of their previous conversation. "Why not?"

"You don't want to hear my long, boring tale," Michael laughed, taking a swig of water and sitting on the grass.

"It's eleven o'clock in the morning. I have another twelve or thirteen hours before I have anything to do. Enlighten me."

"It really isn't interesting."

"You guys knew everything about me before I got here. It makes it hard to fully trust people I know so little about."

"True," Michael admitted, looking away and rolling his neck around his shoulders.

"Look, you don't have to tell me, but I have learned so much about everyone else. I just don't know anything about you."

"It's really not a big deal," Michael said, taking a deep breath, looking at his feet, and rubbing his hands together. "My dad was a highly decorated officer in the Army who was dishonorably discharged or, at least, that's what the government would like you to believe."

"I am sorry to hear that." David could hear the pain in Michael's voice and it bothered him. "What happened to him?"

"As a kid, my family bounced around from base-to-base. I never had a friend for more than a year and any time I developed good friendships, we moved. By the time I was seven years old, I realized I was always 'the new kid in town.' It made it hard to get involved in sports and normal kid stuff.

"One day, I must have been something like eight or nine years old, I started hanging out with the youth pastor over at the church on the base. He taught me about God, Jesus, life, and the world around me. Most importantly, he taught me about responsibility."

"Sounds like a good guy to know."

"He was a great guy," Michael continued, running his hand through his hair. "He really helped me and my dad become best friends. It was hard being an Army kid but over that year, my dad and I really bonded. I believe it was because God was working in my life to straighten out my view of the world."

"Sounds like things were going well for you."

"Well, about six months later, my father was transferred to a new base. I had a new home in a new state, but this time it was okay. Every base had a church and a youth group I could join, and my faith continued to grow. I learned about the world and God, and my relationship with my dad grew stronger every day. For the first time ever, I realized how extraordinary God was making my life."

"I don't understand," David asked, raising an eyebrow because he was confused. "If you had all those great things going for you, why are you here?"

"In 2004, my dad's unit was deployed in Mauryanistan. They came up over a rocky mountainside and started taking heavy fire from the enemy. His unit fought back. When the battle was over and the dust had cleared, they realized they had just engaged another unit on a secret mission.

"Twenty-two men died, and it made for big news back here. They covered up the friendly-fire incident, created a story of heroism for my dad's unit, and handed out a slew of medals to the survivors."

"I'm sorry. That must have been tough."

"It was, and my dad didn't agree with the decisions. He refused the medal they awarded him. He couldn't live with the lie of being a hero when twenty-two of his brothers were dead and quite possibly, some of those men died from bullets he discharged."

"Your dad sounds like an honorable man. He's a hero for standing by his convictions."

"The Army didn't see it that way. They started watching him closely and one afternoon, they caught my dad having a cup of coffee with a reporter who had been embedded in their unit."

"What's wrong with that?"

"Nothing, but when the story broke stateside. It was a big deal to the media. The brass thought my dad told the reporter the truth about what happened up on that mountainside. So they quickly brought bogus charges against him, tarnished his reputation, court martialed him, and after he spent eighteen months in a military prison, they dishonorably discharged him."

"I am so sorry, Michael. I can't imagine how horrible that was for you."

"My dad wasn't even talking to the reporter about the friendly fire incident. He knew better than that. He may not have agreed with their politics, but he knew well enough to keep his mouth shut."

"So why was he talking to the reporter?"

"The reporter was a friend my dad had known in high school. They were reminiscing about friends and family back home."

"That stinks."

"My dad couldn't get regular work because of his dishonorable discharge. So, we moved from town to town as my parents looked for work. They took odd jobs for short money, and we lived in dirty motel rooms. It became too much for my parents, so they started drinking every night.

"One night, in 2010, my mom and dad were on their way back to the motel after a late-night bender at the local bar. My father took the corner wide at sixty miles an hour and drove headfirst into a large oak tree. They both died instantly," Michael recounted, wiping away the tears rolling down his cheek.

"I am so sorry, Michael," David empathized, fighting back his own tears. "I can't even imagine what you went through."

"I was numb, and I was on my own for the first time ever."

"What'd you do?"

"I buried my parents in Potter's field," Michael recounted, pausing to swallow the lump in his throat. "Not one friend or family member, heck, not even one member from his unit showed up to honor his service. And that's when I realized I was all alone. So, I started working for the local church and then about three weeks later, Sebastian showed up."

"He has a way of doing that, doesn't he?"

"I joined The Network immediately, and the rest is history."

"What about the people at the church, didn't they come looking for you?"

"Nah," Michael dismissed, swatting the air with his hand. "They figured I was another wayward teen, and I just took off. And that is why I do the trivial stuff on the other side of the veil. When I vanished from the face of the earth, no one even noticed."

Swallowing hard against the lump developing in the back of his throat, David walked over to Michael, knelt down beside him, and hugged him. The tough guy melted in David's arms. David couldn't imagine what he had gone through in his life, but to have it all taken away in a heartbeat and not have anyone care about his welfare, well, that was more than anyone, nonetheless a child, ever deserved. "I'm truly sorry, Michael. You never should've gone through any of that, especially alone."

"You know, Christ saved us. The stories or reasons may be different, but we found Him," Michael professed, lifting his head, patting David on the back, standing up, and walking back toward the abandoned warehouse. David followed as Michael continued, "I don't know why things happened to my parents the way they did. But Christ saved me from all of it and now, I do everything I can to save people from any kind of pain they might have to face."

"That's not a bad way of looking at it, I guess."

"It's not a bad gig, David," Michael declared, smiling and throwing an arm around his shoulder as they walked. "Besides, it has to be a lot better than writing jingles for a living."

Chapter 23

Millions of stars cascaded across the tapestry of the mountains, accentuating the full moon illuminating the Zephyr family farm. Teams of agents returned from their ill-fated attempt to find David. Eric was talking with a large group of agents a hundred yards from where Nathan was standing in the driveway. Watching the federal agents waltz through his property, he became fed up with the invasion of his privacy.

"I have had enough of this," Nathan pronounced, walking toward Eric as Sheriff Wilkins followed the hulking man across the property.

"Nathan, I wouldn't do this," Sheriff Wilkins advised his friend.

"No, Andy? You wouldn't, but I am."

"They're doing their jobs."

"We've been friends for years, Andy, how could you think David or I could be involved in something like this?"

"I am sorry, Nathan. We all have a job to do. I'm just doing mine."

"That is the dumbest thing you've ever said," Nathan fired back, continuing to march toward Eric. "I am putting an end to this charade."

"Did you search the cabin out by the lake?" Eric asked one of the agents.

"We did, sir, the suspect wasn't there."

"That's because he isn't on my property," Nathan barked, barging into the middle of the conversation.

"Mr. Zephyr, you are interfering with a federal investigation. I am going to kindly ask you to go back to your house."

"The hell I will. Arrest me if you must, but this ends right now."

"Sheriff Wilkins?" Eric looked toward the officer for some assistance.

"I think Mr. Zephyr might be right, Agent. If you want to continue this search, you'll have to do it without the aid of the County Sheriff's office."

"I could have your badge, Sheriff," Eric stated, staring down the officer.

"You can have it," Sheriff Wilkins shot back. "I would rather lose it for doing the right thing than standing idly by and watching you impugn a man's character."

"Special Agent Carmichael," Quyen yelled, running across the yard. "We found something on the far side of the farm that might interest you."

"I think we just found your evidence, Sheriff Wilkins," Eric stated. "What did you find, Agent?"

"I think you are going to want to see this for yourself because I have no idea how to explain it in terms that would make any sense."

"Lead the way," Eric ordered.

Quyen led the group, which included Nathan and Sheriff Wilkins, past a couple of barns close to the house, out past one of the fields, to a group of barns clumped together on the far side of the property at the bottom of a small hill. When he arrived at the renovated barn, he walked around to a side door, opened it, and went inside.

Following Quyen, Eric entered the barn and was perplexed. The lights in the barn were on and in the center of the barn, taking up a large chunk of floor space, was a contraption Eric had never seen before. In each of the four corners stood a twenty-foot post that looked like an old, city streetlamp. Each post had a wide base, a long thin post with a large metal ball on top like a metal light bulb. The floor under each of the lamp posts was made of stainless steel. There was a one-foot raised metal vine connecting each of the four lamp posts around the perimeter of the floor. Another one-foot raised vine running from each lamp post to the corresponding corners of a metal table made of steel in the middle of the room.

Walking around the room, Eric inspected the posts and metal table in the middle of the room. His mind was racing. "Mr. Zephyr, would you mind telling me what this is?"

"I am a farmer, Agent Carmichael," Nathan responded, trying to conceal something.

"I have been around a lot of farms, Mr. Zephyr, and I have never seen anything like this monstrosity. What is it used for?"

"That is proprietary information, Agent."

"You have no right to proprietary information," Eric shouted, placing his hands on his hips and staring at Nathan. "Now answer my question. What the heck is this?"

"You don't need to answer the question, Nathan," Mr. Dewey said, entering the barn with a federal agent escorting him.

"Excuse me?" Eric asked, looking at the gentleman walking into the barn.

"My name is Sam Dewey," Mr. Dewey responded, walking over to Nathan. "Sorry it took me so long to get here, Nathan, I was in court most of the day. I came as soon as I got your message."

"Mr. Dewey, I am conducting an interview here, so if you wouldn't mind…"

"Actually, I do mind," Mr. Dewey interrupted, holding up one hand to silence Eric. "I am Mr. Zephyr's attorney. Based on the copy of the search warrant you executed and was faxed to my office earlier today, the proprietary information contained in this barn is not subject to your search. You're looking for David Zephyr, not trade secrets. Is David Zephyr in this barn?"

"No, he is not," Eric responded, "but I have probable cause to believe this contraption might be aiding and abetting the suspect."

"How so?" Mr. Dewey laughed, walking over to the contraption with his arms wide open. "Is it his hideaway?"

"I have no idea what it is," Eric answered, approaching the attorney. "That is what I am trying to ascertain."

"And I am telling you my client is not going to answer your question."

"We have numerous incidents where David disappeared into thin air without a trace."

Mr. Dewey pointed at the contraption and laughed. "And you think this has something to do with David's ability to escape?"

"I don't know what this contraption is, Counselor, but I would like to know."

"Ludicrous," Mr. Dewey laughed in Eric's face. "You've been working too hard if you're letting your case delve into hocus pocus and magic, Agent."

"I believe I am entitled to answers about what's in this barn."

"And my client isn't going to tell you," Mr. Dewey declared, stepping up to Eric and staring into his eyes. "So, unless you have a reason to charge my client, I believe your search has come to an unfortunate conclusion."

Contemplating his next move, Eric put his hands on his hips. Thinking about how he could connect the equipment to any of the federal crimes David Zephyr was being investigated for was going to be a hard sell. He didn't have much of a legal precedent to continue questioning Nathan. Any argument he tried to make would be easy fodder for a third-year law student, but he didn't want to lose the opportunity to dig deeper into what he had found. He knew the contraption was somehow connected to David; he just couldn't prove it.

"Agent Quyen," Eric ordered, "take Mr. Zephyr into custody."

"What?" Nathan asked, not believing the order that had just been given. "On what charge?"

"Agent Carmichael, you have no grounds," yelled Mr. Dewey, pleading with Eric to reconsider his order.

"Obstruction of justice," Eric shot back at Mr. Dewey.

"Gladly, boss," Quyen said, walking over to Nathan.

"Don't touch me," Nathan barked at Agent Quyen.

"Sir, do you want to add resisting arrest to the charge?" Quyen asked, staring Nathan down. Nathan puffed out his chest to seem intimidating, then relented and placed his hands behind his back.

"You're so far off base, Agent Carmichael. You're making a mockery of your own investigation," Mr. Dewey pressed, not believing what was happening.

"Sam, what is going on?" Nathan asked as Agent Quyen put the cuffs on his wrists.

"Don't say a word, Nathan," Mr. Dewey advised, walking over to Nathan and placing a hand on his shoulder. "This is a witch hunt and Agent Carmichael knows it. I will have you released first thing in the morning."

"I wouldn't be so quick to make promises, Counselor," Eric shot back.

"This is a Hail Mary, Agent. You know and I know it," Mr. Dewey retaliated. "I'd be careful about letting your pride get in your way."

"I won't," Eric smirked, "Agent Quyen, take him away!"

"Sam?" Nathan pleaded, standing there defensively.

"I'll have you out in the morning, Nathan," Mr. Dewey reiterated, staring down Eric while Quyen escorted Nathan out of the barn in handcuffs.

Chapter 24

It had been a long night for Nathan. After enduring the uncomfortable two-hour drive back to Raleigh, he was taken into a cell like a common criminal. He was allowed to sleep on a small, lumpy bunk for about ninety minutes before Eric summoned him to the interrogation room to be questioned.

"We've been here for hours, Mr. Zephyr. The sooner you answer my questions, the sooner we can all go home."

Sitting in his chair and staring straight ahead, Nathan seemed to be in a trance. The room was barren, two chairs on each side of the table, a mirror on the wall behind Eric, a door, and an overhead light. Wishing he had a window to look through while waiting for his lawyer to arrive, he was silent. He knew this was a procedural tactic to obtain information. Sam Dewey told him not to say a word, so he sat there and stared at the mirror.

Eric continued to bombard him, so he filled his mind with other thoughts to drown out the questions. Wondering about David, Nathan wanted to know where he had been hiding out for the past year. And why? When his family needed him most, why hadn't David shown up to protect them?

Nathan was disgusted. David hadn't become the man he had raised him to be. A man stands up for his family, a man stands firm with his wife and children regardless of the situation, good or bad. A man doesn't run away. A man always protects the life he built.

Sitting in his chair and enduring the questions Eric strafed him with for what seemed like an eternity, Nathan lost all respect for David. Because no matter how bad the situation had become, if the circumstances had been reversed, he never would have run out on Monica the way David had run out on Savannah.

"Okay, Mr. Zephyr." Eric sat down in the chair across from Nathan. His tactics hadn't work, Nathan hadn't cracked. He was a formidable foe and as much as Eric tried to cajole answers from him, it wasn't working. So, he decided to change tactics and show some empathy. "I have used every tactic we have. You've had very little sleep, I've played good cop, bad cop, and I've even tried to bully you into answering my questions. But I get it. You don't want to tell me anything that would incriminate yourself or your son…"

"You don't know anything, Agent Carmichael," Nathan huffed, anger coursing through his veins. Breaking his gaze with the mirror and looking straight at Eric, Nathan continued, "I don't know why my son went missing and quite frankly, I don't care. He ran out on his wife and kids. He's a coward and I didn't raise a coward. So, what reason do I have to protect him?"

"Wait, let me get this straight," Eric questioned, sitting up in his chair and rubbing his hands together. "You want me to believe you're angry with your son for running out on his family?"

"Believe what you want, Special Agent, but it's the truth."

"Well, okay," Eric replied, placing his hands on the table. "I believe we are starting to get somewhere, but there is still something I don't understand."

"What?"

"If you want me to believe you're telling the truth about David, why are you still sitting here in my interrogation room? Why didn't you just answer my questions?"

"Excuse me?"

"Why would you sit here all night?" Eric confronted him with contempt. "Why didn't you tell me your feelings earlier?"

"I speak when I have something to say."

"Then why don't you just tell me about the contraption in your barn and we can all go home?"

"You don't need to answer that question, Nathan," Mr. Dewey advised, bursting into the room and walking over to Nathan. "Special Agent Carmichael, I am appalled by your behavior."

Eric's jaw dropped wide open. He couldn't believe the impeccable timing of Nathan's attorney to enter a room at the exact moment he is about to get to the heart of the story. "Excuse me, Counselor?"

"You know very well you have no right to interrogate my client without his lawyer being present," Mr. Dewey reprimanded, sitting down at the table. "Are you okay, Nathan?"

"I'm fine, Sam."

"I am not interrogating your client, Counselor, I'm simply having a conversation with Mr. Zephyr about the strange contraption in his barn."

"I believe my client has made it abundantly clear to you that the item to which you are inquiring is of a proprietary nature."

"Drop the legal jargon, Counselor."

"Mr. Zephyr is a private businessman. He has contributed many wonderful technological advances to the farming industry. He is not required by law to disclose a private business opportunity in a case involving the disappearance of a human being. My client has a right to protect himself as well as his business assets."

"I didn't see farming equipment in the barn, Counselor."

"That's right, you saw a magic spaceship beaming people around the world," Mr. Dewey laughed.

"That's not what I said," Eric corrected the attorney, agitated by his words being twisted.

"You don't know what you saw, Special Agent," Mr. Dewey said with a hint of sarcasm.

"It's not a piece of farming equipment."

"It's not?" Mr. Dewey ridiculed. "Then what did you see, Special Agent?"

"I don't know what it is, Counselor, but considering the missing person in question has an uncanny knack for appearing and disappearing into thin air, I would like to see some proof that what I saw in the barn is a farming device. Without it and based on evidence I have in my possession, the item in the barn raises some serious questions."

"Are you kidding me?" Mr. Dewey laughed out loud at Eric's revelation. "Do you honestly think my client is building some sort of teleportation device?"

"It raises the question, Counselor," Eric stated, frustrated with the direction the interrogation had taken since Mr. Dewey arrived.

"Oh, this is one for the books," Mr. Dewey laughed, slapping his knee with his hand. "You have a few screws loose, Special Agent. You need a really good shrink; may I recommend one?"

"Be that as it may, the device still raises a lot of questions."

"I don't care whether it raises questions or not," Mr. Dewey declared, becoming serious and scolding Eric over the piece of equipment. "The device is of a proprietary nature, and nothing less than a court order will elicit the responses you desire."

"Sam," Nathan offered, facing his lawyer, "does it make sense to just answer the man's ridiculous question so we can all go home?"

"Nathan, wait," Mr. Dewey directed, holding up his hand to stop Nathan from speaking.

"If it means we can all go home, then why not?"

Thinking about the question for a moment, Mr. Dewey looked at Eric and declared, "I would like five minutes alone to confer with my client, Special Agent."

"And if I refuse?"

"Considering the nature of the interrogation taking place here along with numerous other offenses I believe have violated my client's rights, I would have no other choice but to walk down the hall and bury the Area Director in so much legal paperwork that your career, as well as this case, will be tied up in court for years."

"Is that a threat, Counselor?"

"No, Special Agent, it's a promise."

Thinking about his options and the salient points Mr. Dewey had made, Eric didn't want to give David any more leeway while they wrangled over every letter of the law in court. "Five minutes, Counselor. Five minutes."

"And, Eric," Mr. Dewey responded. "Make sure the agents behind the mirror vacate the booth and before they do, make sure they turn off all recording devices. Attorney-client privilege is still in full effect in this room."

Standing up and facing the two-way mirror, Eric made a sweeping motion with his hand to let them know to vacate the observation booth. Then he left the room.

Eric walked down the hall toward his office when he was met by Deputy Director Johnson who was angry. "Agent Carmichael, what have you gotten yourself into this morning?"

"I don't know what you mean, sir."

"I am talking about Nathan Zephyr. Have you charged him with anything?"

"No, sir. Mr. Zephyr is being held for questioning."

"Are you planning on charging Mr. Zephyr, Special Agent?"

"We are still questioning him at the moment, sir. I don't have any plans on charging him with anything yet, but that might change in the next few hours."

"Are you out of your mind? Do you have any idea who Nathan Zephyr is?"

"A citizen like you and me, sir."

"No, he's not," Deputy Director Johnson corrected, pointing toward the interrogation room. "That man is connected to judges, politicians, and community leaders."

"I have an investigation to complete, sir. He is part of the investigation."

"Do you know how many people above your pay grade and mine have been calling all morning to remind us of his connections? The Area Director is not happy about the phone calls he has been fielding."

"I'm sorry for the trouble, sir. I am just trying to do my job," Eric stated, attempting to hold off the brass for a little while longer. "Are you asking me to back off a material person of interest?"

"Eric," Deputy Director Johnson said, leaning in toward Eric and lowering his voice. "I like you. You are my favorite investigator and normally I stay out of your cases, but this one has garnered a lot of attention. So, you either find a solid reason to charge Nathan with something or you let him go home to his wife. Do I make myself clear?"

Staring at his superior officer, Eric stood in the hallway befuddled. The order was clear. If there was a reason to charge Nathan, he wasn't going to be influenced by the powers that be not to follow through with those charges, but there was no reason to charge Nathan. Unless the answer to the question changed the landscape of the investigation when he went back into the interrogation room, Nathan was about to become a free man.

Standing in the hallway, taking the kind of heat from superiors he was encountering at the moment, Eric realized he was on the right track. Innocent men don't lean on influence peddlers for help unless they need assistance in righting a wrong. The only reason for the brass to be dealing with high level phone calls is because somebody who is well-connected needed his or her tracks covered. The only question Eric had as he stood in quiet defiance of his superior officer was *whose tracks were being covered?*

"Do I make myself clear, Special Agent," Deputy Director Johnson repeated with a slight hint of agitation in his voice.

"Crystal clear, sir."

"Good. I would hate to see a stellar investigative career go down the tubes over this case. Carry on, Agent," Deputy Director Johnson smiled, reaching over and patting Eric on the shoulder before walking back down the hall.

With nothing more to go on than a simple crack in the armor of Nathan Zephyr, Eric walked back into the interrogation room and sat down at the table. "Okay, Counselor, your five minutes are up. Mr. Zephyr, would you care to elaborate on the alleged proprietary piece of farm equipment in your barn?"

Looking up from the table, Nathan stared at Eric as a slow, evil smile crossed his face, "No, sir, I would not."

Feeling his body seethe with anger, Eric tried to remain calm, cool, and collected. Five minutes ago, Nathan was ready to tell him everything he wanted to know. Five minutes ago, he was on the verge of breaking this case wide open, but as he sat there and stared back at Nathan, he wondered what went wrong when he left the room. He was back to square one and based on the conversation he had just had with Deputy Director Johnson; he didn't have a lot of time to right the ship.

"Excuse me, Mr. Zephyr?"

"I have nothing more to say, Special Agent."

"So, what you told me about your son was just a lie?"

"Special Agent," interjected Mr. Dewey, redirecting the conversation. "That is enough. You are badgering my client. Either you charge my client, or you release him."

For the second time in less than twenty-four hours, Mr. Dewey had posed the request and once again, Eric contemplated his next move. Any charge he filed against Nathan would be specious at best and ignorant at worst. He knew he had been beaten.

"I don't have anything further at this time, Counselor," Eric conceded, knowing his superiors wanted the interrogation finished, he was out of options. "Mr. Zephyr is free to go."

"Thank you, Special Agent," Mr. Dewey wisecracked, anger dripping off every word, "for wasting everyone's time. Pull a stunt like this again and I will have your badge. Good day, sir."

Nathan and Mr. Dewey walked out of the interrogation room and as the door closed behind them, Eric slammed his closed fist on the table. "Damn it!"

Chapter 25

Sitting in the waiting room, Sebastian was calm, cool, and collected just thumbing through a magazine, stopping every so often to read an article. It always amazed David that very little seemed to bother Sebastian. No matter what they faced or whatever obstacle stood in their way, Sebastian was always able to remain even keeled.

David, on the other hand, never felt calm or secure about any of the adversities facing them every day. He was always nervous about what was going to happen next or how he would face the next battle. He was always looking to the future and what kind of trouble they were going to find themselves in next.

His biggest worry was always his family. Their safety was the most important aspect of his life and as he became more engrossed in his new lifestyle as a warrior of God, he grew even more worried about the safety of his wife and kids because he wasn't there to protect them.

Sitting in his chair, he fidgeted like he always did when he was anxious. The more uneasy he became, the more his foot and knee bounced up and down. Smiling to himself, he thought about how Savannah would reach over and put her hand on his knee whenever his nerves got the best of him. Thinking about his wife's tender gesture of reassurance, he realized his nervous tic had not been bridled for the better part of a year. And now, it was exacerbated by just sitting in an unfamiliar waiting room.

The secretary was typing away on her computer keyboard like she didn't have a care in the world. She could see them because upon entering the building, Sebastian required him to cross back through the veil.

The secretary had been pleasant enough to both of them when they first arrived, but upon learning they didn't require any coffee or water, she resumed her work. She kept peering over her computer monitor and

David felt like she was spying on them. His imagination running wild, his paranoia about being exposed got the best of him. Maybe the incessant clicking of her long, painted fingernails across the keyboard was starting to drive him crazy. Whatever it was, he was becoming antsy.

Putting his head back on the top of the chair, he closed his eyes. Daydreaming, he tried to envision the last Christmas morning he had spent with his family. He tried hard to remember the expressions of joy on the kid's faces as they came downstairs and saw the stockings hanging by the fireplace while a multitude of gifts expanded into the room from underneath the Christmas tree. Remembering they always read from the Bible, he thought about the family having breakfast as they listened. And although he could remember the details like the stockings, the story of Jesus' birth, and the Christmas tree, he was having a hard time picturing the faces of his family members and the smiles that were present that morning.

Opening his eyes and staring at the ceiling, he was hoping for a calm resolve to wash over his body and take away the loneliness. It was moments like these when the gravity of the sacrifice he made sat on his chest like a three-ton weight.

A home body, David wasn't a warrior. He left the active part of fighting for his Christian faith up to those who were better equipped. He was just a normal guy who worked, played with his kids, was still in love with his beautiful wife, and that was okay with him. He didn't need anything more.

He started to count the small little dots cascading across the ceiling tile above his head when the secretary turned from her typing and announced, "Sebastian and David, he is ready to see you now. You may go in."

Who will see us? Why are we here? Where are we? What are we trying to accomplish? What does Sebastian have planned now? And, God forbid, is his crazy plan going to be the one that finally gets me killed?

This time, though, David was prepared. He had learned the two golden rules about going on a secret mission with Sebastian. The first rule was to follow Sebastian's orders without question. The second rule was to be prepared to run at the drop of a hat.

Thanking the secretary, Sebastian led David toward the door behind her desk. Before opening the door, Sebastian stopped, placed his hand on the doorknob, and said, "Today has nothing to do with me, David. Today is about you. Listen closely to every word."

David's nerves went into hyperdrive and he nodded back in agreement. Sebastian smiled, raised his right hand, and patted David on the shoulder. Turning the doorknob, he walked into a large office.

Stepping inside the massive office, David took in the scene. The walls to his left and right, as well as the wall behind him, were covered with pictures of a life well lived. He didn't take a good long look at the pictures on the wall, but they appeared to be of family members.

There was a floor-to-ceiling plate glass window on the far wall. In front of the large wall of glass was a massive desk with an old man sitting in a chair looking over some paperwork. There were two large, plush leather captains chairs opposite the old man that seemed to have been put there just for Sebastian and David.

"Good morning, Sebastian," Alden greeted them, smiling and rising from his chair. Alden stood a little over six feet tall, was thin with a well-defined, rugged face that spoke to the challenges he must have faced throughout his life. His hair was pure white and thinning.

"Good morning, sir," Sebastian responded, walking over to the desk and shaking hands with Alden. "This is the newest member of our team, Mr. David Zephyr."

"It's a pleasure to meet you, sir," David addressed the man, following Sebastian and shaking hands with Alden.

"The pleasure is all mine, Mr. Zephyr. You have no idea how long I have waited to meet you," Alden announced, waving them both toward the two captains chairs. "Please, please, both of you, take a seat and relax."

Sitting down, Alden leaned back in his chair and eyed up David. Nervous, David's leg started to shake again. Not knowing why he was in the office, he stared back at the old man.

"Now, Mr. Zephyr, I'm sure you're wondering why you're here today and well, to be quite frank, you're probably wondering just who the heck I am."

"I apologize, Alden. That is my fault," Sebastian interjected. "I should have told David all about you before we came."

"You worry about yourself, Sebastian," Alden chastened while waving him off, leaning forward and placing his arms on the desk. "It's probably better if David hears all of this from me anyway."

"Hear what from you?" David questioned, sitting up in his chair, looking at Sebastian, and staring, once again, at the old man.

"You're not a patient one, are you, David?" Alden laughed. "Do you mind if I call you David?"

"No, not at all," David chuckled, letting his guard down a little. "I must admit, patience has never been my strong suit."

"Well, David, my name is Alden Fredrickson. To make a long story much shorter, about sixty years ago, I was a young scientist working for the military. It was the height of the Cold War and the military developed a secret unit dedicated to working with emergent technologies."

"Emergent technologies?" David inquired, intrigued, yet confused.

"Yes. Simply stated, the military was interested in weaponizing all technologies against our enemies… Wow, has it really been almost sixty years?" Alden asked himself, reminiscing about how all of this began over half a century ago.

Moving closer to the desk, David hung on every word Alden had to say. Zoe had alluded to an individual who funneled millions into a secret project known as 'The Network,' but sitting face-to-face with the man himself was never a thought David had entertained.

"After mistakenly slipping through the veil one night while I was working on one of my scientific experiments," Alden continued, "I left the military altogether. They could never have this technology."

"They just let you leave the service?"

"Oh no, David," Alden guffawed, clapping his hands together in amusement. "They didn't just let me leave and I knew they wouldn't."

"How did you get out?"

"When you work for the military, especially in the unit I was working in, you have to get creative. I sought sanctuary at a local monastery and although my superiors were not happy, back in those days the military didn't even think about interfering with the church. So, they let me be.

"As part of my agreement with the priests in the monastery, I had to study the Bible. I had always been religious, but after what I saw on the other side of the veil, I wanted to know the Bible inside and out. I had thousands of questions I needed answered and the Bible was the only place to find those answers.

"For two years, I studied every word of my Bible. I continued my work with the technology that had allowed me to cross through the veil. I told the abbot what I was working on and what I had seen when I slipped behind the veil. It terrified him, but he agreed with me. The evil one was using science and technology to corrupt the world, so I was going to use my work to fight back.

"It wasn't easy working with emerging technologies in a monastery. There isn't a lot of money or resources. I tried to improvise, but I wasn't able to achieve the necessary results. Knowing the enemy was using technology and science to advance his stranglehold on the world, I left the monastery and started a small technology company.

"And here we are, fifty-plus years later. I own one of the most successful technology companies in the world. And much like the mafia, my entire company is a shell corporation hiding my true business of spending hundreds of millions of dollars a year on the resources needed to equip a worldwide group of people known as The Network so we can bring the war to Satan's front door."

"Excuse me for interrupting, sir," David interjected, "but what is it?"

"What is what, David?"

"The veil, sir. What is it?"

"Great question, David," Alden smiled, pausing for a moment to reflect while rubbing his chin. "Before you joined The Network, did you own a smart phone?"

"Yes."

"Do you know what the cloud is?"

"It is where my phone wirelessly connects to a backup system, but in regard to the question, I'm not following your logic."

"The veil shields us from the real world, David. It protects us from being able to see the spiritual war going on around us every day. As we go about our daily lives, most of the human race is oblivious to the forces of good and evil around them."

"That I understand. But how is the veil like the cloud?"

"Well, David, when you go to sleep at night, your heart, mind, and soul plug into the veil. Much like a cell phone connects to the cloud to back up your cell phone, sleep is a restorative process for the body and the parts of the brain we do not use connect with the entire world around us."

"So, we connect by having dreams?"

"Some of the greatest stories in the Bible start out with God or an angel of God appearing to someone in their dream. The whole story of Joseph in the Old Testament is predicated on dreams."

"So, we plug into the veil when we are asleep?" David questioned, scratching his head.

"That connection to the entire world around us is why we have good or bad dreams and why we have days when we wake up feeling like something in the world isn't quite right."

"Is that why the Zivlians come at night?"

"Exactly," Alden exclaimed, smiling and shaking a finger toward David. "Except time doesn't exist on the other side of the veil. You've heard that a day is something like a thousand years, well, it's like that on the other side. It's why the members of The Network don't age much, but I digress.

"Evil sees our existence in two measures. Asleep and awake. The most important thing anyone can do before going to bed is to pray for protection against evil. They should pray for good dreams, pure thoughts, and peaceful rest. But we don't, and the Enemy knows it.

"The Evil One knows a bad dream will be passed off as exactly that," Alden continued, shaking his head, "a bad dream. Especially by parents. So, he sends his minions to attack in the middle of the night."

"But a bad dream would lead me to pray," David expressed, baffled by the explanation, "so I don't get the logic."

"A bad dream would lead *you* to pray and to seek solace in His arms, but not everybody will."

"Why not?"

"Do you know the parable of the sower, David?"

"Yes."

"Do you remember Jesus' explanation for the seed that fell on the rocky ground?"

"The seed among the rock is when people hear the word with joy but fall away because of trouble or persecution."

"Those are the people the Enemy attacks. He comes to lie, steal, and kill. He creates trouble for them during the day and attacks their dreams at night. They fall away because of trouble and persecution, but that's where you and our technology come into the story."

"The Hellfire Device?"

"Exactly!" Alden exclaimed with exuberance. "I used an archaic version of the Hellfire Device when I passed through the veil for the first time. Ever since, I have worked tirelessly to create a better device to help us to defeat Satan."

"Pardon me for sounding selfish, Alden," David interrupted, stopping himself and thinking about what he was about to say next.

"Yes, David?"

Pondering his thoughts, David sat there for a few more moments in silence. "I understand everything you are telling me, but even with all of this information, I don't understand what any of this has to do with the safety of my family."

"David…" Alden muttered, letting out a deep sigh, standing up, and walking toward the glass wall behind his desk. "David, I hate to say this, but everything that's happening with the Zivlians and the Fallen Angels is because of you and your family."

"But that's the problem, Alden. Why?"

"David, come over here a minute."

David looked at Sebastian who nodded his head which made it clear to David he should follow the directive he was given. So, David stood up from his chair, walked over to the large window, and stood next to Alden.

"Do you see those men and women working down there?" Alden pointed through the plate glass window at the people working on an assembly line.

Looking through the window, David responded, "Yes, sir, I do."

"Those people come to work every day and have no idea what they are building."

"What are they building?"

"They are assembling the latest version of the Hellfire Device," Alden continued, proud of his latest accomplishment. "It will be a revolutionary upgrade over the devices you are using now and not one of those people have any clue what those devices will be used for when we deliver them to members of The Network all around the world."

"Sorry, sir, what's your point?"

"My point, David, is we won't always have the answers. Those men and women faithfully believe they are changing the world. Abraham faithfully followed God when he almost sacrificed Isaac. Moses faithfully followed God through the desert for forty years. Twelve men left their lives behind to follow Christ through Jerusalem and millions of people have given their lives to Christ all over the world as they follow God's word every day. We don't always understand the reasons why something happens the way it does. We just have to have faith that with God's guidance, our walk through this life will make sense to Him," Alden replied, facing David. "Do you understand what I am trying to tell you?"

"I should be more faithful, and God will reveal the answers in His time, not mine."

"Very good, David," Alden said, patting him on the shoulder, walking back to his desk, and sitting down. After staring through the window at the factory workers for a moment, David went back and sat in his chair. "Fortunately, for you David, today is your lucky day."

"Pardon me? I don't follow."

"Well, Mr. Zephyr, unlike the men and women who work down on the assembly floor, I'm going to explain as much as I can for you. And when I am done telling you what you think you want to know, I'm going to ask you to do some things you're not going to want to do."

Leaning back in his chair, David stared at Alden, "Like what?"

"We'll get to that in a minute," Alden dismissed his question, waving his hand in the air.

"Patience, David," Sebastian added.

"First off," Alden said, "nobody in The Network is here by accident. If you are a part of The Network, you are here for a reason. And you, David, are no different than the rest of us."

"How so?"

"I am glad you asked," Alden replied, smiling. "Did Zoe tell you that you were the first newborn baby we've ever known to have nightmares?"

"She did, but I don't see how that is of any importance."

"Did Zoe tell you your birthmother was her sister?"

"What?" David gasped, looking back and forth between Sebastian and Alden. "Zoe is my aunt? Did you know this, Sebastian?"

"Zoe's parents were part of a cult," Alden interjected before Sebastian could answer. "They raised Zoe and your mother as members of the cult. Zoe doesn't talk much about it. It is too painful, but when she broke free from the cult, she joined a church and gave her life to Christ.

"Zoe's parents didn't take her defection too well. So, they kept a close eye on your mother and forced her to marry a member of the cult. When she became pregnant with you, they ran tests while you were in utero to see if you would be the perfect conduit for their plans."

"What were their plans?"

"Zoe's parents and the cult leaders felt they could bring about a new world order by using you as a conduit to allow all demons to pass through the veil and straight into our world. They firmly believed that once the world had fallen into the hands of darkness, they would be crowned and lifted up as faithful servants of the Evil One."

"Wait a minute," David interjected, leaning forward in his chair with a furrowed brow. "You're saying I was supposed to be used to bring about the end of the world?"

"Not the end of the world, David, a world where the veil is removed, making the predictions of the apocalypse a fallacy. If their plans had succeeded, everything would have changed."

"Alden, this is absolutely crazy," David declared, rubbing his hand on his chin in disbelief.

"David, I know this is a lot to handle right now…"

"A lot to handle. You think?" David argued, growing agitated. "Imagine coming into a room, meeting a guy like you, and finding out your birthmother was part of a cult trying to bring about the end of the world. You would find that a little disconcerting, Alden, wouldn't you?"

"David, I understand your frustration, but there is more to the story."

"Like what?" David challenged, sarcasm dripping of every word. "Pestilence and locusts?"

"Like the fact your birthmother found out what her parents were planning to do, and she wouldn't let them go through with it." Alden paused for a moment and collected his thoughts. He wanted to make sure he was sharing the information in a respectful manner. "After you were born, she secretly brought you to a private Christian adoption agency. You were adopted quickly to prevent the members of the cult from finding you."

"What happened to my mother?"

"She died shortly thereafter," Alden said with a solemn reverence. "The police called it an accident, but Zoe swears her brother-in-law had your mother killed."

"All due respect, Alden. As much as I appreciate you telling me about my birthmother, I still don't understand what any of this has to do with me or my family."

"Because you can't just hide a child from the forces of evil, David. They eventually found out where you were, but by the time they found you, it was too late. You had been saved and had already committed your life to Christ. There wasn't anything they could do to you, so they waited."

"For what?"

"For you to have children," Alden replied, staring at David as the gravity of the statement sunk in.

"No… wait… wait a minute," David interjected, nerves welling up inside him. "Why would they wait for me to have a child?"

"Certain bloodlines are conduits for spiritual interference," Alden continued, lowering his eyes in solemn reverence to the information being shared. "Unfortunately, your family is one of those bloodlines David."

"But if I was given up for adoption and hidden from them, how did they find me?"

"You're dealing with spiritual entities, David," Alden chuckled, pointing at David. "It's not hard for them to find you. You just became untouchable when you became saved."

"This means Jordan is untouchable as well."

"Exactly," Alden exclaimed, waiting for the light bulb to illuminate above David's head. "Which leaves them one last attempt."

"Carissa…"

"Your daughter has had night terrors since she was little, David," Alden conceded, rubbing his hands together. "Carissa is strong willed.

She has fought back and with the strength of the rest of your family, Carissa has remained strong, but she is still in danger."

Realizing what Alden was telling him was farfetched, but if there was any truth to the story, David would do anything to protect his daughter. "What do you need me to do?"

"I like the way you think, David," Alden smiled, leaning forward and crossing his arms on his desk. "They know with you around, especially as a member of The Network, there is no way they can use your daughter to bring their plans to fruition."

"Wait a minute…" David gasped, looking from Sebastian to Alden. "Do you mean they need me out of the way before they can do anything to Carissa?"

"Do you remember the first dream Carissa pulled you into?" Alden asked, reminding David of the night everything started.

"Yes."

"The Fallen Angel was sent to kill you in your daughter's nightmare. Had Sebastian not intervened and pulled you out of the dream, you would have been killed."

David was stunned at the revelation Alden had just shared with him about the initial nightmare. Instead of the dream being a coronation or an initiation into The Network, it was supposed to be his funeral. Pausing, taking a deep breath, and saying a silent prayer to himself, David looked at Alden with a determined look on his face. "What do we do now?"

"We make the hunted the hunter," Alden declared.

"Come again?"

"We have to put you in harm's way as bait and when they take the bait," Alden indicated with a serious look on his face. "We take the war to them on every front."

"And I assume you have a plan for how we do that?" David demanded, nervous about what he was hearing.

"The plan you have with the federal banks is a good start, but I agree with Sebastian, you shouldn't have engaged Agent Carmichael. You made it personal."

"That was my call," David retaliated, anger welling up inside of him. "Besides, I still think he might prove useful, but he can't be our plan to end this once and for all. Please tell me you have something better planned?"

"I agree. I believe the agent will be very useful to us," Alden smirked, winking at Sebastian. "And as far as plans, I have one. I do."

"What is it?"

"I'm not going to lie to you, David. We are going to do a lot of things they wouldn't expect," Alden confirmed, rubbing his hands together. "A lot of dangerous things I can guarantee you are not going to want to do. But, like it or not, you are going to have to do them, David,"

"I understand," David replied, a solemn expression on his face as the gravity of the situation sunk in.

"Can you live with that, David?" Alden questioned, skeptical that David would be able to follow through with their plans.

"Do I have much of a choice?"

"At this point, David," Alden asserted, leaning forward on his desk, "no, you really don't."

<h1 style="text-align:center">Chapter 26</h1>

Eric had eaten very little on his plate. He was engrossed in his work. It was late and he had to eat, so he went to a diner near his office. There were only a couple of patrons sitting at the counter, so he sat at a booth that overlooked the street. Most of the task force had gone home, but the Zephyr case consumed him. He was focused on it twenty-four hours a day. It was his obsession and his cross to bear. Catching David Zephyr had become a fixation that would not be exorcised until the suspect was in custody and he had the answers he desired.

The failed interrogation of Nathan bothered him. *Why was the brass taking high level phone calls?* Eric thought to himself. *And from whom? What was the purpose of derailing my investigation? And who scared Deputy Director Johnson to the point of threatening me? What is so important about the contraption that influence peddlers came to his defense?*

"Are you done?" the waitress asked, standing beside the table.

"Yes," Eric replied, dropping the file on the table, sitting back, and looking at her. "I'm sorry. I was lost in my work."

"Fifth night this week," the waitress smiled, clearing away the plates, "you're becoming one of my regulars."

"Guess I am," Eric joked, cracking a smile and winking at her. "Hope you don't mind."

"Not at all, especially since you tip well," she chuckled, winking back at him.

"Do you mind getting me another cup of coffee?" Eric asked, sliding the cup across the table. "It's going to be another long night."

"Back in a minute," the waitress replied, taking his plate to the kitchen.

"Thank you." Eric picked up the file on the table and continued reviewing the case when she walked off to get him another cup of coffee.

Eric pulled out his notebook, opened it to a blank page, and started reading through the file. As he came across new information or something he found interesting, he wrote it down in the notepad he carried with him at all times. It's how he kept all of the relevant information with him. It was an old school method, but it worked.

"Isn't your wife going to get jealous if you keep working late every night?" the waitress asked, picking up his cup and filling it with more coffee.

"Not married."

"Really? A handsome man like you," The waitress expressed, putting the cup on the table and eyeing Eric up. "Is there a girlfriend somewhere waiting up for you?"

"No ma'am," Eric acknowledged, taking a sip of the coffee. "Married to the job. No time for anything else."

"If you don't mind my saying," the waitress continued, "life is too short to waste it at work. My Bobby and I have been married twenty-five years and one thing we have always agreed on, don't let work rob you of the one life you live."

"Twenty-five years? Congratulations," Eric praised, tapping on the file in front of him. "Maybe one day, but my work is all consuming. No time. It wouldn't be fair to anyone I was with."

"I can see that," the waitress scoffed. "I hope you find her one day."

"Me too." Eric was lying. The idea of having a family was foreign to him. He would never be able to find a work, life balance that would produce a healthy relationship with someone he truly loved.

"Well, if you need anything, I am here until 3 a.m.," the waitress informed Eric before walking over to the customers at the counter.

"Thank you," Eric replied, smiling to himself.

Eric picked up the file and continued thumbing through it and taking notes. While writing down a piece of information, something caught his eye. Pausing and staring at the page for a moment, he looked through the window and saw David standing on the sidewalk staring at him. Looking back down at the file and dropping the pencil, Eric looked again, and David was gone.

Eric shook his head from side to side while rubbing his eyes, because he was now seeing things. Maybe he was working too hard, and his mind was playing tricks on him. So, Eric stood up and walked toward the front door. "I'll be right back"

"Okay," the waitress responded, watching him leave.

Eric opened the door and stood in front of the diner. Looking to his right and left, he didn't see anything. He laughed. His mind was definitely playing tricks on him because he was working so hard. *Maybe the waitress is right,* he thought to himself, *I need something more than just work in my life.*

Eric was about to go back into the diner when something caught his eye again. Looking down the street, David was standing halfway down the street just staring at him. As Eric faced him, David waved and stepped into an alleyway.

"David, stop," Eric yelled, running down the sidewalk to the alley.

Pulling his gun out of his holster, Eric peered around the corner. The alley didn't have an exit, it ended at a brick wall. He also didn't see anyone in the alley, so he stepped into the alley and methodically worked his way down the corridor with his gun drawn in front of him. His heart pounding against his chest, Eric looked behind every object to make sure David couldn't overtake him.

"You can't hide, David," Eric declared, inching his way down the alley. "There's no way out, except through me."

"Are you sure about that?" David asked from behind Eric.

Whipping around with his gun drawn, Eric didn't see anyone. He was perplexed. He didn't know how David had gotten behind him. He worked his way back toward the opening of the alley looking for David.

"I'm not there either," David yelled from the end of the alley.

"Stop playing games." Eric spun around and trained his weapon on the end of the alley. He didn't know how David was pulling off the trick, but he knew David was in the alley and he was going to arrest him. "Show yourself."

"I'm not playing games," David declared.

"And neither am I," Sebastian yelled from the fire escape. Eric trained his weapon on the fire escape but didn't see anyone.

"Or me," Michael proclaimed from the opening of the alleyway. Eric spun and looked for the accomplice and saw nothing.

"None of us are playing games," Zoe yelled, standing behind Eric by the dumpster. When he turned to look for her, she was gone.

"You only see what you want to see, Special Agent," David explained from the opening of the alley by the street.

Whirling around to confront David, Eric saw no one in the alley. "I don't know how you are doing this, but I will catch you, David."

"Will you?" Zoe asked from the roof.

"Are you sure?" Sebastian questioned from behind the dumpster.

"You can't even catch us in an alley," Michael declared from the fire escape.

"We know what you're going to do before you do it," Peter yelled from the end of the alley.

While they bombarded him with commentary, Eric spun in the direction of the voice every time they spoke and saw nothing. His heart beating faster and sweat starting to bead on his forehead, he turned and faced the opening of the alley to see David standing there alone. He trained his weapon on David and ordered, "Stay right where you are. You're under arrest."

"You will catch me," David declared, unflinching and calm in his resolve, "if and only if I let you catch me."

"Don't move, David," Eric repeated, inching up the alleyway with his gun trained on the suspect.

"Look beyond the facts, Special Agent," David warned, smiling at him. "Look for what you cannot see, believe in what you don't believe in, and open your mind to the possibilities. Then and only then will you find me."

"Don't move, David," Eric ordered, moving up the alleyway. "Put your hands up."

"Good night, Special Agent. See you soon." David smiled, waved, and ran down the street.

"David, no," Eric yelled as he gave chase. Running out of the alley into the street, Eric couldn't see David anywhere. He disappeared into thin air again. Throwing his fist in frustration, Eric yelled, "How are you doing this?"

Chapter 27

Sitting on the beach, Savannah listened to the waves crashing on the sand. Sipping her coffee just a few feet outside of the hotel room she had rented, she took solace in this moment of solitude. Coming to the coast for the weekend was the best decision she had made in a while. It was the happiest her children had been in months, and she didn't want to wake them. Even if it was only for a couple of days, she was bound and determined to let the cares of the world dissipate while they enjoyed the surf and sand of Wrightsville Beach.

Joy washed over her as she recalled how the innocence of her children had returned just a few hours earlier when they arrived. Splashing around in the Atlantic Ocean and building sandcastles until the tide rose brought more laughter than she had heard in months. Swimming until the sun disappeared and letting the tapestry of stars illuminate their path to the local clam shack for dinner, they topped the evening off with banana split sundaes before calling it a night.

Smiling, her heart grew tenfold because Jordan and Carissa were able to be kids again. No one was staring at them. The finger pointing was miles away. The pity people felt for their lot in life was gone. Most importantly, there wasn't anybody asking them about David.

She wanted to say this trip was for her children, but she realized this trip was just as much for her. She was tired of the constant intrusions from the authorities, of having to rely on Nathan and Monica, and of being treated like an outcast. As rumors of David being a criminal circulated, friends and neighbors shunned her and her children.

She had had enough of the rumors and the lies. She didn't want to cry herself to sleep anymore as a dark emptiness crept into the Zephyr home. She wanted to take the pain away from Jordan and Carissa as they tried to make sense of the world. She wanted to answer their questions; *"Where was their dad? Why did he leave? Was he a criminal?"*

She contemplated her marriage to David. She had been in love with him since elementary school but over the last year, she had weak moments when she thought long and hard about her wedding vows. She understood good and bad times, being sick or poor was easy, but where was the line about a spouse disappearing into thin air? What was she supposed to do? When was he going to prove his innocence so they could start the hard work of repairing their life?

Staring at the sun rising over the ocean with a warm cup of coffee in hand, though, Savannah gave thanks to God for everything she had in her life. She asked God for His grace, wisdom, and clarity. But most of all, she asked God to give her the strength to get through the trials and tribulations she had to face in the future. She knew it wouldn't be easy but with His love and strength, she could conquer any mountain standing in her way.

Feeling her strength return, she realized her prayer lifted her spirits. She didn't know why they had to travel this path. All she knew was God had a plan and whatever the plan was, they would find a way to work it out together when this nightmare was over.

Standing up and walking over to the sliding glass door of her hotel room, Savannah opened the door a crack and listened. Not hearing the kids making any noise inside the hotel room, she decided to let them sleep a little longer. Closing the door, Savannah went back to her chair on the beach.

Sipping her coffee, she closed her eyes and rested. Facing the sun and listening to the sound of the waves, her memories wandered to previous vacations when she and David brought the kids to the ocean for long weekends. Remembering long walks, hand-in-hand, along the shore with David made her smile. Tears of joy tugging at her heart brought back memories of playing in the surf as a family. She longed for those moments again because she had learned over the past year, there was nothing better than spending precious time with the ones you loved.

"Excuse me, ma'am," Sebastian interrupted her peaceful bliss while walking across the beach toward Savannah. "Do you mind if I sit here for a moment?"

Opening her eyes and looking at the teenager dressed in black, Savannah smiled to herself. Ignoring his apparent advances, she closed her eyes again. "I am very flattered, but I am married. Plus, I might be a little old for you."

"You are very beautiful, ma'am," Sebastian stumbled over his words as he was caught off guard by her response. "But I'm sure David might take it personally if I tried to hit on you."

Savannah was startled by his response. This was more than a young man on the prowl, he knew who she was. More importantly, he knew who David was. Opening her eyes and staring at the young man standing in front of her, she sat up in her chair and prodded, "Excuse me?"

"David would be extremely upset if he thought I was hitting on you."

"How do you know who my husband is?" Savannah pressed, concerned for herself and her children.

"I know a lot of things, Mrs. Zephyr," Sebastian replied. "Like, I know there are two federal agents in a blue sedan directly across the street from your hotel."

"Are you kidding me?" she grumbled, looking toward the street. "They followed me here, too?"

"Unfortunately, they follow you everywhere, Savannah," Sebastian acknowledged, pausing for a moment as he caught himself being rude. "Pardon me. What I meant to say, is do you mind if I call you, Savannah, Mrs. Zephyr?"

"Apparently, you know more about my life than I do, so you can call me whatever you want if you have answers."

"I might have some answers for you, Savannah," Sebastian responded with a boyish charm she found endearing. "Do you mind if I sit down?"

"Please, sit." Savannah sat up in her chair while a wave of butterflies fluttered in her stomach.

Sebastian looked around to make sure no one was watching before removing the bag hanging over his shoulder and sitting down on the sand next to Savannah. Placing the bag in his lap, he resumed, "Savannah, I'm sorry for what you have been through over the past year. I am partially to blame for everything your family has faced. I hope you can forgive me."

"You?" Savannah chuckled, raising an eyebrow at the insinuation. "How are you to blame? You're just a kid."

"Well, be that as it may, I am sorry. If those federal agents weren't out front, David might actually be sitting here with you."

"Is David here?" Savannah's heart jumped into her throat as she looked around for her husband. She hoped he would show himself. She wanted to hold him in her arms and melt into him.

"He is nearby, Savannah, but he couldn't come."

"I want to see him," Savannah demanded, continuing to look up and down the beach for him.

"It isn't safe for him to be here."

"I want to see him."

"They're watching," Sebastian declared with a stern demeanor. "You can't. It's not safe for him."

"Bring my husband here right now," Savannah insisted, grabbing Sebastian's wrist and staring him down.

"Savannah, if we can't be civil, I am going to leave," Sebastian warned, staring at her.

"I'll follow you."

"You won't be able to," Sebastian responded, chuckling.

"That's what you believe."

"It's what I know." Sebastian smiled at her, activated the Hell Fire device, and slipped behind the veil in front of her eyes.

"What the heck?" Savannah gasped, jumping up from her chair and staring at the empty space where Sebastian had been sitting. Panicked, she looked around for him, scared. "What is going on here?"

Reappearing in the same spot, Sebastian sat on the sand and smiled. "Can we talk now?"

"How did you do that?" Savannah insisted, stepping back from him, afraid.

"We don't have time for me to explain everything. Please sit down."

"Are you an angel?" Savannah asked, goosebumps welling up on her skin.

"I am human."

"But how?" Savannah questioned, moving back to her chair and sitting down slowly.

"That's a long story we don't have time for."

"Can David see me?"

"Yes, he is close by."

"What can I do to help?" Savannah was freaked out by what she had just witnessed, but she wanted her husband to come home. "I'll do whatever it takes to bring my husband home."

"Before we get started, everything they said about David is false. He has remained faithful to his family, and he isn't involved in any sort of criminal activity."

"I want to believe you… but I don't even know your name," Savannah stammered, eying up Sebastian. "Do you have one?"

"Pardon me for being rude," Sebastian chuckled, holding out his hand. "My name is Sebastian Fredrickson; it's a pleasure to meet you."

Shaking hands with him, Savannah pressed, "Pardon my curiosity, but how do you know my husband?"

"That's a hard question to answer."

"Why don't you try?"

"Rather than waste our time trying to make sense of the last year, why don't I do something better?"

"Like what?"

Reaching into the bag on his lap, Sebastian pulled out a couple of items and handed them to Savannah. "This picture of David was taken about an hour ago. As you can see, we are holding today's newspaper in our hands."

"Who are these other people?"

"I'll get to them in a moment," Sebastian replied, pointing at the items she was holding. "That is the copy of the newspaper we are holding in the photograph. We all signed it."

Savannah was frozen. A plethora of feelings washed over her. Staring at a picture of David, she wished he had come, but she also knew the agents would take him away in cuffs. Knowing he was so close made her heart ache. She wanted to hold him. She wanted to kiss him. And, yes, a part of her wanted to slap him across the face for everything he had put her through. But most of all, she wanted him to come home.

"I assume you came here to tell me something other than my husband took a picture with you," Savannah interrogated with purpose, staring Sebastian down, hoping for some information.

"I did," Sebastian countered, pausing to collect his thoughts. "We need you to do something for us."

"Me?" Savannah was astounded by the request. "What do you need from me?"

Handing the bag to Savannah, Sebastian explained, "In this bag are pictures of David with each of the people he has been with for the past year. We need you to take these pictures to Special Agent Carmichael and tell him David has reached out to you."

"No." Savannah held up her hands in protest and refused to take the bag. "I won't do it."

"You have too," Sebastian pleaded, "you're our only hope."

"You're absolutely nuts if you think I am going to do that, Sebastian," she declared, shaking her head in disagreement. "You can tell David I won't do it. If he doesn't like it, he can come find me himself."

"You have to take those pictures to Special Agent Carmichael, Savannah," Sebastian cajoled, hoping to find a crack in her outright defiance. "It is critical to everything we are trying to do."

"And what are you doing, Sebastian?"

"We're trying to make it so David can come home."

Stunned by his pronouncement, she stared at the teenager sitting in front of her. "No."

"You have to," Sebastian persuaded, pausing for a moment to collect his thoughts. "This is the first step in ending all of this."

"I can't," Savannah uttered, tears rolling down her cheeks. "This doesn't make any sense, Sebastian. Why? Why do I have to give these pictures to that horrible man. He'll use them to prove David is guilty."

"You're absolutely right, he will."

"What is wrong with you?" Savannah threw her hands up in frustration. She was concerned about the logic of making David look guilty. It didn't make sense to her. "Now you want him to think David is guilty? How does that help? What am I missing here?"

"He already thinks David is guilty," Sebastian explained without any change in his intonation or demeanor. "With these pictures, he'll also think you're involved, so don't go alone. I would take a lawyer with you, because as soon as you deliver these photographs, I can guarantee the interrogation will start immediately."

"Are you out of your ever-loving mind?" Savannah bellowed, staring at Sebastian in disbelief at what he was proposing. "You want to take both parents away from my children?"

"Oh, right. I forgot," Sebastian deadpanned, "a babysitter might be a good idea, too."

"This isn't funny, Sebastian, this is my life you're playing with."

"Do I look like I am laughing?"

"No. I can't," Savannah muttered to herself. She put her hands in front of her, facing Sebastian, moving them back and forth in a show of defiance. "This is crazy. You're crazy. I won't do it."

"I need you to trust me, Savannah."

"Trust you? Huh! I don't even know you."

"But you do know David," Sebastian countered, "and he is asking you to do this."

"You're a hundred percent right, I do know my husband," Savannah confirmed, growing angrier by the moment. "Look around, Sebastian, do you see my husband? Because I don't."

"Calm down, Savannah."

"Don't tell me what to do," Savannah exclaimed, pointing a finger at him. "The answer is no. This is ridiculous, I'm not doing it."

"David thought you might feel that way," Sebastian conceded, reaching into his pocket and pulling out a sealed envelope. "David told us there's no way on God's green earth you would do this unless he came with me and begged you to do it himself."

"Sounds like David to me," Savannah softened before pausing for a moment. "He's not wrong."

"You know why he can't be here," Sebastian resumed, handing her the letter. "He gave me this letter. It doesn't explain much, but it is the best he could do on short notice."

Holding the letter in her hand, she began to tremble, tears streaming down her cheeks. Recognizing David's handwriting on the envelope, she wanted to tear it open and read it, but she wanted to wait until Sebastian was gone.

"I'm not agreeing to anything," Savannah bargained, wiping the tears from her eyes. "But if I decide to help you, how do you want this done?"

"If you decide to help us," Sebastian directed, "take these pictures to Special Agent Carmichael. Tell him David is not a thief and we would like him to back off his investigation."

"He's never going to stop chasing David."

"I know, we don't want him to," Sebastian smiled, standing up and wiping sand off of his pants. "That's why it's so important for you to give him the pictures."

"Is David ever coming home?"

"If everything goes according to plan, David will be home soon."

"And if everything doesn't go according to plan?"

"It would be better if none of us think about that possibility."

"Thank you, Sebastian," Savannah acknowledged. Standing up, she gave him a hug. "Tell David to be safe and to come home quickly."

"I will."

"Good luck."

"Thank you." Sebastian nodded his head in silent solidarity with Savannah and walked down the beach.

Sitting back down in her chair, Savannah pulled the pictures out of the bag. She didn't recognize any of the people in the photos. Putting the pictures back in the bag, she paused for a moment and stared at the letter David had written.

Holding the envelope, her heart began to race. Her mouth was dry. Putting her fingernail under the flap of the sealed envelope, her finger started to shake as she ripped it open. Pulling out the piece of paper, she unfolded the note and read it:

My Dearest Savannah,

How ticked off are you right now? I bet if I were there, you would have a hard time choosing between hugging me and slapping me. I hope when the time comes, you choose to hug me. I miss holding you in my arms.

I know I will never be able to apologize enough for the pain I've caused you and the children. Please realize how truly sorry I am. I love you. And one day soon, I hope to sit down and explain all of this to you.

Please believe me, I am doing all this for our family. I miss you all every single day and if all goes well, I will be home soon. But before I can do that, I need you to do something for me first.

In your hand, you hold a stack of pictures. These pictures are very important and, although I know you don't want to do this, please take the pictures to Special Agent Carmichael. Give them to him. Tell him about meeting Sebastian on the beach. And if you want to rub it in his face, you can tell him I stood next to the car his agents were in outside the hotel. I signed my name in Sharpie in the wheel well while his agents slept on the job. That will drive him sufficiently up the wall.

I need you to bring these pictures to Special Agent Carmichael. I know you're angry with me, Savannah, for asking you to do this for me and after you deliver those pictures, you're going to be much angrier. My prayer is that I will be able to come home soon. And God willing, those pictures will help me do that. Please trust me.

I love you with all of my heart, mind, and soul. I thank God for you and the kids every day of my life. Kiss the kids for me.

Love,
David

Chapter 28

Officer Wilson walked the city streets of Zion Corners like he had for the past twenty-five years. A throwback to an era when police officers walked the beat in order to remain close to the city and the community, he believed the close connection offered a level of protection most cities had lost. There had been opportunities for Officer Wilson to move up through the ranks of the Zion Corners Police Department, but he always declined because to serve and protect meant remaining close to the heartbeat of the city.

Taking his lunch break, he stopped into Betty's Diner and ordered the roast beef combo with an endless cup of coffee. It was a typical calm and uneventful evening, so he took a few extra minutes to joke with the regulars who worked the night shift.

It was quiet when Officer Wilson headed back onto the streets of Zion Corners to finish his patrol. Passing the entrance of the Zion Corners Federal Bank, Officer Wilson heard a disturbance. Pulling out his flashlight, he started walking down an alley when he heard a loud crash from inside the bank. Running to the plate glass door of the bank, Officer Wilson pointed his flashlight. He couldn't see anything beyond the long hallway that turned into the lobby.

Hearing another loud crash, Officer Wilson reached for his shoulder and spoke into his two-way radio, "This is Officer Pete Wilson. I am at the entrance of the Zion Corners Federal Bank, and it appears we have a robbery in progress. Send backup."

Officer Wilson listened for the muffled response, "Copy that, Officer Wilson. Backup is in route."

Standing at the front door waiting for backup to arrive, Officer Wilson heard a loud crash and a distant voice that seemed to be yelling out in pain. *What if there is an innocent bystander in the bank? I can't wait for back up while an innocent person gets hurt.*

Casting aside protocol, Officer Wilson drew his service revolver, lifted his leg, and kicked the plate glass door of the Zion Corners Federal Bank. Covering his head while glass shattered all around him, he ducked under the door handle and crept down the hallway while the alarms sounded.

Officer Wilson's nerves were on heightened alert as he heard the voices growing louder. Goose bumps popped up all over his body, his breathing became elevated, and his heart pounded away inside his chest. Moving down the hallway toward the perpetrators, he was running on pure adrenalin. Reaching the end of the hallway, he pressed his back against the wall, brought his service revolver up to his chest, took a deep breath, and prepared himself for what was waiting around the corner.

Popping around the corner, Officer Wilson pointed his revolver with the flashlight on top of the barrel in front of him. Pointing his weapon at the back of David who was standing in the middle of the bank, Officer Wilson barked orders, "Freeze! This is police, turn around slowly, and put your hands where I can see them."

Ignoring the order, David braced himself for another attack from the Zivlian which raced at him at a speed that evaded being seen by the video monitors and the eyes of Officer Wilson. Raising his left arm, David caught the beast by the leg, threw his right hand full force into the demon, spun ninety degrees, and launched the vile creature across the lobby into the wall of the bank.

Following his instincts, Officer Wilson ducked when David spun and launched something in his general direction. Hearing something he never saw hit the wall, Officer Wilson stepped into the opening, trained his weapon and his flashlight on David, and shouted his orders, "Freeze and put your hands where I can see them… Hands where I can see them."

Standing there motionless, David stared at Officer Wilson. He took pity on the officer. He knew something bad was going to happen and there wasn't anything he could do to stop it.

Taking another step toward David, Officer Wilson smelled sulfur permeating his nose and burning his eyes. He found it difficult to breathe.

Struggling to keep his eyes and weapon trained on David, he yelled, "Hands where I can see them."

The heat from the sulfur was so intense Officer Wilson started sweating. Taking another step toward David, out of the corner of his eye, he saw the beast charging at him with blood red eyes, jagged teeth, razor sharp claws, and wings spread wide across its jet black, wart-laced torso. He tried to face the entity, but it was too fast for him. The demon collided with Officer Wilson as he discharged his weapon in the proximity of the creature and he found himself hurtling backward into the bank wall.

Slamming his head against the wall, Officer Wilson collapsed on the floor. Standing over the officer, the Zivlian breathed on his lifeless body. Looking for signs of life, the demon pushed and pawed at Officer Wilson's body.

Stepping toward the entity, David taunted the creature, "Come on you worthless beast, come get me… Fight me."

Staring at David, the beast felt a blast of wind rushing down the hallway. Sensing an exit, the beast ran toward the open door.

"No," David yelled, preparing to fight it in the streets.

Crashing against the wall in front of him, David was startled when the beast was thrown back into the bank by someone or something in the hallway. He stepped back into a defensive position as the beast struggled getting to its feet. "Come on you gnarly, nasty looking, piece of burnt meat, fight me like the inferior dog you are."

The Zivlian became enraged. Weakened from being battered around the bank, the Zivlian made one last charge toward David. Meeting in the middle of the bank lobby, David pinned the beast on the floor, jammed the Hellfire Device into the torso of the entity, and delivered electrical charges into the demon. Feeling the creature starting to lose the battle, he sent it off with a message, "In the name of Jesus Christ, I send you back to the depths of Hell."

Delivering one final blast, the Zivlian disappeared underneath him. Sitting on his knees in the middle of the bank, David said a prayer of thanks for surviving another battle. Taking a deep breath, wiping the sweat off his forehead, and standing up, David walked over to Officer Wilson.

Bending down on one knee, David made sure the officer was not dead. He was relieved to see there was only a scratch on the officer's arm that was barely bleeding. Checking for a pulse, Michael whispered from the darkened hallway, "He's fine, David, you need to get out of here. He called for backup, and it should be arriving shortly."

"Why are you here?"

"Peter alerted me when the officer showed up," Michael answered, making sure to stay hidden from the cameras. "Now get out of here."

"I need to know the officer is okay," David replied without looking as he knelt beside the officer, because he knew every action was being recorded by the security cameras.

"He's fine, but if you don't leave quickly, you won't be."

"The officer getting hurt wasn't part of the plan," David shot back, checking the officer out for injuries.

"You can't plan for everything. But if you stay, the whole plan goes out the window."

"What about you?"

"I have steered clear of the security cameras," Michael answered, "I was never here."

"Get out of here, Michael," David barked, still checking out the officer. "I'm leaving in a minute."

Taking David's warning to heart, Michael didn't need to be reminded twice. He made his way down the hallway to the broken front door of the Zion Corners Federal Bank and slipped out, disappearing into the darkness.

Hearing sirens blaring in the distance, David picked Officer Wilson's service revolver from the bank floor and returned it to his holster. "You're going to have one heck of a headache in the morning, Officer. Sorry about that."

Chapter 29

Entering the lobby with the task force after the three-hour drive to Zion Corners, Eric yelled, "Who's in charge here?"

"I am," Detective Parkinson yelled, raising his hand as he crossed the lobby toward Eric.

"Who are you?" Eric asked, standing face to face with the detective.

"Detective Parkinson, Zion Corners Police Department," the rotund detective responded, dressed in a fifty-dollar suit and sporting a pencil thin mustache. "And you are?"

Flashing his badge, Eric declared, "Special Agent Eric Carmichael, FBI. I am claiming jurisdiction over this crime scene. Tell your men to stand down."

"Well, Special Agent," Detective Parkinson laughed, placing his hands on his hips. "I am glad you boys showed up. Have fun with this one."

"You heard him, Agent Quyen," Eric barked, turning to give his orders. "Meet with their forensics team and see what they have gathered so we can get to work."

"We're on it, Boss," Quyen responding, leading the team into the bank.

Facing Detective Parkinson, Eric pressed for information "What can you tell me so far?"

"Nothing. This case doesn't make any sense." Detective Parkinson ran his hand through his hair and looked at Eric with a vacant stare. "Nothing was stolen."

"That's his M.O."

"What kind of criminal doesn't steal anything?"

"That will be the first question I ask when I apprehend the suspect."

"And you said this is his M.O.?"

"Yes."

"Good riddance then. I'm glad you boys showed up." Detective Parkinson laughed and slapped his hands together symbolizing washing his hands of the case.

"Since you caught the perpetrator in the act, do you have any eyewitnesses?"

"Yes, but…"

"But nothing," Eric interrupted, looking around the lobby. "Are they still here? I want to speak with them."

"To be honest, Agent, the eyewitness is worthless," Detective Parkinson declared, fidgeting and avoiding eye contact. "His story doesn't make any sense."

"Really?" Eric prodded, shooting a side glance at Detective Parkinson. "Why?"

"You have to hear his story." Detective Parkinson rolled his eyes. "I can't do it justice."

"Try me. What's his story?"

"Sorry, Agent, you'll have to hear it from him," Detective Parkinson announced, becoming agitated with Eric's impatience. "It'll make you scratch your head in disbelief."

"Please don't tell me the witness is crazy."

"To the contrary, Agent, he's one of our finest."

"He's a cop?" Eric was surprised at the response, furrowing a brow, he compelled the detective for more information. "What happened?"

"The officer stood in the lobby, his service revolver firmly fixed on the suspect and somehow, he got thrown across the room into a wall. Knocked him clean out."

"How do you know he had his weapon pointed at the suspect?"

"Surveillance video," Detective Parkinson confirmed. "He had his service revolver drawn. He was approaching the suspect, he turned briefly, and flies backward into the wall."

"An accomplice?"

"Nobody was in the room."

"And he got thrown into the wall?"

"Wouldn't have believed it if I hadn't seen it myself."

"Really?" Eric was perplexed, staring at Detective Parkinson in disbelief. "How?

"I don't know. The impact knocked the officer clean out."

"And the suspect?"

"He checked on the officer, put the service weapon back in the holster, and got away."

"How did the suspect get away?" Eric questioned, wondering the manner in which the suspect escaped the authorities.

"Disappeared."

"Hm, interesting." Eric crossed his arms and processed the information he had just learned. "I need to speak to the eyewitness. Is he available?"

"Be my guest." Detective Parkinson pointed in the direction of some cubicles. "He's being treated by EMTs."

"What's he being treated for?"

"Hopefully, for a traumatic brain injury."

"Why would you hope for that? Isn't that a little harsh, detective?"

"It's either a TBI or one of us is going to have to tell a twenty-five-year veteran with a sterling service record, he's being placed on leave pending a complete psychiatric evaluation."

"I'll leave that part up to you local boys."

"I hope it doesn't come to that," Detective Parkinson responded, patting Eric on the shoulder. "Good luck, Agent. I think you're going to need it."

"Thank you, Detective." Eric walked across the lobby, deep in thought.

Stopping just outside the cubicle where Officer Wilson was being attended to by medics, Eric noticed the ice on the back of his head and the bandaged arm. Sitting in a chair, Officer Wilson was muttering to himself under his breath. Eric noticed similarities between the behavior of Officer Wilson and many of the men he had shared the battlefield with who had gone through traumatic situations.

Eric could see the faraway look in Officer Wilson's eyes when he sat down in the chair next to him. "Do you mind if I sit down?"

"Let's cut the small talk, sir. Internal Affairs? Or the Feds?"

"Pardon me?"

"You're not wearing a cheap suit, so you're either with Internal Affairs or the Feds," Officer Wilson responded, straightening himself up in the chair.

"You're pretty observant, Officer."

"Been my job for twenty-five years," he stated, staring at Eric nervously. "So, which one are you?"

"Feds."

"Knew it."

"My team and I have been investigating a case involving the man standing in the middle of the bank tonight. His name is David Zephyr. Any information you can give me about him would help us greatly in our attempt to apprehend him.

"I know you have had quite a traumatic night," Eric continued, pulling out his notebook and flipping to a blank page. "But if you don't mind answering some questions, we will try to make this quick so you can go home."

"I'd appreciate it."

"What can you tell me about the suspect?"

"Nothing."

"Come again?"

"He didn't do anything," Officer Wilson responded, staring into Eric's eyes. "He just stood there staring at me the whole time."

"He had to do something, Officer."

"Nope." Officer Wilson shook his head in disagreement. "He just stared at me."

"Stared at you?"

"It was more like he pitied me."

"Pitied you?" Eric asked, raising an eyebrow. "Why would he pity you?"

"He knew what was about to happen and there was nothing he could do to stop it."

"I'm lost, Officer." Eric looked at the officer for a moment. Sitting back and rubbing his chin with his fingers, he paused to collect his thoughts. "What did he know was going to happen?"

"The beast."

"The beast?"

"He knew he couldn't stop the beast from attacking me."

"What?" Eric stared at Officer Wilson in disbelief. "What are you talking about? What beast?

"The one that attacked me," Officer Wilson declared, holding up his bandaged arm.

"Your statement doesn't make any sense, Officer. Walk me through what happened."

"I had my gun trained on the suspect," Officer Wilson continued, "told him to keep his hands where I could see them. That's when I smelled it."

"Smelled what?"

"Sulfur."

"Sulfur?"

"Yes. Sulfur. It was thick. It burned. Oh, how it burned. I thought I was being poisoned."

"The suspect attacked you with sulfur?" Eric scratched his head, trying to follow the story the officer was telling. He was beginning to understand why the detective was so eager to pass off this case to him.

"I continued to approach the suspect. That's when I saw it."

"Saw what?" Eric was becoming frustrated with Officer Wilson's fanciful tale.

"The creature."

"What creature? What are you talking about?"

"It was a doglike creature," Officer Wilson continued, ignoring Eric's utter contempt for him. "Its skin was covered in warts. Its eyes were blood red. Its teeth were long and razor sharp. Its claws were like knife blades, and it had a wingspan at least six feet wide."

Tears rolled down Officer Wilson's face as he continued recounting the story, "I saw my life flash before my eyes. It was on top of me before I could react. I fired my weapon, but I missed. It knocked me clear across the room and I hit my head against the wall."

"How are you not dead then?" Eric wasn't willing to show the officer any empathy.

"I don't know." Officer Wilson lowered his head into his hands. "I believe the suspect saved me."

"The suspect saved you?"

"Yes, sir, he saved me."

"From what?"

"The hands of the Devil." Officer Wilson lifted his head with solemn reverence and stared into Eric's eyes. "From the hands of the Devil."

Eric was dumbfounded. Watching Officer Wilson being reduced to a stark raving lunatic was more than he could bear. "Thank you, Officer, I think we have enough."

"You don't believe me, do you?" Officer Wilson questioned, reaching out and grabbing Eric's wrist.

Staring at the bandage on the officer's arm, Eric locked eyes with Officer Wilson. He had met many honest people before and Officer Wilson seemed like an honest man, but Eric was a black-and-white kind of guy; believing something to be true and knowing something to be true were two different things. Without concrete evidence to back up Officer Wilson's story, he dismissed the story as nothing more than post-concussion syndrome.

"I think you had a rough night," Eric responded. "Concussions have a way of messing with a man's head."

"I know what I saw. Look at the tape, Agent. The suspect never moved. How do you explain that?"

"I don't know yet, Officer." Eric stood up and walked out of the cubicle.

"May God have mercy on your soul if that's what you are chasing," Officer Wilson yelled after Eric. "May God have mercy on your soul."

Walking away while Officer Wilson kept yelling things, Eric felt bad for the officer. But the only thing that mattered to him was what he could prove. And for the time being, what he could prove was that David Zephyr had been standing right in the middle of the Zion Corners Federal Bank just a few hours earlier and now he was gone.

Where did you go, Zephyr? Eric thought to himself. *How did you get in? Why didn't you take any money? What really happened to Officer Wilson when he came face to face with you? Was Officer Wilson telling me the truth? Or is the officer a stark raving lunatic? I'm going to find you, David, and you better have a good explanation for all of this.*

Chapter 30

Driving down the street, looking for a parking spot to open up, Savannah kept glancing over at the bag Sebastian had given her. She felt she must be crazy for considering this idea, but if it brought David home, it was worth the risk. She felt as though she should be nervous, but she wasn't. She was calm. She had a resolute action plan. Knowing everything in her life was going to change again when she handed over the bag, she was prepared to go on the offensive. It was the path she was willing to walk.

Seeing a parking space open up in front of her, the time to act had come. Putting her fears aside, she pulled her car into the space and parked. Bowing her head, she prayed, "Father God, give me the strength to get through the trials of this day. Give me the wisdom to make the right choices. May your grace flow over me as I stand face-to-face with my adversary. With you by my side, no one can stand against me. In Jesus's name, I pray, Amen"

Taking a deep breath and grabbing the bag from the passenger seat, Savannah exited the car and slammed the door. "Here goes nothing."

Crossing the street with confidence and purpose, she was unsure of why she was bringing the evidence to Eric, but she knew it was the right thing to do. The days of living in doubt and fear were behind her. She had a new purpose that started the moment she decided to turn the pictures over to the authorities.

Walking into the coffee shop, she ordered a coffee, found a table, and sat down. Pulling out Eric's business card, she dialed the number on her cellphone.

"Special Agent Carmichael's office, how may I help you?" said the voice on the other end of the line.

"I'd like to speak to Special Agent Carmichael, is he available?"

"Is he expecting your call, ma'am?"

"No, he is not, but I know he will take my call."

"Well, I am sorry, ma'am, Special Agent Carmichael is in a meeting. May I take a message?"

"Interrupt him."

"I can't interrupt him, ma'am. He is a very busy man. If you leave your name and number, I will have him call you back as soon as possible."

"I see how it is," Savannah responded, becoming irritated with the conversation. "Y'all can bother me when you feel like it, but God forbid anyone bother him. He's too busy."

"Ma'am, I'm very sorry. He's in a meeting. May I take a message?"

"Tell Special Agent Carmichael Savannah Zephyr is in the coffee shop downstairs. I have important information for him. I will be here for thirty minutes. When the thirty minutes is gone, so am I."

Disconnecting the call without waiting for a response, Savannah set the timer on her cell phone, grabbed her coffee, and pulled a book out of her bag. Thinking about everything that had happened over the past year and how much strength God had given her, she was proud of herself. A year ago, she never would have honored David's request, but with God's care, compassion, and comfort, she realized she was strong enough to face any challenge and conquer it.

Trying to read her book, she could feel God sitting next to her. Regardless of what happened next, it wasn't anything she couldn't overcome. She whispered, "Thank you, Lord."

Eric raced into the coffee shop. Looking for Savannah, he saw her sitting at a table. He straightened his tie, walked over to her, and asked, "Reading anything good, Mrs. Zephyr?"

Picking up her cell phone and looking at the timer, Savannah smiled when she responded, "You made it with four minutes to spare, Special Agent Carmichael, cutting it kind of close?"

"I apologize. I was in a meeting. Do you mind if I sit down?"

"Please do." Savannah put away her book and folded her hands in front of her.

Sitting down across the table from Savannah, Eric asked, "So, what prompted your call this morning?"

"You don't waste any time with small talk, do you?"

"Should I?"

"Most people would be polite and ask how my day was, or how my weekend was, or how my kids are doing," Savannah responded, contempt pouring off each comment.

"Would you like me to engage you in small talk, Savannah?"

"Mrs. Zephyr to you, Agent. And no," Savannah responded, rubbing her hands together. "I wouldn't. This is not a social call."

"I didn't think so."

"I have come across something that might help your investigation."

Sitting up in his chair and placing his elbows on the table, Eric asked, "What is it?"

"As you already know, since you followed me, I took my children to the beach over the weekend."

"Come on, Mrs. Zephyr, you had to know we were going to follow you."

"What you don't know, Special Agent Carmichael, is that I was visited by a young man on Saturday morning," Savannah said, smiling and taking a sip of her coffee before taking a shot at the competency of his men. "While your men were dozing off in their car, he handed me some very interesting materials."

"What kind of materials?"

"Pictures."

"Pictures?" Eric was confused. He wondered what kind of pictures she could have and why she thought they might be of any importance to him.

"He also told me a story about how my husband isn't involved in the high crimes and misdemeanors you claim he has been perpetrating."

"You know I can't speak with you about the details of an active investigation, Mrs. Zephyr."

"That's ironic, Special Agent," Savannah laughed, taking another sip of her coffee, "because you've popped up so many times to share details of your ongoing investigation when it seems to suit your agenda."

"Touché, Mrs. Zephyr," Eric replied, nodding slightly at Savannah. "You're absolutely right. I apologize for being smug. You came here in good faith. I should return the favor. Please accept my apologies."

"Keep your apologies," Savannah responded, aggravated with Eric's attitude; she had no time for vapid apologies. "To be honest, I wouldn't be sitting here right now if my husband hadn't asked this young man to plead with me to do so."

Eric stared at Savannah with a bit of skepticism. "Have you seen David?"

"No, I have not."

"But you just said…"

"David asked this young man to come speak with me," Savannah interrupted, holding up a finger to silence him. "Let me finish, please."

"You're right, please continue."

"This young man," Savannah continued, ignoring Eric, "answered questions and told me David wanted me to come down here today so I could share some information with you."

"And how do you know this person has ever had anything to do with your husband?"

"Because he's in the pictures David asked me to bring you," Savannah responded, dropping the bag containing the photographs on the table. "Because he is in the pictures with David, Agent Carmichael."

Grabbing the bag, opening it, and thumbing through the pictures, Eric stared at each picture. This day was turning into a nightmare for Eric. He had a sworn affidavit from Officer Wilson wreaking havoc on his investigation with stories of monsters, and Savannah showed up with pictures of four new possible suspects.

"Pardon me, Mrs. Zephyr," Eric asked, placing the photos on the table in front of them, "which one of these individuals brought you these pictures?"

"He did." Savannah pointed at the picture of Sebastian. "He sat with me on the beach and we had a nice chat where he told me my husband isn't a crook."

"I'm sure he did," Eric responded, thumbing through the pictures again. "And did he explain to you in detail why we have the facts of the case all wrong?"

"No, he did not, but he did say he would prove you wrong."

"Mrs. Zephyr, your timing is impeccable." Eric looked up from the pictures and stared at Savannah with a stoic expression. He contemplated his next response while looking at the photos. "I'm not sure if you're aware of this but recently, your husband violently attacked a local police officer in the Zion Corners Federal Bank."

"You're lying… David wouldn't do that."

"Well, he would, and he did."

"And what does that have to do with me?"

"Up until a few minutes ago," Eric smiled, holding up the pictures. "I had no plausible explanation for how he was able to knock out the police officer and escape. Now I have a pretty good idea how your husband pulled off his little trick."

"You're incredible, do you know that?" Savannah scoffed, shaking her head. "You'll find any reason possible to crucify my husband, won't you?"

"Mrs. Zephyr, whether you think your husband would or wouldn't be involved in the commission of this crime is irrelevant. I have a surveillance video contradicting your personal beliefs," Eric responded, standing up from his chair. "Mrs. Zephyr, I need you to come with me. I have to take these photos back to our command center and review them with my team of investigators, and then I have a bunch of questions I need you to answer for me."

"And if I refuse?"

"I will take you into custody and hold you in a cell while we decide whether or not to charge you with obstruction of justice."

"Guess you're going have to take me into custody," Savannah responded, placing her hands on the table in front of her. "You'll have to bring me in in handcuffs."

Shaking his head in disbelief, Eric took out his handcuffs and placed them on Savannah, "Suit yourself."

Chapter 31

Standing in the dusty, cob-webbed filled attic, David and Peter were staring at the latest design of the spear which Peter called the Lightning Bolt. Lost in thought on how to improve the fourteen-foot spear laid out on the table, David scratched his head. "I think you need to make two critical modifications."

"Like what?"

"It has to be longer."

"Really?" Peter asked, looking at David. "You really think so?"

"A Fallen Angel stands eighteen feet tall."

"And the spear is fourteen feet long."

Picking up the device and moving around the room, David demonstrated the mobility he had while wielding the spear. "When I hold the spear by the handles, the spear is shortened to eleven feet."

"You can stretch out and strike with it."

"I'll lose my balance or my grip on the spear," David responded, demonstrating for Peter. "If I stretch too far, I am off balance."

"But you still have a good ten to eleven feet to strike."

"When I faced the Fallen Angel, its wingspan had to be about eight feet wide. It can still strike me because I am too close."

Demonstrating how close he would have to be to a Fallen Angel in order to hit one of the demons with a kill shot, David showed him how dangerous it was. Peter questioned David about everything as they walked through the process of how long the Lightning Bolt device needed to be in order to be an effective weapon.

Done demonstrating how the device would be used in battle, David placed the spear back on the table as Peter asked, "What was the second thing?"

"More power."

"Still?"

"Yes." David was emphatic about this fact. "I don't want to be in a position to destroy a Fallen Angel and not have enough juice."

"I added two more Hellfire Devices," Peter said, leaning over the weapon and showing David the placement of the four devices.

"In theory, four might be enough. But we don't know how much juice we will need. I would rather have more power than I need."

"Because not enough is guaranteed death?"

"Exactly," David stated, pointing at Peter.

"How much power do you think it needs?"

"Ten, maybe," David responded, staring at the spear and rubbing his chin.

"Ten?" Peter raised his hands in frustration. He was concerned about how many devices David had suggested. "You don't think ten's going overboard?"

"It's kill or be killed. I don't want to be the one who bites the dust."

"Hmmm," Peter muttered, thinking about what to do next.

"Looks like you have some work to do."

"Uh-huh."

Peter was lost in his thoughts. David watched Peter tinker with the spear for a few minutes, and then he left the attic and made his way back to the living room.

"There you are," Sebastian said as David walked into the living room. "I have some news for you."

"What is it?"

"Savannah delivered the pictures and, just as we suspected, the feds took the bait."

Walking over and staring out the window, David asked, "Have they started interrogating her?"

"They have."

"I know this is part of the plan, Sebastian, but I still don't like using my loved ones as pawns."

"I know you don't," Sebastian admitted, walking over and standing next to David. "But at this point, the wheels are in motion. Go get some rest. You have an extremely long night ahead of you."

Chapter 32

"Come on, Mrs. Zephyr," Eric said, pacing the interrogation room. "We've been at this for hours. Stop playing games with me and tell me the truth."

Eric was trying to intimidate her, but Savannah wasn't buying into the act. She just sat in her chair staring at him. She had been in the interrogation room for hours and the more he asked the same questions, the more she gave him the same answers. It was becoming futile at this point. He pressed her for answers she didn't have and as a result of his tactics, she became stronger in her resolve. And the stronger she became, the more unraveled Eric became.

Putting his hands on the table, grabbing the pictures, and holding them up in front of her face, Eric pushed forward, "Mrs. Zephyr, I am going to ask you this one more time. How did you come into possession of these pictures?"

"You're not going to like my answer."

"Then tell me the truth."

Smiling, Savannah started to tell the story again, "I took my kids on a trip to the beach. On Saturday morning, I woke up early…"

"For a cup of coffee," Eric interrupted, seething with frustration. "You went to the beach to listen to the waves when this young man dressed in black came up, handed you the pictures, and told you some fanciful story about your husband…"

"So, you've heard this story before?" Savannah responded, chuckling to herself.

"Why are you playing games with me?" Eric was getting nowhere. He couldn't understand why she would give him the pictures and then stonewall him when he started asking her about them. It was infuriating.

"I am telling you the truth."

"See, I don't think you are. I think you are hiding something."

"Then enlighten me, Special Agent," Savannah challenged, growing calmer by the moment, settling back in her chair, and crossing her legs. "What do you think the truth is?"

Pacing the room, Eric stopped in front of the two-way mirror. Staring past his reflection and watching Savannah at the table, his blood started to boil. "I think David visited you."

Watching Savannah's facial reactions, he noticed her demeanor never changed especially when she said, "I wish he had. I would've loved to have seen him but as I told you before, the young man came to visit me."

"And how old would you say the young man is, Mrs. Zephyr?"

"I don't know, nineteen, maybe twenty years old."

Leaning his back against the two-way mirror, and crossing his arms, Eric said, "He was born in nineteen eighty-two. Making him more than thirty years old. How do explain that Mrs. Zephyr?"

"Well," Savannah said, raising her eyebrows and shrugging her shoulders. "He does look good for his age, I guess, doesn't he?"

"Is this a joke to you?"

"No, Agent, it's not," Savannah responded, smirking into the palm of her hand. "I don't know what to tell you about why he looks so young. Good genetics? All I know is he was the young man I spoke with."

"I have time, Mrs. Zephyr," Eric said, grinding his teeth. "Sooner or later, you will tell me the truth."

"There you go again, Special Agent, alluding to some sort of truth you seem to think exists, but you're never willing to share. If you think there is another explanation, please enlighten me. I'd like to hear it."

"I think you Photoshopped some pictures in order to manufacture a story."

Laughing at his suggestion, she regained control of her emotions when she saw him get angry. "Why would I do that, Special Agent?"

"To create plausible deniability."

"Is that what I'm doing? I'm creating plausible deniability. Why?"

"Sebastian Fredrickson wasn't a person of interest until you showed up and handed me these photos."

"So?"

"You have motive," Eric stated, pausing for a moment. "The only person who has ever shown up on a surveillance video is your husband. So why should I believe these pictures have anything to do with this case?"

"You can believe whatever you want to believe, Agent. The young man in the photos asked me to bring them to you. My husband asked me to bring them to you via a handwritten letter. So, I brought them."

Eric paced the room because something didn't add up. Skeptical of her motives and wanting to poke holes in her story, he continued, "Look at this from my point of view. You and I don't necessarily get along, do we?"

"No."

"If I had to guess, you probably hate me. Is that a fair assessment?"

"I don't hate you, Agent" Savannah sighed, repositioned herself in her chair, crossed her legs and folded her hands, placing them on her knees. "I don't know you, so hate is a strong word."

"Then how would you describe me to your friends?"

"Friends, ha," Savannah laughed, staring at Eric pacing the room. "Your investigation has left me pretty isolated. It's not like my besties and I are having gossip days to discuss your stellar detective work. Although, you're probably vain enough to think we are."

"Is it safe to say, you don't like me very much?" Eric asked, stopping and raising his arms.

"You're more of an annoyance, Agent. You're misguided, self-centered, and conceited. You're never wrong and even if the facts pointed in another direction, you would probably manipulate the evidence to fit your narrative. That's what I would tell anyone who asked me about you."

Eric was taken aback by her direct, unflattering description of him. "Thank you for your candor."

"Don't thank me," Savannah responded. "I don't find any joy in any of this or your investigation."

"You don't trust me, Mrs. Zephyr. I am the bane of your existence," Eric stated, pausing, leaning against the wall, and crossing his arms. "Why on earth would you bring me these photos? It doesn't make any sense."

"Faith."

"Faith?" Eric was perplexed. "I don't follow."

"Sometimes, you have to believe blindly in something and do it."

"Is that why you're here? Because of faith?"

"Yes," Savannah replied. "I believe God wanted me to bring the pictures to you. I don't know why or for what reason. Maybe He is trying to get your attention."

"Why would God want to get my attention?"

"Because He loves you."

"And what does that have to do with your husband's case?"

"Maybe He needs you to look beyond what you think you know and accept the possibility of another explanation, Special Agent."

"So now God is in the middle of this case?" Eric asked, dripping in sarcasm.

"God is in the middle of everything we do every single day of our lives."

"Why would He get involved now?" Eric asked, approaching the table, and staring Savannah down. "Why did He wait almost a year?"

"I don't know. He works in mysterious ways."

"Ironically, Mrs. Zephyr, so does your husband."

"That was uncalled for, Special Agent" Savannah was shocked at his insinuation. Taking a deep breath to calm herself down, she continued, "You might not have any faith, but I believe bringing the photos to you was what I was supposed to do."

"And even with your heartfelt admission, I still don't believe you."

"You can believe whatever you want," Savannah admonished, crossing her arms and sitting back in her chair. "At this point, I frankly don't care."

"Why not, Mrs. Zephyr?" Eric asked, trying to taunt her into a confession. "Don't you ever want your husband to come home?"

Staring at the wall, she choked back the tears. "You have no idea what this has done to our family. I wanted David home a year ago, but if that means helping you frame him for some crime he didn't commit, then no, I don't want him to come home until the truth is revealed."

Sitting down in the chair across from Savannah, Eric asked, "Why you, Mrs. Zephyr? Why are you here defending your husband? Why doesn't he come see me himself?"

"I thought about that." Savannah paused for a moment to fight back the tears and swallow her anger. "I see it like this; I've had the opportunity to get to know you and I think you're a very short-sighted man. You only see what you want to see."

"Thank you for your brutally honest character assessment of me, but you're wrong. I do not see only what I want to see, Mrs. Zephyr. I see what the facts and the evidence tell me."

"The facts are wrong," Savannah stated, smiling at him. "Why can't you see that?"

"The facts are never wrong, and the facts tell me your husband has illegally entered a bunch of federal banks."

"He hasn't stolen anything."

"Yet," Eric interjected. "And I refuse to let him get away with taking anything from the hard-working people who put their money and trust in those banks."

"And there it is," Savannah responded, pointing her finger at him.

"What?"

"You only see what you want to see." Putting her hands on the table, she continued, "You have no proof David is there to steal anything, but that's the conclusion you have drawn. You, not the facts, leapt to that conclusion."

"That's not my problem, Mrs. Zephyr. Without any proof to the contrary, that's your husband's problem."

"No." Savannah shook her head in disagreement. "He's innocent until proven guilty."

"Not with the evidence I have, he isn't."

"And that's why I'm here instead of him."

Pushing his chair back from the table and standing up, Eric smiled and walked out of the interrogation room. A few seconds later, Quyen and two other agents stepped out of the observation booth where they had been watching Eric interrogate Savannah and joined Eric in the hall.

"What do you want to do now, boss?" Agent Quyen asked.

"We have nothing right now," Eric admitted, running his fingers through his hair and releasing an exasperated sigh. "Between Officer Wilson's sworn statement and the bombshell Mrs. Zephyr dropped in our lap today, we took a huge step backwards in our case against David Zephyr. I need something credible that helps us find him before this case gets away from us.

"The clock is ticking," Eric continued. "We have a few hours left before Nathan and Sam Dewey are in my office making my life miserable. At which point, we'll have to let her go."

Chapter 33

Standing at the bottom of the stairs, David peered into the living room and watched Nathan argue with his attorney on the phone. Hidden by the cloak of invisibility the veil provided, it felt weird standing inside his house watching his father fight with his lawyer about having Savannah released from custody. He had never seen Nathan so angry. Face turning red, veins pulsating in his forehead, his arms swinging around, and his muscles bulging and rippling, he lambasted the gentleman on the other end of the receiver.

The gentle giant David had known was showing off his angry side and David felt a tinge of fear. He felt the malicious intent and volatility emanating from his father's usual calm demeanor. Looking into Nathan's eyes, he noticed his glare was laser focused and intent. Nathan's eyes were wild with anger and brimming with the fire raging inside of him. David had never seen this side of Nathan before, and it was one he never wanted to see again.

Standing motionless at the bottom of the stairs, David watched for a few more minutes. He didn't like his father's anger, but he was brimming with pride watching his father defend his family in his absence. It brought him some satisfaction knowing his wife and children could count on his parents in their time of need.

David crept up the stairs, he had a mission. He had work to do. Reaching the top of the stairwell, David avoided the top two steps to keep them from creaking underneath him.

At the top of the stairs, he could still hear his father yelling downstairs and his mother's snoring coming from Carissa's room. Creeping down the hallway to Jordan's room, he opened the door, slipped inside, and walked over to the side of Jordan's bed.

His son was sleeping without a care in the world, and he was hesitant to wake Jordan up. He knew it was in those moments of restful sleep, Jordan was able to escape this nightmare. That somewhere in the middle of the dreams, Jordan was able to find some semblance of tranquility. Sitting down on the bed, David shook Jordan's shoulders.

Rolling around in the bed and rubbing his eyes, Jordan whined. "Not now, Mom, give me ten more minutes of sleep."

"It's not Mom."

Rubbing his eyes and trying to adjust his vision in the darkness, Jordan sat up and looked at his father. "Dad? What are you doing here?"

"I love you too, Jordan." David wrapped his son up in a big old bear hug and kissed the top of his head.

"I love you, Dad. Are you home to stay?" Jordan asked, melting into his father's embrace.

"Not yet."

Pulling back and staring at David, he asked, "Then when?"

"Soon," David smiled, winking at him. "But first, you and I have some work to do."

"What kind of work?"

"Important work, Jordan. The kind that lets me come home sooner." David scoured the side table for a few items. He leaned over and picked up Jordan's cell phone. "Come on, we don't have time to waste."

Not knowing whether or not he was dreaming, Jordan didn't hesitate. He was spending time with his dad and he was going to savor every minute. "Do I need to change my clothes?"

"Nah, Son, keep your shorts and T-shirt on," David responded, tussling his hair. "You might want to put on a pair of shoes, though."

Grabbing his sneakers and putting them on his feet, Jordan bounded out of the chair. "Let's go, Dad."

"You sure you're ready?"

"Come on, Dad, let's go."

"Then we're off," David smiled, holding out his hand. Taking Jordan's hand in his and placing his other hand on the Hellfire Device, he activated the device.

"This is so cool," Jordan squealed in amazement, looking all around and asking, "Where are we?"

They were standing in the entrance to Grand Central Station in New York City when Jordan ran to the top of the grand staircase and stood wide-eyed as he gawked at the architecture of the building. David watched as his son spun around, engrossed in the sights and sounds of the famous terminal in the heart of the greatest city in the world.

"Grand Central Station in New York City, Jordan."

"How did we get here?"

"That is a story for another day," David answered, walking down the stairwell.

Following close behind, Jordan asked, "Where are we going?"

"There is a kiosk across the lobby selling the best bear claws and hot chocolate in the world. You want to try them while we get caught up?" David strolled through the lobby.

"Sounds great," Jordan exclaimed, taking his father's hand and walking across the lobby.

Smiling, David listened to Jordan's adventures. It was a moment of pure bliss for both of them. After all of the chaos they had endured, they reveled in spending some time together, just the two of them, catching up about everything under the sun.

Nearing the far side of the Grand Central lobby, they walked up into one of the hallways and headed toward the coffee stand. Reaching the counter, David made sure he and Jordan were standing in front of the security camera while they waited to be served.

An older gentleman stood across the counter from them. "What can I get you?"

"Two cups of hot cocoa and two bear claws."

"Whipped cream on those hot chocolates?"

"Yes, please," Jordan responded.

"Two hot chocolates with whipped cream and two bear claws, coming right up," the attendant repeated, turning around and making the drinks. Grabbing two bear claws from the display case, he put them into a bag with some napkins. Coming back to where David was standing, he put the items on the counter and rang up the order. "That'll be seventeen fifty."

Taking a crisp twenty-dollar bill from his pocket and handing it to the cashier, David made sure he was in front of the security camera. "Keep the change, but can I please have a receipt?"

"Yes, sir," the cashier responded, taking the bill, ringing up the order, and handing the receipt to David. "Thank you."

Placing the receipt in his pocket, David grabbed the food and walked over to a small table in the corridor. Sitting down at the table with his son, he handed him a cup of hot chocolate and a bear claw, took a sip of his cup, and asked Jordan about everything happening in his life.

Jordan regaled his father with stories about football games, about Mom making him do well in school, about making the basketball team, about family holidays, and about the wild adventures he had with his friends. Grinning and enjoying the stories being shared, David took pictures of the two of them with Jordan's cell phone.

After thirty minutes of talking and taking pictures, David asked, "You almost done with the hot cocoa, Jordan?"

"Almost."

"Good," David said, standing up and cleaning off the table. "We have more work to do."

"Is this what you do for work, Dad?" Jordan was impressed. "Because I am having the best time of my life. It sure does beat going to school."

Throwing away the garbage, David laughed, "I am glad you feel that way, Jordan, because there is more fun to be had."

"Really?"

David held out his hand and Jordan took it. They both walked down the hallway toward the 42nd Street exit. After they passed through the doors, David led Jordan into a nearby alley, placed his other hand on the Hellfire Device, and activated it again.

Standing outside the entrance to the iconic Opera House in Sydney, Australia, David watched Jordan's jaw fall open. "No way! How did you do that, Dad? Where are we now?"

"We're at the Sydney Opera House in Australia."

"Am I dreaming, Dad?" Jordan asked, pinching himself.

"That's an extremely complicated question to answer, Jordan," David chuckled, putting his hand on Jordan's shoulder.

"What are we doing here?"

"We're going to take a tour."

"We are?" Jordan was confused. "Why?"

"You have always been interested in drawing, so I wanted to show you some of the amazing architecture around the world."

"This is awesome," Jordan exclaimed, running toward the Opera House. "Last one to the ticket booth is a rotten egg."

"Not this time."

Running after his son, David caught up to him, but he didn't pass him. Laughing while they jockeyed for position, Jordan cut off David, sprinted the final fifteen feet to win the race and danced while celebrating his victory. David strode in behind him, laughing as the cares of the world washed away in a finite moment of pure joy. "Guess I'm the rotten egg."

Dancing around and reveling in his win, Jordan teased, "Good race, Dad."

"You too, Son," David replied, catching his breath. "You're getting faster."

Joking around with each other and laughing while they waited, David purchased two tickets for the tour. He made sure to position both of them in front of the security camera, and he requested the receipt along with the tickets.

For the next few hours, David and Jordan toured the Sydney Opera House, learning about the history and the architecture of the building. It was the best time they had shared in over a year and neither of them wanted the evening to end, but David knew he had more work to do before morning. As much as he wanted to stay longer, he knew it was time to face reality.

"I hate to say it, Jordan, but it's time to go home."

"I don't want to go home, Dad."

"I know you don't, Jordan, but this chaos is almost over. If things go well over the next few days, I will be home before you know it."

"How soon, Dad?"

"That depends on a few things," David answered, putting his arm around Jordan's shoulders. "And one of those things involves you."

"Me?"

"I need you to do something for me, Jordan." David stopped walking and faced his son. "Can you do a favor for me?"

"What is it?"

Putting his hand in his pocket and pulling out the receipts, he handed them to Jordan with the ticket stubs, and Jordan's cell phone. "Tomorrow morning, ask your grandfather to drive you to the federal building."

"I don't want to go there." Jordan was emphatic in his protest.

"I know you don't, Son, and I wish you didn't need to. But if you don't, it will be harder for me to come home."

"Why?"

"It is vital to get your grandfather to take you to the federal building tomorrow so you can hand Agent Carmichael the receipts and the ticket stubs I just gave you. Show him the pictures on your cell phone."

"But what if he takes my phone?"

"Let him." David knelt in front of Jordan and put his hand on his shoulder. He was asking a lot from Jordan. No kid should ever be put in this position, but he didn't have much of a choice. He had to show Eric he was capable of doing what he claimed he could do. "And when he asks you questions, you tell him the truth. You tell him where we went and what we did. Do not lie to him. Do you understand me?"

"Yes, Dad," Jordan said, lowering his head. "But what if he doesn't believe me?"

"He won't believe you, Jordan. He will tell you it is impossible to travel from New York to Sydney in the time those receipts are stamped."

"Is it impossible?"

"With God, Jordan, anything is possible," David responded. "I mean, anything is possible. So, when he presses you to tell the truth, you tell him to look at the footage from the security cameras."

"Really?"

"It's very important you tell him to look at the security footage. Without viewing that footage, he will never believe you."

"What will that prove?"

"It will not only prove it was possible," David responded, smiling, "it will prove we were in both places. Now can you do that for me, Jordan?"

"I will, Dad."

"I love you so much, Jordan." David wrapped his son up in a bear hug while tears started to roll down his son's cheeks. "I'm sorry you have to go through all of this. I promise I will be home soon."

Chapter 34

Burning the midnight oil, Eric had the Zephyr case files strewn across his desk. Pulling together all of the information they could find on Sebastian, Michael, Zoe, and Peter, he was trying his best to find a connection between them, but he couldn't. It bothered him. Nothing made sense. Every time he thought he had the investigation figured out, the rules changed, and everything went right out the window.

There was a knock at the door. He looked up from the file. "Come in!"

"This is the rest of the information we were able to gather on the alleged accomplices," Quyen said, walking into the office with an arm full of manila folders.

"Does anyone have a plausible reason to tie these five people together?"

"Nothing, sir. It doesn't make sense." Quyen stacked the folders on Eric's desk. "Sebastian is an eccentric recluse, two of the other three are kids who are missing persons, and the woman should be over 60 years old if we got her identity right."

"And the final accomplice?" Eric was just happy to have some information on the people in the pictures Savannah had given him. Maybe now he could find a connection between them and David. "What's his story?"

"Nothing, a drifter, son of a dishonorably discharged soldier."

"Send the team home." Eric realized his team was exhausted. They had been putting in eighteen-hour days and needed a break. "We'll pick this up in the morning."

"Will do, sir," Quyen said, opening the door. "What about you? You heading home?"

"No. I have a few more hours of work to do."

"What are you working on, sir?"

"See this?" Eric pointed at an opaque object in the picture he was holding of one of the banks lobbies. "It is blurry and looks like it has defined edges."

"What is it?"

"I'm not sure." Eric paused for a minute and handed to photo to Quyen who inspected the image closely. "One of the forensic scientists was examining the individual frames from the surveillance videos. He noticed this same phenomenon in each bank. It's almost like something is moving so fast, the camera can't pick it up."

"What could move that fast, sir?"

"And now you know why I am stumped. Some of the photos," Eric pulled one from his desk and handed it to Quyen, "almost look like they have features. I can almost make out an eye in that photo."

"None of this makes sense."

"And that is why I am tethered to my desk every night," Eric smiled, leaning back in his chair. "At some point, it all has to make sense. I just haven't figured it out yet, but I will."

Quyen put the pictures down on Eric's desk. "You need sleep, sir."

"I'll sleep when David Zephyr is finally behind bars."

Chapter 35

Sitting in front of the computer screen, Peter studied the data. Michael came into the room, sat down next to him, and watched the computer screen, waiting for his cue.

Peter was watching David battle a Zivlian inside the dream of a college student. He was waiting for the perfect moment to initiate the plan which relied on the sophisticated computer system relaying accurate information back in real time. Tensions were high amongst the members of The Network. If they were late, David would be long gone when the authorities arrived. If they were too early, David would be in custody and everything they had worked for would be ruined.

Giving Michael a thumbs up, Peter said, "Go ahead, Michael, make the call."

"Are you sure?"

"Positive," Peter replied, pointing at the computer screen. "David just pulled the Zivlian into the bank. Make the call."

Picking up the burner cell phone and dialing the emergency number, Michael heard a voice on the other end of the line. "Nine, one, one, what's your emergency?

"I am outside the Ferndale Federal Bank. It sounds like there is a robbery going on inside. Please, send the police." Michael pleaded. Then he hung up the phone, stood up from the table, and went out into the neighboring streets to dispose of the burner cell phone.

Miles away, standing in the middle the Ferndale Federal Bank, sweat poured down David's face. The Zivlian was much larger and stronger than most of the beasts he had faced. He could feel the blood rolling down his left bicep from the scratch the demon had given him before he pulled the evil creature out of the dream and into the bank lobby. Breathing hard, David taunted the beast. "Come on you vile, clueless creature, come and get me."

Out of the corner of his eye, David saw the Zivlian charging at him. Turning to face the monster, bracing himself as the beast lunged, he grabbed it by the arm and with his right hand delivered a punishing blow with the Hellfire Device, swinging the Zivlian around and launching it across the bank.

"That's right, beastie, looks like we have evened up the fight. Now what are you going to do? Come on you dumb mutt… Come and get me." David derided the entity to get the Zivlian angrier. *If the beasts only knew that anger made them weaker,* he thought to himself having learned over time their anger was the Zivlian's downfall. *What would they do if they knew their anger was the true enemy?*

Staggering to its feet, the beast steadied itself. The creature stared down David with an angry snarl, the burning stench of sulfur emanating from the beast. Although, David never thought he would acclimate to the eye burning, throat-choking smell of sulfur that these creatures secreted, the sulfur didn't bother him as much as it once had.

Lowering itself to the ground in an attack position, the demon growled and stared at David with an anger that sent chills down his spine. Lunging forward and charging at David, it leapt at him. Grabbing the front paw of the creature with his left hand and delivering another punishing electrical blast with his right hand, David sent the entity flying across the room into the far wall of the bank.

"It's almost over, now. You can feel it, can't you?" David mocked, feeling the end of the battle was near. "You're angry… Mad… Beyond insane… Now come on, you worthless beast, come get me."

The creature was weakening. The demon struggled to stand. It was panting and sulfur poured out of its veins causing the bank lobby to feel like the smoldering fires of hell. David could feel the beast staring him down and panting against the wall of the bank. It wanted to kill him. It wanted to destroy him where he stood. It wanted to shred him into little pieces and for that reason, he didn't take his eyes off the Zivlian.

Attacking at full speed, the demon leapt at him. Grabbing the creature and pinning it to the ground, David placed the Hellfire Device on the beast and delivered electrical charges as it let out the vile, blood-curdling evil screams.

"In the name of my Lord and Savior, Jesus Christ, I send you back to the depths of hell," David yelled, the Zivlian disappearing back into the farthest reaches of the Netherworld.

Sitting on his knees in the middle the bank floor, he could feel the searing pain from the cut on his left bicep. He wiped the sweat off his forehead. His body ached. He felt like he had just run a marathon while being pelted with ice.

Taking a deep breath, he stood up. Dragging his aching body across the bank lobby, he heard a voice behind him scream, "Freeze! Police… Don't move."

David hesitated for a moment. He was too far away from an exit. He thought about passing through the veil in the lobby, but it was against the rules. It would also mess up the plan. So, he contemplated running. Maybe the officer would shoot, maybe he wouldn't; but David didn't want to take the chance.

Taking a couple more steps toward the manager's office, the police officers confirmed his worst fear when one of them yelled, "Freeze! Or I'll shoot."

David had a decision to make. Stay put and get taken into custody, make a run for the manager's office and risk being shot, or jump through the plate glass window about three feet to his left.

David didn't contemplate his options for very long. The plate glass window was his best option, so he took a step toward the window and leapt, making sure the Hellfire Device was the first thing to contact the glass. Hitting the window with the Hellfire Device, he could hear shots being fired.

Being shot was the furthest thing from his mind. He landed in a large puddle on the sidewalk with broken glass crashing down around him. Then David felt himself floating. Not floating, falling. The sidewalk wasn't underneath him. He was falling through the darkness of the night when he heard a familiar sound below. Before he could figure out what the sound was, David splashed down into a fast-flowing river.

Trying to keep his head above water, David surfaced, gasping for air. He fought the swirling water while the current forced him down stream. He smacked into rocks. He tried to brace for impact, but he had a hard time seeing rocks on the in the pitch black darkness of a moonless night. He screamed as his left arm dragged against the hanging branches of a fallen tree. His gash reopened and started to bleed again. He yelled out in pain when his body crashed full force into a rock that just cleared the level of the water.

Ten minutes of being forced down the river took a toll on his battered body. The water slowed down and David was drifting in a calm part of the river. Tired from the battle and his ride down the rapids, he doggie paddled to the side of the river, crawled up the riverbank, and collapsed on dry land.

Laying in the dirt and leaves, trying to catch his breath, he realized he had lost his Hellfire Device in the river. His eyes adjusted to the darkness, but the lack of moonlight was not good. It was going to make the ability to make it back home a more daunting task. He could hear cars off in the faint distance. He still had work to do before dawn, so he picked himself up off the riverbank and started walking in the direction of the cars.

Stumbling onto an old dirt road, he had no idea where he was or where he was going but the dirt road had to lead somewhere. The road had to end up somewhere in the civilized world. So, after a moment of consideration, he picked a direction and walked down the dirt road.

Walking for a while, he saw headlights from an old pickup truck heading his way. *Thank God,* he thought to himself. David stopped walking and waited with his thumb out to his side as the truck raced down the dirt road like a bat out of hell. The driver locked up the brakes and came to a screeching halt while dust and small pebbles pelted David's body.

Walking over to the passenger side of the truck and peering inside the cab, he saw Zoe smiling at him. "Going my way."

"How did you find me?"

"Peter was able to track the signal from your device."

"I dropped it when I was falling."

"Peter figured as much. So, he hacked into some satellites and conducted a heat signature scan of the area."

"And that worked?"

"There aren't many people in the forest at night," Zoe laughed while David climbed into the passenger seat. "Besides, you're the only person with traces of sulfur."

"It's crazy how he is able to do that."

"Trust me, Peter can find you anywhere if you give him enough time."

"Well, I'm glad he did." David put his seat belt on, ran his hands though his hair, and let out a loud sigh. He was tired, but he had work to do. The plan required him completing many tasks before daybreak. "Did you bring me a new Hellfire Device? I still have work to do."

"I did," Zoe responded, handing it to him. "But it won't do you a lot of good out here."

"Why not?"

"Spotty Wi-Fi."

"Are you kidding me?"

"Our equipment runs on technology," Zoe answered, smiling and shrugging her shoulders. "We need to get closer to civilization before you'll be doing anything else tonight."

"Great. Are there any other rules I don't know about?"

"A ton," Zoe laughed, throwing the truck into gear and flooring the gas pedal.

"You know, you're a horrible driver."

"I know," Zoe laughed, continuing to race down the dirt road at high speeds.

They had been driving for a while and the wind whipping through the window on David's face felt refreshing. "Can I ask you a stupid question?"

"Shoot."

"How did I end up in a river?"

"You broke through the glass just fine, but you landed in a puddle left behind after the rain earlier today. You must have still had the device engaged, because if the Hellfire Device touches water, you're going for a swim."

"Why didn't anyone tell me that?"

"No one ever thought you would need to know." Zoe winked at David. "Now sit back and rest. It's been a long night."

"Thanks, but it's about to get longer," David said, leaning his head against the door and feeling the wind rush against his face. "I still have one more thing I have to do tonight."

Chapter 36

Eric was passed out, face down on his desk in a small puddle of drool that was developing underneath him. David was sitting in the chair across the desk from him, watching him sleep. Then David leaned over and shook Eric's shoulders. "Are you going to sleep all night? No wonder you haven't found me yet."

Opening his eyes, trying to adjust to the light in his office, Eric lifted his head from his desk. David smiled and gave a little wave. "Good morning, Special Agent, how are you today?"

Trying to push back from the desk and grab his gun, Eric realized he was handcuffed to the desk, "What's this all about?"

"Just a little precaution. I want to make sure we get a chance to talk."

"How did you get in here?"

"That's a long story." David chuckled and paused for a moment. "Besides, if I told you, you wouldn't believe me anyway."

"Try me," Eric replied, making a move for his gun.

Noticing Eric reach for his weapon, David smiled. "Don't worry about your gun. I took out the magazine and the one in the chamber."

Staring at David for a moment, Eric settled into his chair because there was nothing else he could do. Resting his handcuffed arms on the desk in front of him, he quipped, "Doesn't seem very fair."

"Fair, Special Agent?" David laughed. He looked at Eric for a moment and shook his head at the incredulous notion of fairness between the two of them.

"I'm cuffed and you're not."

"Considering the manpower and the firepower in this building, I think the handcuffs are a great equalizer."

"How did you get into the building, Mr. Zephyr?"

"Maybe I'm here. Maybe I'm not. Maybe you're sleeping." David raised an eyebrow and smirked. He was loving every minute of messing with Eric's psyche.

"Are you trying to tell me I am dreaming?"

"I'm not going to tell you what to believe. You can make up your own mind," David responded, leaning into the desk and whispering, "Last I checked, you're good at that."

"You're ridiculous," Eric stated, rolling his eyes.

"Am I?"

"You're trying to convince me of all of this hocus pocus."

"And you wouldn't believe in that," David laughed, clapping his hands together and pointing at Eric. "because you're a man who believes in absolutes. Black and white. Right and wrong."

"Seems like you have it all figured out, Mr. Zephyr."

"I am far from having any of this figured out," David responded, settling back into his chair. "I live in the gray area and until you allow your own intellect to accept the gray area in this investigation, you're never going to solve the case and I will never get to go home to my family."

"Sounds like we're at impasse."

David swallowed hard, trying to keep his composure. He looked at Eric and rubbed his chin. "But do we need to be?"

"We don't have to be," Eric countered, lifting his hands. "We could take the cuffs off, go down to an interrogation room, and videotape our conversation. If you prove to me you're not a thief, you can go home tomorrow."

"Really?" David laughed. He was amused at the thought of being a thief. He wished he was a thief. He wished it was that simple. He also pitied Eric. He was so far off base and unless David was able to set Eric straight, he might never go home. "You think I am a thief?"

"You break into banks."

"You think this is about theft? Now that's absolutely hysterical."

"Are you telling me you're not a thief?"

"Open your eyes, Detective," David said, leaning into the desk. "Look at the tapes again and tell me what you're missing."

"Why don't you tell me, David? What am I missing?"

"You're missing the truth."

"Then prove it to me. Give me proof. Make me see it."

"That's the problem. I can't make you see anything you're not willing to see for yourself first. You have to be open to the possibility first."

"That is the most ridiculous thing I have ever heard," Eric responded, sitting back in his chair and giving David a look of disapproval.

"Jesus is the way in life. He is the truth. Nothing in this life means anything without Him. Have you accepted Him into your life, Special Agent?"

"What does that have to do with anything, Mr. Zephyr?"

"Everything," David responded. "I have always followed the truth. It frees the heart, mind, and soul."

"Jesus told you to rob those banks?"

"If you still think this is about robberies, you are so missing the point."

"So, what is the truth?"

"The truth has always been right in front of you, you just have to open your eyes and see it. If you only believe in the possibility, it will set you free."

"Which file, David?" Eric asked, lifting his cuffed hands and pointing at the manila folders. He believed the truth was in one of the files on his desk and if David showed him which one, maybe he would believe David. But without physical proof to the contrary, he still thought David was a thief. "Tell me which file to look in for the answers."

"That's the irony, Special Agent. There is no file."

"Then how can I find the truth?"

"You have to look inside your heart and believe what you know to be true."

"How does that solve this case?" Eric asked, getting frustrated. "How does that help solve anything?"

"These files won't tell you anything more than facts about Peter, Sebastian, Michael, Zoe and myself."

"Isn't that a start?"

"They won't make any sense until you can find the one reason, we are all linked together. And you won't find the reason until you look past the black and white of our lives and see the gray area where we all live."

"How do you get into the banks without setting off any alarms?"

"It's part of the gray area." David knew he wasn't getting anywhere. Eric was close minded. Eric's heart was hardened and unless it softened, even the truth wouldn't help to take the blinders off Eric's eyes. "It's part of the riddle. Look closely. You'll see it."

"This isn't real," Eric mumbled, closing his eyes, shaking his head and opening his eyes.

"Still here." David smiled, waving at Eric again.

"There is no way this is real. We are not having this conversation right now."

"Believing you are dreaming is more plausible than the fact I am here?"

"There is no way you walked into this building without being arrested. It's not possible." Eric believed he was still dreaming because David never could have gotten to his office without being apprehended. He was working too much. He conjured up a dream with David to help him resolve he unanswerable questions.

"I didn't walk into those banks either." David could see the wheels turning in Eric's mind. He couldn't rectify his own truth with the fact that David might be sitting in front of him. "So, if I can get into those banks, what makes you think I can't get into your office?"

"This isn't real, David, you're not here," Eric continued, opening, and closing his eyes while shaking his head back and forth.

"If that's the way you want to play it," David responded, standing up from the chair. "I thought you wanted answers, but I guess you're not ready yet."

"I don't want answers. I want the truth."

"That's what I have been trying to show you."

"You're a lunatic."

"How can I be a lunatic, Special Agent? I'm not here," David shot back, holding his arms out wide. "Look around. None of this is real. So wouldn't that technically make you the lunatic?"

"This is just a dream," Eric repeated, trying to wake himself up. "When I wake up, you'll be gone, and everything will be back to normal."

"It will be," David stated, walking over to the door. "Two things you might want to remember from this dream when you wake up, Special Agent."

"Yeah?" Eric was defiant in his tone. "What are they?"

"I am not done showing you things, yet. So, pay attention to every detail."

"And the other thing?"

"The spiral ends in Raleigh."

"What does that mean, Mr. Zephyr? What spiral?"

"It's nothing, Special Agent, because I'm not really here. This is all a dream."

"What does it mean?" Eric shouted.

"If you figure it all out, I'll see you next Thursday night, Special Agent," David said, slamming the door behind him.

Waking up, jumping up from his seat, and looking at his wrists, Eric wasn't cuffed to the desk. Checking his holster and finding his weapon safely inside, he looked around the room. David wasn't there.

Sitting down at his desk, he mumbled under his breath, "I must be working too hard. I'm dreaming about my suspects now."

Eric looked at his watch and went back to reviewing the case files. Picking up a file on David Zephyr, he started to review the evidence. As he turned the page, a handwritten note fell out of the file onto his desk. Picking up the handwritten note, Eric read it:

Good morning, Special Agent,
Sorry I had to leave so abruptly. I was hoping we could have had a real dialogue.
For your sanity, it was real. I sat across from you at your desk last night. Keep looking, Detective. The truth is right in front of you. Follow the spiral. Believe what you know to be true, and you'll find the answers you seek.
David Zephyr.

<h1 style="text-align:center">Chapter 37</h1>

Jordan woke up and sat on his bed. He looked at the receipts underneath his cell phone. Picking up his phone and opening the photos, he knew he had work to do. He had promised his dad he would take the receipts to Eric.

He showered, dressed, and ate breakfast before arguing with his grandfather about contacting Special Agent Carmichael. Nathan wanted Jordan far away from the cockamamie investigation being conducted. He may not have been able to keep his son and daughter-in-law out of the line of fire, but he refused to let his grandson inject himself into the middle of the fracas.

The more Jordan argued, the more resolute Nathan became in his refusal. He puffed out his menacing chest and blurted out, "You aren't going anywhere but to school today… and that is final!"

Standing in the middle of the kitchen, staring dumbfounded at his grandfather, Jordan realized the discussion was over. He stomped up the stairs, slammed his bedroom door, and locked the door behind him. He sat down at his desk and searched through the drawers. Opening the last drawer, he saw the crumpled-up card. Picking up the business card, he dialed the number listed. "Special Agent Carmichael, my dad, David Zephyr, is in our house right now."

Jordan sat in the interrogation room for more than two hours before Eric was calm enough to speak with the boy. Jordan saw the humor in the situation. Special Agent Carmichael had deployed two tactical teams to the scene and when they stormed the house, the scene turned ugly when Nathan lost his cool and had to be restrained by members of the tactical teams.

When Jordan emerged from his room to confront Eric about the bogus tip, the situation went from bad to worse. After listening to Jordan's impossible story of the travels, Eric confiscated his cell phone and the receipts and had taken Jordan into custody. Escorting him from the home, Eric showed a rare sign of compassion and allowed Jordan's grandmother to ride in the car with Jordan.

When they returned to the federal building, Eric spent the first hour being yelled at by his superiors. It wasn't the finest moment in his career and if he felt he could have gotten away with it, he would have thrown the book at Jordan and charged him with every applicable crime. But with Nathan's attorneys swarming the offices of his superiors, he knew his hands were tied. Jordan was going to walk out of the building at the end of the day with nothing more than a slap on the wrist.

But Jordan wasn't budging. He refused to leave until he had a chance to have a conversation with Eric. Seething with anger, Eric went into the interrogation room and sat across the table from the boy. He suffered from lack of sleep, was unshaven, was still wearing the same clothes he worn the day before and, although, he had consumed many cups of coffee, he was exhausted. He had spent a very long night pouring over case files. He was in no mood for games when Jordan had called his cell phone and lied about David.

Eric didn't want to hear anything more about the far-fetched tale Jordan had spun at the Zephyr residence. His patience was growing thin. He was in no mood to the debate the merits of the fanciful yarn being spun by the middle schooler sitting across the table from him.

"Jordan, I am very disappointed in the prank you played earlier today. You put a lot of people's lives in danger, including your own."

"It wasn't a prank."

"I could charge you with a crime, but after speaking with your grandfather and various attorneys in our office, we are going to forget today's events ever happened."

"I don't want to forget it," Jordan yelled, slamming his hand down on the table. "You're not listening to me."

"Before you go, you have to promise never to file a fake report with the police or federal authorities again. Do you understand, Jordan?"

"I had good reasons," Jordan whined, slumping back in his chair. "You just won't listen."

"You don't lie to the authorities," Eric yelled, losing his composure.

"I had to speak with you."

"Jordan, somebody could have gotten seriously hurt today."

"It was the only way I could get your attention."

"Not by lying, Jordan."

"I was only half-lying. My dad was at our house. He just wasn't there when I called you."

"Your dad wasn't at your house," Eric responded, gritting his teeth and clenching his fists. "You've been under a lot of stress, and you wanted to believe he was there. The mind…

"He was there!" Jordan interrupted.

"No, he wasn't!" Eric erupted, slamming his hands against the table, popping up from his chair, and leaning against the mirror on the wall, trying to reign in his anger.

"He took me to New York and Sydney."

"There is no way you were in New York City and Sydney last night. End of story."

"How do you know?"

"Because it is physically impossible," Eric laughed. He was beyond frustrated with the boy.

"I gave you proof. What about the pictures and receipts I gave you?"

"You know, Jordan," Eric stated, taking a deep breath. "I am a patient man, but I think it would be best for everyone involved if your grandmother took you home."

"I'm not going anywhere." Jordan crossed his arms and shook his head. He promised his father he would share the information about their travels. He had shared the receipts and the pictures, but Eric wasn't budging, so Jordan decided he wasn't budging either. "I'm not done showing you things yet."

Struck with a vivid flashback of David uttering those exact words, Eric paused and looked at the boy with a weird expression. "What did you just say?"

"I'm not done showing you things yet."

Déjà vu sent a chill up his spine, he remembered the note David had left for him; "*The truth is right there in front of you. Follow the spiral. Believe what you know to be true, and you'll find the answers you seek.*"

Maybe it was the fatigue setting in because Eric had no reason to continue the conversation, but he wanted to see this game play out. He wanted to know if Jordan really knew something or if the boy was just missing his father and creating stories in his head. Whatever the reason, Eric was willing to play along. "Okay, kid, show me."

"Did you check the security tapes? If you want proof, look at the security videos."

"Jordan," Eric walked over to the interrogation room door and opened it, "follow me."

Eric escorted Jordan down the hall to the task force command center. Looking around the room, Jordan saw a big picture of David on a wall with strings connected to various people and places. On another wall, there was a huge map with a bunch of large, colored pushpins stuck into the map. He was also amazed at the number of agents working in the room.

"Agent Ramirez, can you do me a favor and put up a world map?"

Walking across the room with Jordan, they stopped in front of a large screen where the map of the world was displayed. Putting his finger on the map, Eric stated, "Jordan, this is New York City."

Running his finger across the map to Sydney, Eric continued, "This is the flight path from New York to Sydney. It would take twenty-two hours to cover this distance in a plane."

"This would be a whole lot easier if you just looked at the security cameras," Jordan remarked, raising his eyebrows and shaking his head. "A lot easier."

"It's not that I don't want to believe you, Jordan, because I do," Eric stated with empathy. "I want nothing more for you because I know how painful this must be, but as you can see, it would be physically impossible to travel to all of these places in one night."

"If you just look at the security tape, you will believe me," Jordan uttered under his breath.

"I requested the security footage hours ago, Jordan, because it is my job to run down all of the evidence." Eric put his hand on Jordan's shoulder. He felt sorry for the boy. He couldn't imagine the feelings Jordan and Carissa must be feeling because David left and, in his place, he left a federal investigation. "In the end, you're going to realize you had a dream about your dad. But that's all it was, Jordan, just a dream."

"It's too bad you can't see the truth, Special Agent Carmichael," Jordan stated, walking toward the door. "My mom is right. You only see what you want to see."

Watching the boy walk across the room, Eric's heart broke for the young man who wanted nothing more than to spend time with his father. And for the first time, he became angry with David for skipping out on his family.

"Cool spiral," Jordan said, pointing at the map on the wall.

Having another flashback to the dream he had about David, Eric remembered David said *the spiral ends in Raleigh* and *follow the spiral*. Eric yelled across the room, "What did you just say, Jordan?"

"I was pointing at the spiral on the wall," Jordan reiterated, pointing at the map. "It looks like it ends in Raleigh."

Looking around the room, Eric was befuddled. This was the second time Jordan reminded him of the dream he had had the night before. This couldn't be a coincidence. He looked at the boy and asked, "Where Jordan? Where's the spiral?"

Walking over to the map of all the banks David had entered over the past year, he pointed, "Right there."

"It's just a map, Jordan," Eric said, walking over and staring at the map. "Where's the spiral?"

Picking up a red sharpie from a desk, he climbed up on a chair and drew a red line on the map. He started at Nashville, Tennessee and drew a line up to Frankfort, Kentucky. He drew a line to Columbus, Ohio to Pittsburgh, Pennsylvania and then to Philadelphia. He continued down the map to Norfolk, Virginia and Wilmington, North Carolina before he headed over to Columbia, South Carolina and Atlanta, Georgia. He drew his line up to the pin at Knoxville, Tennessee and around to Roanoke,

Virginia before drawing the line over to Richmond. He turned the pen down and drew a line to Greenville, North Carolina before continuing south down to Fayetteville. He spun his line into Zion Corners and Charlotte before he hooked it around to Ferndale and ended up in Durham.

When Jordan finished connecting all of the dots on the map with the red sharpie, he stepped back and looked at the drawing. "If you continue the spiral, it looks like it will end in Raleigh."

"That it does, Jordan," Eric muttered in disbelief, staring at the map and rubbing his chin. He was dumbstruck. "I believe you're onto something, kid, the spiral does end in Raleigh."

Chapter 38

The command center was buzzing with activity all day long. They ran down every lead, new and old, because Eric was committed to finding the truth. Having always been a facts guy, black-and-white made sense to him, but as the investigation had dragged on, the facts didn't add up.

Looking at each document again, he was seeing the information in a new light. Reviewing each video file was like looking at them for the first time. Seeing what was there, he was committed to also looking for what wasn't obvious. *If David Zephyr was going to steal something, why hadn't he done it by now? Why would someone break into nineteen banks just to look around? It didn't make sense.*

"We got the security footage from New York and Sydney," Quyen yelled across the room.

"Put it up on the screen," Eric responded, butterflies fluttering in his stomach. "I want to see what we've got."

"First up is New York City."

A hush settled over the room. Stopping their work, every agent on the task force looked at the screen. Quyen scrolled through the video file and stopped it just to a few minutes before the stamped time on the receipt. No one was surprised to see David and Jordan on the video when they appeared. It was conceivable. David could've picked up his son, taken him to New York City and back in one night. It was a quick flight.

"Record the time stamp on the footage," Eric barked, pointing at an agent. "I want to make sure the receipts match."

"Tuesday night at 10pm, Boss."

"Well, I'll be," Eric mumbled, writing down his observations in his notebook.

The video bothered Eric. It proved the pictures on Jordan's cell phone hadn't been faked, which also made him wonder if the pictures Savannah had given him were real as well. And if they were, her story about Sebastian Fredrickson walking up to her on the beach was true. It would also mean Sebastian had asked Savannah to hand over the photos. *But why? Why would someone who was unknown to investigators hand over information incriminating themselves? And what is the connection between David and the four people in those pictures?*

Writing down his observations and questions in his notebook, Eric was back at square one again. The facts never answered the questions, they only added more. Eric stopped writing and scratched his chin. "Show me the Sydney footage, please."

"Are you sure you really want to see it?" Quyen asked.

"I've got to rule out everything, don't I?"

Quyen loaded the video and scrolled through the film until they reached a mark about ten minutes ahead of the stamped receipt. Watching the footage, a bad feeling overtook Eric. He wasn't sure why, but he started to feel sick to his stomach. When he was about to excuse himself from the room, David and Jordan appeared on the screen. The room fell silent, and all eyes stared at Eric.

"What the heck? Can't be," Eric mumbled, writing in his notebook. "Record the time stamp, please."

"Wednesday afternoon at 2pm."

The room erupted with a buzz of conversations. David and Jordan had pulled off the impossible. No rational explanation would put them in a location fourteen time zones away from Grand Central Station, one hour after they were seen in a New York City.

"That's not physically possible," Eric stated. "Has the footage been doctored?"

"The videos have been verified and authenticated. These are the actual videos."

Staring at David and Jordan on the screen, Eric wracked his brain to come up with a plausible explanation before adding more questions to his notebook. *How did David get into the banks without setting off the alarms? How was David Zephyr able to get his son from Raleigh to New York to Sydney and back again in the span of a few hours?*

Reviewing what he had just written, Eric pulled out the note David left in his office. *How had David gotten into my office? Was it a dream? Was it real?* Staring at the note, the words jumped off the page: *Believe what you know to be true, and you'll find the answers you seek.*

Eric knew David had been in his office the night before, hours after being in Sydney, Australia with Jordan. He didn't know how David had pulled it off, but at the moment, it didn't matter. David told him to accept the gray area in this investigation or he would never solve the case. Closing his eyes, Eric focused on the details of his conversation with David. Playing back the conversation in his mind, he scoured each word for information that would help him solve the case.

Freeing his mind from the facts, Eric opened his eyes, walked over to the map on the wall, and stared at the spiral Jordan had drawn earlier in the day. Focusing on the map, he yelled, "I know where and when David Zephyr is going to strike next."

Chapter 39

Gathering the team together, Sebastian went over every detail of the plan one last time. The gravity of the situation could be felt throughout the room. No one joked. No one made idle chatter. They were focused. They all knew the consequences if a mistake was made.

Sebastian worried about the details of the plan more than any member of his team. Their lives were in his hands. It was his responsibility to make sure they were prepared. He had lost friends before and he carried the weight of their deaths as a daily reminder that fighting evil was always a life-or-death situation.

Putting his hand on David's shoulder, he asked, "Are you good with this plan?"

"I'm ready," David responded, giving him a look of reassurance.

"It's not what I asked," Sebastian stated, looking into his eyes. "Once you walk out of here, we don't have any control over what happens to you."

"I know the consequences."

"We can come up with another plan," Zoe added.

"I've made my choice." David once had lived his faith as a passive participant, but being a part of The Network had changed his life forever. He believed God had it all worked out. Whatever was going to happen he was willing to accept. If it was His will, then David was willing to accept the outcome. It was his destiny.

"Peter has updated and double checked all of the new equipment," Sebastian continued.

"Are we going to be able to track David once they take the Hellfire Device from him?" Michael asked.

"I have some tricks up my sleeve," Peter interjected, cracking his knuckles and rubbing them against his chest in a cool, calm, collected manner. "I have put a few tracking devices on David."

"Will they work?" Michael asked.

"I tracked Savannah using just her biorhythms after she met with Sebastian. I had a few hiccups, but for the most part, it worked. I am hoping to do the same with David."

"Were you able to pinpoint why those blips occurred?" Zoe asked.

"I have," Peter continued. "I lost track of her when she was around anything with lead in it."

"Are you confident you will be able to find me if all else fails?" David asked.

"Confident? Yes," Peter hesitated. "Absolutely positive? I can't make that promise, David. Sorry."

"I trust you," David assured Peter, patting him on the shoulder. "You've never let me down before."

"But what if Peter can't track, David?" Michael asked.

"We'll see the plan through to the end," Sebastian responded, confident and resolute. "Regardless of what happens to David, we still have a job to do."

The room fell silent. They all knew the risks. Death was always an option, but no one wanted to admit it because this mission was different. They were leaving a friend exposed without any protection, and that alone was cause for silent reflection.

"One last prayer before we go?" Sebastian asked.

Stepping to the center of the room, the entire team stood shoulder to shoulder, holding hands, in a circle. Sebastian led them in prayer. When he had finished, he paused. Then in unison, they all said, "Amen."

Waiting inside a staging area in the building next to the Raleigh Federal Bank, Eric went over the plan in his mind one more time. Time passed slowly. Sitting against the wall and closing his eyes, he reminisced about his days in the military.

He missed his combat days, but he didn't miss the hollow feeling of not knowing what waited for him around each corner when he was out on patrol. Sitting in the staging area, those hollow feelings returned as the hours dragged on into the darkest hours of the night.

The tactical commander walked over and asked Eric, "How long are we going to sit here?"

"We'll sit here all night if that's what it takes," Eric ordered, sensing the tactical commander was losing confidence in the mission.

"At least we'll get to see the sunrise," the tactical commander joked as his men snickered.

Giving the tactical commander an icy stare, Eric could tell the rest of the team was restless. They had been sitting in the cramped office for hours and there hadn't been a hint of movement inside the bank.

"Have you guys ever seen action?" Eric asked.

"We see action all the time," one of the team members responded.

"Nah, man, have you seen any combat action overseas?" Eric was making small talk to kill time. He figured if he could keep their minds off the boredom, the minutes would tick by faster.

"I was in Iraq," another member of the tactical team added. "But by the time I was deployed, I spent most of my time on street corners trying to keep the peace."

"What about you, Carmichael?" The tactical commander was aggravated and wanted to challenge Eric's authority. He thought this mission was a waste of his time. He didn't understand why they were sitting around waiting for something than might never happen. So, he decided to show his men that his federal counterpart was a pencil pusher with no real tactical experience. "You ever seen any action?"

"I did two tours in Afghanistan and one in Iraq."

"Peace keeping?"

"I was one of the first units on the ground after September 11th. I was involved in some pretty big skirmishes."

"You sound like you miss it."

"I miss the rush of adrenaline you get when you're carrying out the mission. I don't miss the waiting between missions." Eric paused and reflected, looking at each of the men in the room. They reminded him of the men he had served with, many of whom never came home and some who came home irreparably changed. "I don't miss the killing. We lost a lot of good guys over there."

"I still get nightmares from my tour in Afghanistan," another guy stated. "It was a hell hole."

"And yet, you ended up on the tactical team?" Eric was baffled.

"This is different," he responded. "Most of my targets deserve to be taken out. Over there, you never knew who was evil and who was a human shield. The enemy always used human shields. Too many innocent people died."

While they were reminiscing about their days in the military, the radio came to life with the pronouncement, "I think we have movement in the bank lobby."

Readying their assault weapons, the team got ready to cross the alley to breach the bank before Eric interjected, "We go on my order and not a second before."

"Give the order, Carmichael," the tactical commander yelled.

"Not yet," Eric responded, picking up the radio and speaking into it. "Agent Quyen, do you have eyes on the suspect?"

"No, sir," came the reply. "We do not have eyes on the target."

Taking their positions, the tactical team waited for the order to storm the bank and takedown David Zephyr. They had prepared for the mission at hand and were waiting for the final order. They could hear him screaming from inside the bank and knew something was happening.

"I'm going in," said the tactical commander.

"Stand down, Commander," Eric barked. "We go on my order."

"I can hear it from across the alley," the tactical commander responded, staring down while holding up his fist so his men would stay put. "Someone's inside the bank, Agent."

"We have eyes on the suspect, Agent Carmichael," Quyen's voice crackled through the radio.

"Go! Go! Go! Go!" Eric ordered, deploying the tactical team.

The tactical team ran across into the alley and headed in four directions as they converged on each entrance to the bank. Methodically making their way to the bank lobby, dozens of red lights were trained on David's body as he sat on his knees on the lobby floor covered in sweat. He didn't move just in case one of the agents was trigger happy.

"Place your hands on top of your head," the tactical commander ordered, his weapon trained on the bridge of David's nose, right between his eyes.

Raising his hands and interlocking his fingers on top of his head, David stared ahead into the darkened room. Eric walked up to David and slapped cuffs on his wrists. "I've been expecting you, Mr. Zephyr. What took you so long?"

"Actually," David smiled, looking up at Eric. "It's the other way around, Special Agent. I have been waiting for you. What took *you* so long?"

Chapter 41

David was tired of being away from home, tired of the battles with the Zivlians, and tired of hiding from everyone he loved. He was tired. Beyond tired, he was exhausted.

Sitting in the interrogation room, David felt a calm resolve wash over him. His chance to clear his name had come and it was only a matter of time. And once he cleared his name, he would have to find a way to exist in a world in which he was living but was no longer a part of anymore.

Adrenaline overtaking his body, David couldn't sleep. So, he kept himself focused in the small room. Spending the hours praying and thanking God for his blessings rejuvenated him and gave him the energy to forge on in the face of adversity.

"Good morning. How are you today, Mr. Zephyr?" Eric burst into the room with a cup of coffee in hand while whistling a tune that David couldn't quite recognize.

"Peachy," David smirked. This was going to be a game to Eric and David knew it. He dug deep inside his exhaustion and maintained a positive attitude. "How are you, Special Agent?"

"The birds are singing, the sun is shining, the air has a sweet, succulent smell to it, and one of the most wanted fugitives on my docket is sitting in custody. So, I am having a great day." Eric smiled, put some files on the table, and sat down.

"Glad to hear it," David held back his laughter, "I wouldn't want to inconvenience you."

"Inconvenience me?" Eric rolled up his sleeves and tried to figure out how David thought any of this was an inconvenience. This was the job. This is what he lived for, catching the fugitive and holding David to account for his crimes. "It was an inconvenience when you weren't here. So, I'm good."

"So, tell me, Special Agent," David continued the banter, hoping to have a little fun with Eric because it was part of the plan for him to be in custody. He wondered if Eric would be dismayed if and when he found out. "Is this when you play good cop, bad cop in order to coerce a confession out of me?"

"That's funny, Mr. Zephyr," Eric snickered, sipping his coffee. Folding his hands on the table, Eric smiled at David. "But no. I have something a little bit more benign planned for us today."

"It's your house; deal."

"So, David, where have you been for the last year?"

"Right here in town," David responded, downplaying the year he had. If Eric had known about the battles he had been through, the interrogation might turn into a different kind of conversation. "Just hanging out, doing my thing."

"And what is your 'thing'?" Eric mimicked the final word by making quotation marks with his fingers.

"Beg your pardon?"

"What is your 'thing', David?" Eric asked, shrugging his shoulders. "I'd love it if you could provide some context, some details to your view of your year."

"Nothing much." David sat back in his chair and smiled. This was going to be fun for David. He liked being the thorn in Eric's side. "A little of this, a little of that."

"This is cute. Are you available for kids' parties, too?"

David laughed at the comment before sitting up and staring at Eric. "No one told me you were a funny guy."

"As much as I would love to play word games with you all morning, I'm going to move this conversation along." Eric opened a file on the table and started reviewing the information on the pages inside. He took a while to look at each page, hoping the silence would start to irritate David. He cleared his throat and closed the file. "How did you get into all of these federal banks?"

"I'll tell you," David said, leaning into the table and lowering his voice. "But quite frankly, I don't think you're going to believe me."

"Why not?"

"Because I didn't believe it at first and I was actually doing it."

"Try me, David." Eric lost the smile. This was getting serious. He wanted answers and he was tired of playing games with David. "Let me decide what I believe and what I don't."

"Where do I begin?" David sat back in his chair and folded his arms. Taking a moment to think about the previous year, David rubbed his fingers over the tip of his chin. A moment later, locking his hands in front of him, he put them on the table. "Special Agent, I'm part of a select group of people spending their time fighting demons from Hell in order to make the world a safer place."

"Insanity defense, Mr. Zephyr?" Eric laughed. Eric loosened the top button on his shirt because David's cavalier attitude was starting to aggravate him. "Not going to work this time."

"I said you wouldn't believe me," David chuckled, rolling his eyes, moving his tongue against his cheek, and shaking his head.

Taking a deep breath and another sip of his coffee, Eric stared at David and decided to continue. He wanted to see where the current line of questioning might take him. "I can do weird, Mr. Zephyr, but it still doesn't answer the question of why you ended up in those banks."

"I tell you I'm involved with a group defending the world from demons and you want to know why I was in a bunch of banks?"

"As odd as it sounds to you, Mr. Zephyr, I am in law enforcement, not the priesthood. So, unless the Devil needed a quick infusion of cash and you were there to stop him from robbing the bank, I couldn't care less about demons."

"Interesting," David smirked, eyeing up Eric. He found it interesting that Eric had no interest in pursuing the story in its entirety. He thought knowing everything about his opponent was Eric's standard operating procedure, but passing over the crux of the story without a hint of interest was surprising.

"What is?"

"Sarcasm as a defense mechanism."

"We can play this game as long as you would like, but at the end of the day, I need to file a report detailing what has happened for the better part of the last year." Eric paused and took a sip of his coffee. Rubbing his hands together and leaning into the table, he smiled. "As I see it, you are either (a) planning a major bank heist or (b) you are guilty of multiple counts of breaking and entering."

"Those are two very different charges."

"They are," Eric agreed, taking another sip of his coffee. "But what I decide will dictate the charges filed against you. Believe it or not, these charges will have a big impact on the rest of your life."

"You make it sound as though you have a choice."

"You always have a choice, Mr. Zephyr."

David chuckled, shaking his head and staring at Eric. "That's not what I said…You make it sound like you have a choice."

"Listen, Mr. Zephyr, I have a job to do. You can choose to do whatever you want to do, but you don't have the right to choose the consequences. You chose to illegally enter federal banks, now I have to sort out the consequences."

"Ah yes, Special Agent," David remarked, trying his best to contain his laughter. "Natural consequences."

"Then you understand what I have to do, whether I like it or not."

"Look." David grew serious in his tone and his intent. Eric was not taking the bait, and this concerned David. The plan depended on Eric taking interest in the truth, the gray area of the investigation. "If I violated some trespassing law, save the court time. Call my lawyer and work out some agreement for community service so we can all get on with our lives."

"I want to know how you got into the banks," Eric yelled, slamming his hand down on the table and pointing at David.

"Temper, temper, Special Agent." David sat back. He was calm and that irked Eric. He could see it and he figured if he could bait the hook long enough, Eric might bite. Or, David thought, Eric might just lock him up and throw away the key.

"Why were you there?"

"Fighting demons."

"Stop playing games."

"I'm not. You're not listening."

"You're lying." Eric was hot under the collar. He expected this behavior from your standard criminal element, but David was supposed to be an upstanding Christian man and Eric thought David would be honest when being interrogated. "How did you get out of the banks?"

"Magic." David barrel laughed. This was fun. He didn't want to make a career of it, but he was having fun watching Eric lose his cool while he provided honest answers.

"I hope you have some left for court, Mr. Zephyr."

"We're not going to court, and you know it."

"See, I believe you were doing more than trespassing and I am going to prove it."

"You have no evidence to the contrary." David dismissed the accusation. He knew Eric was grasping at straws and he hoped it would lead Eric to listen to at least some of what he was saying.

"Are you sure about that, David?"

"I never stole anything, so you have nothing on me except trespassing."

"And what about the police officer you assaulted in Zion Corners?"

"Is that your prosecution?" David laughed, clapping his hands. "I never laid a hand on him. The surveillance video will exonerate me on any trumped-up charge you try to make in regard to assault. Please tell me this case doesn't rest on Zion Corners."

"How did he get knocked out?"

"The beast rushed him." David paused and stared at Eric to gauge his reaction, but Eric remained unfazed by his declaration. "He never saw the Zivlian. It was too fast for him."

"You're sitting in a federal building facing multiple charges pending the outcome of our conversation, David," Eric stated, standing up and pacing the room. "Don't you think it's time to play ball?"

"I understand the gravity of the situation," David admitted, watching Eric closely. "By the way, your bad cop needs work. I like the unhinged demeanor and rapid-fire questions, but I'm not confessing to anything except the truth."

"Shut up, David," Eric yelled before pausing to recompose himself. He didn't want to let his emotions lead the interrogation. Swallowing hard, Eric grimaced while staring at David. "You don't control this situation. Your control ended the second you sat down in that chair. I decide what happens next, because I have a prosecutor who wants to throw the book at you."

"Let him. It won't stick in court."

"If he does," Eric stated, placing his hands on the table, "you'll never see your wife and kids outside of a visitation room ever again."

"Whatever decisions you decide to make, make them." David was unfazed by the threat and the accusations. He knew they had him on breaking and entering. Nothing else would stick without a confession and the only story he was willing to tell was one of a supernatural nature. "You're really not in charge here."

"I'm not?" Eric was taken aback by the statement. "Then who is?"

"God will decide what happens to me when the time comes."

"You're facing real jail time here, David."

"If I go to jail, I go to jail. It only means God has a plan for me in there."

Agitated, Eric was beyond baffled by David's composure and how nonchalant he was toward the charges facing him. David wasn't scared, he didn't squirm in his seat, he didn't act like he had done anything wrong, and Eric was dumbfounded by it. Sitting down, looking at David, he paused to collect his thoughts. "What game are you playing?"

"I'm not," David paused and stared at Eric for a moment. "Look, you have already established you believe in facts. What I have to tell you is so far off the beaten path, you'll probably order a psych consult by the end of the day."

"You don't know that."

"Don't I?" David laughed, winking at Eric and making quotation marks with his fingers. "Remember? The insanity defense… Right, Special Agent?"

"Let me be the judge of that. You can trust me."

"Trust you?" David laughed again, shaking his head in disbelief at the lengths Eric would go to make it seems like they are friends. "No, I can't. But I know God wants you to know the truth, and I am the one who is supposed to tell you. So, what do you want to know?"

Staring at David with skepticism, Eric decided to play the game and asked, "Who are the other people in the pictures Savannah gave me?"

"They're the other members of The Network."

Taking a sip of his coffee, Eric continued, "What is The Network?"

"A worldwide group of people fighting against the forces of evil."

"Why?"

"Satan sends demons to terrorize people who haven't decided which path in life to take. As long as they haven't been saved, these demons try to keep them from finding faith in God."

"What does this have to do with how you ended up in a number of federal banks?"

"Since Adam and Eve were created in the Garden of Eden, we've been in a spiritual war. The devil, along with the Fallen Angels aligned with him, tried to make the world their own. God gave man free will to choose between Him and the world. It's the reason Adam and Eve were cast out of the Garden. Satan uses every tactic possible to turn us away from God. Dreams are one way evil can deceive people."

"You still haven't answered my question, David? How did you end up in the federal banks?"

"We can't kill demons." David rolled his head around his neck while rubbing his hands together in disgust. "I'm not happy about that, but we can't kill any of the beasts. We can only send them back."

"How do you get into the banks?" Eric's patience for David's rambling was starting to wear thin. He allowed David some latitude to prove his innocence, but the story was now turning into a far-fetched tale rooted in the recesses of a warped mind and Eric didn't have time for it. He wanted answers. Real answers.

"We cross through the veil back into this world. We can't defeat the Zivlians behind the veil because they're too powerful. They draw on the energies of the Fallen Angels and other demons. So, we pull them back into our world where their anger, hate and vile contempt for us works against them. They slowly become powerless on this side of the veil, so we can wear them down, and send them back to Hell to be punished."

"How do you get inside the banks, David?"

"The circular device you took from me allows me to move freely through the veil. By holding the device and activating it, I can pass through the veil. I can reappear anywhere. In the next room, down the hall, or miles from here. Thousands of miles even."

"That's not possible," Eric said, staring at David with skepticism.

"It is possible, Special Agent." David smiled at Eric while shrugging his shoulders. "How else do you think my son and I got from New York to Australia in a matter of minutes?"

"How does it work?"

"That I can't answer." David laughed while raising his pointer finger toward the sky and shaking it next to his ear. "I don't know how the device works. It has many uses and although I don't understand the technology, trust me, Special Agent, it is very real."

"You expect me to believe all of this?"

Pointing toward the door, David answered, "If you want me to demonstrate how the device works, bring me mine, and I'll show you."

"What?" Eric was taken aback by the comment as he opened the file and looked for the picture of the device they had taken when they apprehended David.

Eric wondered how David would show him how the device worked. For argument's sake, if he allowed David to show him how it worked, would David use it to escape custody? He wasn't ready to believe the fanciful tale, but he couldn't have his reputation tarnished by handing David the means to escape. Hocus or pocus or not, Eric had seen enough to know David had some solid tricks up his sleeve and for that reason alone, he would not be handing David the device.

"It's synced to my biorhythms. If you bring it here, I can show you how it works."

"That's impossible, Mr. Zephyr, nobody has the technological capabilities to dematerialize a person and rematerialize them on the other side of the world."

"We aren't dematerialized," David laughed, shaking his head. "We just step out of this world and into the real world. We remove the veil that exists between the two."

"You're crazy," Eric stated, slamming the file shut.

"If you don't think it's possible, Special Agent, bring me the device."

"I am not bringing you the device."

"Why not?" David coaxed, needling Eric to see if he would bring the device. "If you are so sure I don't have the technological ability to do what I say I can do, why won't you bring me the device?"

"You're delusional."

"I can prove it… Bring me the device." David stared at Eric with purpose. He knew he had Eric on the ropes. If he could convince Eric of the story, the first part of his mission would be accomplished.

Eric stared back, paused, and dismissed the conversation. He was tired of playing this game with David. "You ramble on about demons like they're real, Mr. Zephyr."

"Oh, they are real, Special Agent," David lamented, pointing to a scar on his hand. "Very, very real."

"No, they're not, David. None of it is real. You're making it up." Eric was done with the mockery David was making of the interrogation.

"I promise you. It is more real than you can ever fathom. I found out the hard way when the demons attacked my family." David emphasized and resigned himself to understanding how Eric felt. He too had been angry about the absurdity of what he thought wasn't real a year ago. "For that, I joined the war. I will do whatever it takes to protect them. Even if that means fighting demons in the middle of a federal bank."

"You really do believe all of this, don't you?" Eric asked, worried for David's sanity.

"I do."

"You're not trying to build an insanity defense. You're actually crazy."

"Bring me the device, Special Agent, let me show it to you," David replied, staring into Eric's eyes. "Because there is so much more than meets the eye."

Staring back at David, Eric tried to make sense of the information before he conceded, "You're right. I don't believe you."

Laughing in frustration, David let out a deep sigh. "Keep telling yourself that, Special Agent. Ignorance makes the world safer to live in, but there is a spiritual war going on. We have the technology to fight back. So, all due respect, whether or not you believe me is irrelevant."

"Stop lying to me, Mr. Zephyr."

"It's how I got into your office and told you exactly where I was going to be last night."

"I caught you using solid detective work."

"Now look who's delusional," David chuckled, clapping his hands together. "Do you really think I am here because you caught me?"

"You're not that bright, Mr. Zephyr."

"I have been entering banks in a spiral fashion for a year and I had to send my seventh-grade son in to point it out to you. But somehow, I'm not the bright one. Comical."

Eric seethed at the insinuation. If he had been a lesser investigator, he might have reached across the table and punched David. But he wasn't. He was the kind of man who played by the rules, even when the person sitting across the table from him was spitting on the rules.

"Mr. Zephyr, stop making a mockery of the law and get comfortable. We're going to be here until I know how you got in and out of those banks."

"You do what you have to do, Special Agent."

"I intend to," Eric said, standing up and leaving the room.

David waited in the interrogation room for hours. Fatigue overtook David, and he took a nap. He felt someone shaking his shoulders. Opening his eyes, shooting up in his chair, and acclimating to his surroundings, David stared at the man across the table. "Who are you?"

"Agent Quyen," he responded, setting a cup of coffee on the table. "I brought you some coffee."

"Are you supposed to be the good cop?"

"If bringing you coffee makes me the good cop," Quyen chuckled, sitting down, "then I guess I am."

"Maybe," David responded, picking up coffee and sipping it. "Maybe not."

"To be honest, I'm neither the good cop nor the bad cop." Quyen leaned back with a devilish grin on his face.

"Then who are you?" David asked, taking another big gulp of the coffee. "Are you the person who comes to gain my trust?"

"Nope."

"Do you play nice while Special Agent Carmichael stands on the other side of the mirror hoping to catch me in a lie?"

"Have you been lying, Mr. Zephyr?"

"No." David leaned to the side so he could look around Agent Quyen and yell at the mirror. "I have been telling you the truth, Special Agent Carmichael. You'll see."

"You don't need to yell, Mr. Zephyr." Quyen smiled while David kept taking big gulps of the coffee. He realized David must be tired after spending his entire time in the interrogation room. "Special Agent Carmichael is at a meeting. He will be for a while. And the agent in the observation room has probably fallen out of his chair by now."

"Why would he have fallen out of his chair?" David was perplexed. He wasn't sure what was happening, but Quyen's admission about the agent behind the glass falling out of his chair was cause for concern.

"Passed out," Quyen shrugged his shoulders. "Who knows? Maybe he's just slumped over the desk. Either way, I doubt he's watching us."

"Why would he pass out?"

"Because I drugged him." Quyen smiled while watching David trying to figure out what was happening.

Taking another large gulp of his coffee and putting the cup on the table, David was confused. "You drugged your own guy? Why would you do that?"

"Don't worry, I drugged you, too. It's just a matter of time before you feel it."

"Why would you drug me?"

Leaning into the table and folding his hands in front of him, Quyen admitted, "Because I believe you, David. I know what you're doing in those banks. I know all about The Network."

"You're supposed to be one of the good guys," David said, shaking his head trying to fight off the effects of the drugs as they started taking effect in his body.

"Not me, Mr. Zephyr," Quyen chuckled, raising his eyebrows and putting his hands on his chest. "Special Agent Carmichael and the rest of his team? Yes, but not me."

"Why are you doing this?" David could feel his muscles being weighed down like a ten-ton weight. The drugs were slowing down his thoughts and his movements.

"Because I also know your daughter is being brought to a very special place, so we can open a portal and unleash a new world order."

"If you touch her, I swear I'll kill you," David threatened, struggling to stand on his own two feet as the room was spinning.

Quyen stood over David as he fell to his knees and held his head trying to shake off the groggy feeling and announced, "Not if I kill you first."

Punching David in the side of his head, Quyen watched him collapse unconscious on the floor.

Chapter 42

David was lying on a cold, wet concrete floor when he started fluttering his eyes. He could still feel the lingering effects of the drugs. He tried to shake off the heavy feeling in his head. Lifting himself to a kneeling position, he rubbed his eyes trying to adjust to the darkness. The outside world illuminated the gaps in the frame, and he noticed the outline of a door across the darkness.

Standing up, he stumbled over to the door and tried to open it. He attempted to open the door by fighting with the doorknob. It was futile. He was locked inside the darkened prison. *Time to shake this off and get back in the game,* he thought to himself as he weighed his options.

He walked backwards until he reached the wall behind him. Then, he steadied himself and bolted toward the door. Turning his body and slamming into the door with his shoulder, he let out a loud, painful shriek and was knocked backward from the force of the impact, but the door didn't budge.

He wasn't deterred as he prepared himself for another run at the door. He took a deep breath, said a small prayer, and looked at the light around the door. He let out a guttural, primal scream while racing across the room and slamming into the door. He felt waves of pain radiate through his body from the force of the impact before collapsing on the floor. He was imprisoned. There was no way out of the darkened cell and unless he found help, the team would have to continue without him.

He picked his aching body up off the floor and walked to the door. He peered through the cracks to see if he could figure out where he was or if anyone was outside. "Is there anyone out there? Can you hear me? Help."

He yelled for help for a while before he realized he was wasting time. No one could hear him. Pressing his ear against the structure, he listened for noise just to be sure.

"Okay," David muttered to himself while pacing the small, dark room. "Think, David, think."

He was helpless without his Hellfire Device to help him break out; he was trapped. Help wasn't coming and time was the enemy. Whoever was behind the plan to capture and imprison David was putting his daughter in danger. He had to escape, but he didn't know how.

He let out another guttural, primal scream in frustration and raced at the door, slamming into it again. The pain was secondary to the anger overcoming him. He pounded on the door while anger coursed through his veins. "Let me out. Let me out. I swear, if you harm my daughter, it will be the last thing you do… Do you hear me? Let me out."

He backed away from the door and started kicking it with his foot. "Let me out."

He stepped away from the door and started pacing the room. He mustered up the strength to break down the door. He took a few more laps around the structure, becoming enraged, he raced at the door. He leapt into the air and karate kicked the door with his right leg. The door swung open, and he crashed down on his back in the leaves outside the structure. He was exuberant as he laid on the ground pumping his arm in the air. "Yes!"

"Hi, David," Michael said, standing over David and staring at him celebrating.

"Michael?" David was perplexed as he stopped celebrating and looked up at his friend.

"You might want to conserve some of that energy." Michael held out his arm and pulled David to his feet. "You might need it later."

"When did you get here?"

Michael rolled his eyes and walked away muttering in sarcasm, "Sure… great to see you, Michael. Thanks for letting me out of the concrete prison. Thanks for saving my life. It sure is great to see you."

"You're right, Michael," David replied while looking around at the shed which had been built in the middle of the woods. "Thanks for finding me."

"Come on," Michael yelled, walking away through the woods. "We haven't got time for sappy reunions. We've got work to do."

"Why did it take so long to find me?" David asked as he raced through the woods to catch up.

"The cinder blocks are filled with solid lead."

"Really?"

"Whoever is behind all of this knows the weaknesses of our technology."

"How?"

"Don't know," Michael said, picking up the pace. "Don't care. All I know is they carried you out of the federal building in a lead covering and placed you inside a building made of lead."

"So, Peter wasn't able to track me?" David asked, trying to keep up with Michael.

"Nope."

"Then how did you find me?" David grabbed Michael by the shoulder and the both of them stopped walking.

"Sebastian."

"Sebastian?"

"In classic Sebastian style, he changed the plan at the last minute. He had me follow you after you were arrested in the bank."

"Why?"

"He had a gut feeling something wasn't right," Michael said, looking at David. "Be glad he did. When Peter told me he lost track of you, I was able to follow the white van when it left the federal compound."

"So why did it take so long for you to find me?"

"I had to stop following when they turned down the dirt road he took to get here," Michael answered before heading down the trail away from David.

"Huh?"

"The same dirt road is a quarter mile in that direction," Michael said, pointing in the direction of his car.

"Let's go." David started jogging in the direction Michael pointed and when he caught up to Michael, the two upped the pace through the woods.

Racing back to the car, they made up lost time. Starting the engine, Michael floored the gas pedal, pulled a 180, and raced down the dirt road at top speed. David felt the rush of the wind against his face in the passenger's seat through the open window. "You got a cell phone?"

Michael grabbed a throwaway cell phone from between the seats and handed it to David. Taking it from Michael, David dialed a number and waited while the phone rang.

"Hello?" came the voice on the other end of the line.

"Savannah."

"David?" Savannah questioned, relief washing over her body. "Where are you?"

"I don't have time to explain, Savannah. Where is Carissa?"

"Monica took her to the farm so they could ride horses tomorrow."

"Darn!"

"David, what's wrong?" Savannah was worried because she could tell by the intonation in his voice that something wasn't right.

"Savannah, I don't have time to explain." David was short on details and quick with directives. "I need you to take Jordan to the neighbors."

"Why?" Savannah could hear the worry in his voice. "What's going on?"

"You have to just trust me," David pleaded into the phone. "Then, I need you to wait on our front step. I'm sending someone to pick you up. You need to go to the farm and bring Carissa home as soon as possible."

"David, you're scaring me, what's going on?"

"There's no time to explain. I need you to trust me. Can you go get Carissa?"

"Yes." Savannah's heart was racing as her eyes filled with tears. She had always trusted David and even though she was mad at him for the past year, she knew he would never do anything to put his family in harm's way. She trusted that whatever David had planned must be important because whatever was happening forced him to call home to ask for help.

"This will all be over soon, and I will explain everything." David swallowed hard against the lump in the back of his throat. "I promise."

"I trust you, David."

"And Savannah…"

"Yes, David?"

"I love you."

"I love you, too," she said, a smile rippling across her face while she wiped the tears away. She had waited a year to hear him say those words again and they melted her heart.

Hanging up the phone, David felt his heart pounding in his chest. Fighting against his emotions, he dialed a second number and waited while the phone rang six or seven times. The answering machine picked up and he listened to the message, "You have reached the cell phone of Special Agent Eric Carmichael. Please leave a message and I will get back to you soon as possible."

Hearing the beep, David spoke, "Special Agent Carmichael, it's David Zephyr. Your agent took me hostage, but I escaped with a little help from my friends. If you want to see me again, go to my house and pick up Savannah. She is expecting you. Then go to my father's farm. Find my daughter. Protect my wife and daughter, Special Agent. Protect them with your life. It's all going down tonight. If we survive, I will tell you everything you want to know in the morning."

David hung up the phone.

"Really?" Michael raised an eyebrow because he was aggravated with David's message. "You're going to tell him everything he wants to know?"

"It won't matter, he won't believe me anyway," David laughed, staring at the road in front of them. "But if he keeps Savannah and Carissa safe, he can lock me up for life if he wants to."

"You married people are willing to do the strangest things for your loved ones."

"You will too one day, Michael," David said, dialing a number on the cell phone.

"It's good to have you back, David," Peter said, answering the call.

"How's it going?"

"Everything is quiet right now."

"Where is she?"

"At the farm, sleeping." Peter checked the computer system to confirm the information. "She seems to be safe for now."

"She is far from it," David said, shaking his head and pausing. "If we make it to morning, she'll be safe."

"We're here." Michael pulled into a gas station, slammed the brakes, and slid across the parking lot to screeching halt. Shutting down the engine, he turned to David and asked, "Ready?"

"Give me a moment?"

"Yeah, I'll wait outside." Michael exited the car, walked to the trunk, and popped it open.

David returned to his phone call, "Peter, you still there?"

"Yeah, David, what's up?"

"I don't know what is going to happen tonight, but I need you to make sure Special Agent Carmichael is on his way to the farm to protect Savannah and Carissa. If we have eyes on her, we can stop whatever is about to go down."

"Nothing is going to happen, David." Peter tried to reassure him that everything was going to go according to plan, but his voice wavered. He knew the danger involved in the mission, and while he hoped David would come back alive, he knew there were no absolutes in their line of work.

"I love your enthusiasm, Peter, but whoever is behind this wanted me out of the way. When I show up, all bets are off. They will do everything in their power to kill me."

"They won't succeed…"

"Peter, I don't need a pep talk," David yelled, interrupting. "I know the risks."

"We got this."

"I got a bad feeling about tonight, Peter." David paused to choke back his emotions. It was one thing to go out in battle, it was another to miss out on the last year with your family and then go down swinging. "They can do what they want to me, but promise me, Peter, promise me you will protect my wife and daughter for me tonight?"

There was a long pause as the gravity of what David said sat heavy upon his heart. Peter mustered up the strongest whisper he could, "I promise."

"Thanks," David said, taking a deep breath, and letting it out slowly. "God bless you, Peter. You're a great man."

"Stop talking like this, David."

"I expect amazing things from you when the time comes," David said, smiling to himself. "Take care of yourself."

Hanging up the phone, taking a deep breath, and getting out of the car, he destroyed the cell phone. David walked to the back of the car, where Michael had the trunk open. Michael asked, "Ready to go?"

"I need some gear."

"That's what I thought," Michael said, pulling out a black belt with a Hellfire Device attached to it and handing it to David. "It's been synced to your biorhythms."

"Good," David said, putting the belt around his waist.

"Is the Wi-Fi strong enough?"

"I wouldn't have stopped if it wasn't."

"Let's get to work."

Throwing the car keys of into the trunk, they both activated their Hellfire Devices and stepped behind the veil.

Chapter 43

Working in front of the computer terminal connected to the steel altar in the center of the barn, Quyen was excited because all the work, preparation, and planning was coming to fruition. He was going to open a portal into the spiritual realm and release the demons of Hell. He was smiling because the thought of his reward as a ruling member of the new world order the Prince of Darkness was about to create. The world would know who he was.

Nathan carried his granddaughter into the room and laid her down on the altar. The four lampposts hovered above Nathan while he strapped her arms and feet into the restraints on the metal bed. Picking up the electrodes on the side of the altar and placing them on Carissa's forehead, wrists, arms, and ankles, he turned and said to Quyen, "These will allow us to control her REM activity and, in essence, her dreams for the rest of the night."

"Are ready to go?" Quyen asked, surveying Nathan's work.

"Yes." Nathan stepped down from the altar and walked over to the control panel. "The hour is almost upon us."

"And the girl?"

"She is sedated," Nathan stopped in front of the control panel and pushed some buttons, "as is her grandmother back in the house. Neither one of them should disrupt our plans."

"Then let the new world order begin," Quyen announced, raising his hand and giving Nathan a high-five.

Nathan made a few more adjustments to the control panel before placing his hand on a large power switch and turning on the machine. There was a loud noise when the generators in the other rooms of the barn fired up. Loud cackling noises echoed throughout the barn while the machines created enough energy to open the veil and create a portal between both worlds.

The globes at the top of the posts became hotter and brighter. Small branches of electrical charges stretched out from the top of each lamppost. The electrical charges from each lamppost inched toward each of the others high above the altar. Quyen stepped backwards toward safety. It took about fifteen minutes before the electrical charges joined each of the metal posts together.

"Wow," Quyen uttered, staring in awe at the amazing power he was witnessing. "It is more magnificent than I ever imagined, Nathan."

"And the best part is still to come," Nathan replied, cackling in an eerie manner. "When the time comes, the lightning bolts will join together and open a portal in the veil which will allow spiritual entities to cross freely into our world. And then our plans will be complete."

Chapter 44

Waking up from a deep sleep, Carissa looked around her bedroom. She was scared. It was quiet. Quieter than most nights. Sitting up in her bed, she felt weird. She was cold and her stomach was bothering her. Queasy and nauseous, she had a headache.

"Mom?" Carissa called out with the weak whine she made whenever she wasn't feeling well. "Mom, I don't feel well."

The house was silent. Maybe her mother didn't hear her. Maybe she was downstairs watching television. Ignoring the way she felt, she laid down again, putting her head on the pillow and closing her eyes. Her stomach pain grew worse, and her head started throbbing. She couldn't ignore the pain anymore. "Mom? Jordan? I'm sick."

She heard the door open, and someone walk to foot of her bed. Rolling over, Carissa opened her eyes, "Mom, I don't feel well."

"Sorry," an eerie voice hissed, "Mommy's not here."

"Ah," Carissa screamed, crawling backward in fear across the bed into the wall behind her. "Help! Daddy Help!"

"Daddy can't help you," the creature hissed, reaching out to grab her.

The closet door flew open, and Sebastian crashed into the room. "Leave the girl alone."

"Pick on someone your own size," Zoe interjected, kicking open the bedroom door.

The Fallen Angel rose up to full size and towered above them. It burned hot with anger, the smell of sulfur emanating throughout the room. Sebastian and Zoe fought off the burning sensation in their eyes, noses, and throats while the creature stared at both of them waiting for either one to attack.

Crawling off the far side of her bed, Carissa hid while Sebastian circled the Fallen Angel. Zoe circled around the beast at the same time while looking for an opening to attack. They had been taught not to tangle with a Fallen Angel. They had been taught to run, hide, and pray for survival, but tonight was different. Humanity hung in the balance. There were no options. They were going to stand their ground and fight.

Sebastian charged at the beast. Following his lead, Zoe attacked the Fallen Angel from the opposite side. Swinging its winglike arm, the Fallen Angel knocked Sebastian across the room into the bedroom wall. Swinging its other wing behind it, Zoe found herself flying across the room. She hit the wall with a loud crash and collapsed on the floor. Lifting her head and looking around, she saw Carissa hiding under the bed. Holding her finger up to her lips, she made a gesture for the girl to be quiet. Carissa acknowledged the quiet sign by nodding her head and curled up in a ball underneath her bed.

"Are all you Fallen Angels a bunch of wusses?" Zoe taunted, standing to engage the Fallen Angel. The Fallen Angel stared at her. "Why don't you pick on me instead of picking on a little girl, you vile gnome?"

"My pleasure," the Fallen Angel hissed, letting out a demonic chuckle.

Stepping toward Zoe, the creature had her trapped. Knowing she was cornered and with very few options at her disposal, Zoe raised the Hellfire Device and charged the Fallen Angel.

The Fallen Angel grabbed Zoe under her arm. The monster had a full grasp of one side of her body. He tightened his grip which caused her to drop her Hellfire Device before it lifted her off the ground. She felt her ribs cracking in its grasp, so Zoe fought to free herself.

Immense pain radiating throughout her body, Zoe saw her Hellfire Device on the floor. Wishing she hadn't dropped it, she fought for her life. Zoe saw the other arm of the demon in front of her face. She watched it unwrap its fingers and show its claws. Moving a sharp claw to the skin above Zoe's eye, the evil entity pressed against her forehead until it saw blood start to trickle down her face. She screamed in pain when the creature moved its claw across her forehead. Her skin ripped open, and blood poured down her face.

Pulling its arm away from her face, straightening up, and dropping Zoe from its grasp, the monster let out a bloodcurdling screech. Holding the Hellfire Device to the lower back of the demon and delivering a series of electrical blasts to the torso of the beast, Sebastian attacked. Moving with the Fallen Angel in order to avoid being struck by its winglike arm, Sebastian yelled, "Zoe… get up and attack."

Lying on the floor in pain, Zoe scampered across the room on her knees and grabbed her Hellfire Device. She watched the demon writhing in pain. Standing up, charging, and placing the Hellfire Device on the demon's torso, she delivered another set of electrical blasts to the front of the creature.

Letting out more violent, bloodcurdling screeches, the Fallen Angel reached down and knocked Zoe across the room. She steadied herself and watched as the demon swung at Sebastian while he moved in a symbiotic motion with the Fallen Angel to avoid being hit. It was like watching a synchronized dance.

Sebastian continued to deliver blow after blow of electrical charges, when he noticed a slit developing in the veil. It was growing bigger. He couldn't believe what he was seeing. A Fallen Angel getting through the veil would have catastrophic consequences. He had to keep the Fallen Angel from going through the opening into the world.

Zoe braced herself against the wall and charged at the demon. Sebastian saw her and tried to stop her, "Zoe, No!"

It was too late. Delivering a powerful blow to the torso of the Fallen Angel, she knocked the demon backward. Zoe grabbed onto the left arm of the demon so she could deliver more blasts from the Hellfire Device. Sebastian followed suit and grabbed onto the right arm of the demon while praying for help as the beast dragged both of them through the opening in the veil.

<h1 style="text-align:center">Chapter 45</h1>

Eric slammed on his brakes and came to a screeching stop across the gravel driveway about ten feet in front of Nathan's farmhouse. He shut down the engine and jumped out of his truck. Eric and Savannah, who climbed out of the passenger side of the truck, ran to the front door. It was locked. Banging on the front door, Savannah screamed, "Nathan, let me in."

"Nathan, open the door," Eric yelled, standing behind Savannah.

"Let me in, Nathan." Savannah leaned against the door and looked at Eric, "I don't think he's in there."

"He has to be." Eric moved around Savannah and tried to force it open. "David told me to pick up both you and Carissa. You said she was here for the night, so Nathan has to be here watching her."

"Well, obviously, he's not, Special Agent."

"What the heck is going on?" Eric raised his arms in frustration and started looking through the windows. The house was dark. It was quiet, too quiet. "Something doesn't add up."

"I don't know." Savannah forced back her tears. Refusing to give into her fears, she started looking through the windows of the house. "David called me, told me to drop Jordan off at the neighbors, to wait for someone to pick me up… never thought it'd be you… but he told me to go with you and to bring Carissa home as soon as possible."

"So, where's Carissa?"

"She's supposed to be here," Savannah answered, terrified. "She's having a sleepover with her grandparents."

"Someone has to be home." Eric tried to pry the door open again.

"Obviously, they're not. This doesn't make sense. It just doesn't."

"There's no way David would put you and me in the same car if he was trying something," Eric said, thinking out loud while pacing the front porch while peering into the windows. "No, he would never risk you becoming caught up in all of this."

"Something's wrong, Special Agent," Savannah said, looking at Eric with tears in her eyes. "I'm afraid something bad has happened."

"Stand back." Eric drew his weapon and kicked the door. The door flew open and hit the wall with a loud crash. Eric moved inside with his gun raised while he searched for any signs of life inside the house. "Stay here, Savannah."

"Over my dead body," Savannah responded.

"I don't have time to argue, Savannah. It may not be safe."

"My daughter may be in danger; you can't stop me from coming in with you."

"Fine. Stay behind me." Eric was breaking protocol, but he didn't have time to fight with Savannah; a child's life might be in danger. He would do his best to protect her while canvassing the house. "We don't know what's in there. I don't want you getting hurt."

"I will," Savannah said, staring into his eyes and realizing he was serious. "I promise."

Eric swept through the lower floor of the house in a methodical fashion. He went from room to room looking for foul play while Savannah followed behind. The house was quiet, eerily quiet.

"Wait here until I get to the top of the stairs," Eric whispered, creeping up the stairs with his gun raised, scouring the scene for clues.

Ignoring his command, Savannah followed him up the stairs. The methodical process Eric employed amped up her nerves. Her heart pounding against her chest, she was desperate to find Carissa and take her home.

When Eric reached the top of the stairs, he continued sweeping the house as he went from room to room looking for intruders or foul play. He didn't find any. He didn't find anything. The house was calm, and the silence was deafening. Opening the door to the master bedroom, he saw a lifeless body on the bed.

"Monica," Savannah yelled, racing past Eric, trying to wake Monica, but her mother-in-law just laid there limp in her arms. "Is she dead?"

Holstering his weapon, Eric walked over to the bed and checked for a pulse. "She is alive."

"What's wrong with her?"

"She appears to have been drugged."

"Who would do such a thing?"

"Where's Nathan?" Eric continued to question what was happening. David had asked him to take Savannah to retrieve Carissa. He told him to keep his family safe. He said everything was going down tonight and if he survived, he would tell Eric everything in the morning. Red flags started flashing in his brain. Whatever is happening is happening now. "And more importantly, where is Carissa?"

"You don't think Nathan has anything to do with this, do you?"

"All I know is your husband told me to protect you and your daughter." Eric looked around the room for clues. Going into the hallway and checking the other rooms for Nathan and Carissa, Eric returned to the bedroom. "There is no sign of them anywhere."

"You don't think her grandfather would hurt her, do you?"

"I don't know what Nathan is capable of," Eric stated, searching the room before staring out the window at the farm in the distance, "but if he were involved in any of this, I have a pretty good idea of where he might be."

Chapter 46

Flying through the opening of the veil above the metal altar, Zoe and Sebastian were still holding onto the arms of the Fallen Angel. Landing on the floor of the barn, the creature let out another bloodcurdling scream. Unfurling its wings, Sebastian and Zoe were launched in different directions across the room before the Fallen Angel hunched over in pain and remained motionless.

Landing on the floor a few feet from the wall, the force of the throw caused Zoe to fall backward. Her bottom landed on the concrete floor as her body hit the wall behind her. She screamed in agony when a rusted metal hook that once housed a piece of barn equipment drove through the back of her left shoulder and popped out of her chest just below her collarbone.

Wincing in pain, she looked down at the metal hook she was impaled on and labored to take a breath. The blood rolling down her face from the gash above her right eye started to spread across her clothing. Leaning her head back against the wall and closing her eyes, she didn't dare pull her shoulder off the hook. She didn't know how much internal damage the hook had caused. So, sitting on the floor in pain, she prayed for wisdom and guidance.

Sebastian crashed to the floor after being thrown into the wall. He was breathing hard as he was lying on the floor. Bracing the palms of his hands against the concrete floor underneath him, each breath felt like a million tiny spears stabbing him in the chest. Positive he had cracked a rib or two, he knew he didn't have a choice. He had to stand up and fight.

Catching his breath, pushing himself up, and bracing himself on his knees, he surveyed the room. Carissa was strapped to the metal altar, the Fallen Angel was hunched over motionless, and Zoe sat against the wall with a metal hook protruding from her body.

He scurried around the barn floor toward Zoe, doing his best to avoid the detection of the Fallen Angel. He was perplexed by the Fallen Angel's behavior, but he didn't care. He was concerned about Zoe's welfare. Reaching Zoe's side, he knelt beside her and looked over her injuries. "This doesn't look good, Zoe."

"I've had better days." Zoe smiled and grimaced in pain at the same time.

"Let me help." Sebastian took hold of Zoe's shoulder and tried to pull her body off the hook.

"Ooouuuccchhh!" Zoe cried, reaching over with her right hand, grabbing Sebastian's arm while writhing in the pain. "Stop, Sebastian. Please stop."

"Gotta get you off this spike."

"I'm fine, Sebastian. Leave me be." Zoe put her head back against the wall and fought off the pain. The situation was not good, but there were bigger issues facing them. Like the Fallen Angel that had passed onto this side of the veil. They had to stop it. Her welfare had to wait. "The only way you can help me is by killing that thing, Sebastian. Destroy it. Then come back and get me."

"I'm not leaving you, Zoe."

"Good old Sebastian, always doing the right thing," Zoe laughed, wiping the blood off her forehead. "You have to leave me. You've got work to do, and you know it."

"Argh," Michael screamed, flying through the opening in the veil, tucking his shoulder and rolling over as he hit the floor. He popped up in a defensive position and surveyed the room. Charging at the Fallen Angel, he delivered a charge of electricity. The minion of darkness screeched in pain before stretching out its arm and swatting Michael ten feet to the right.

It started to unfurl itself as it made a frightening, demonic sound. It stood up and rose to its full eighteen feet. The Fallen Angel stared down at Michael, so he charged at the demonic entity once again and delivered another electrical surge to the body of the monster. Letting out another bloodcurdling screech, the Fallen Angel swung its arm and launched Michael into the door of the barn. The door fell backwards off its hinges and into the barnyard. The enraged Fallen Angel went after him.

"You've got to help him, Sebastian," Zoe pleaded, staring into Sebastian's eyes. "He can't do it alone and even if I could pull this hook out of me, I'm too weak to fight."

"I'm not happy about this, Zoe."

"When have you ever been happy with me, Sebastian?" Zoe asked, forcing a smile. "But you've got work to do. Go."

"I'll be back for you shortly. I promise," Sebastian said, running after the Fallen Angel.

Zoe leaned her head back against the wall and winced. She felt the throbbing pain where the metal had gone through her body. She tried to relax and calm herself down by praying under her breath for relief from the pain.

Nathan walked out of a back room where he had been observing everything, reveling in the success of his plan. He was elated because evil was going to triumph over good. While he was walking across the barn floor toward Zoe, Quyen, who was scared by what he had just witnessed, followed Nathan out of the backroom and ran like a coward out of the barn seeking safety. Nathan stopped ten feet in front of Zoe. "Well, well, well, we meet again, Zoe. How many years has it been now?"

Opening her eyes because she could not believe she was hearing the vile voice she had erased from her life years ago. "Why am I not surprised you had something to do with this?"

"Yes, dear sister-in-law," Nathan replied, pulling a long knife out of a sheath hanging from his side and kneeling next to Zoe. "You messed up my plans when I married your sister, but not tonight. The veil is open. Evil has passed through."

"You won't get away with this."

"I already have, Zoe," Nathan snickered, staring at her with contempt. "I released one Fallen Angel. I'm just sorry you won't be around to see the rest of them come through the wormhole and take over the world."

"It'll never happen." Tears formed in Zoe's eyes. She was in unbearable pain from the hook protruding through her body. It hurt to breathe. It hurt more to speak. Pain radiated through her body when she shuddered at hearing Nathan's voice.

"It's already done. Embrace it." Nathan opened his arms wide and smiled at her. He was proud of his plans coming to fruition. It had taken a long time, but the hour was upon them. He would take his rightful place as one of the rulers in the new world order.

"You're incredible," Zoe chuckled, wincing as the hook moved inside her body. "You still think you can control the world."

"I'm glad you find this funny, Zoe, because it's taken me years to get back to this point," Nathan lamented, playing with the knife in his hands. "After we failed last time, I had to take care of your sister…"

"You killed her!"

"Unfortunately, Zoe, yes," Nathan said with a solemn reverence, a hint of sadness in his voice. "I had to kill the only woman in my life I have ever loved."

"You didn't love my sister," Zoe sneered at him.

"You have no idea how I felt about her."

"The only person you have ever loved is yourself."

"Be that as it may." Nathan stared at her with an evil look while smacking the side of the blade in an up and down fashion in his open hand. "Once I found out where you hid the boy, I had to kill Monica's husband, too. It was brilliant, really. They both collided head on with one another in a high-speed crash."

"What?" Zoe was shocked. "You killed David's adopted father?"

"It took a long time to get Monica to fall in love with me." Nathan reminisced about his courtship before an evil smile crossed his face, "but she eventually did."

"So, you're the reason the dreams stopped," Zoe said to herself, thinking about why she lost track of David as a child.

"They had to. I couldn't have The Network snooping around. Not if I was going to pull off all of this." Nathan smiled, opening his arms wide and looking around.

"You're a horrible person, Nathan."

"Maybe, Zoe, but I've got to hand it to you. You did a good job finding a nice Christian family to adopt him. By the time Monica fell in love with me, the boy was already saved. Not much I could do at that point but wait for him to have children of his own."

"Are you that heartless?"

"Heartless?" Nathan asked, laughing. "Of course not. I will share all of my power with Carissa. She's earned it, she's doing all the hard work."

"You used your own grandchild, Nathan," Zoe said in disgust.

"It had to be done," Nathan responded in anger, the vein in his forehead pulsating. "I needed her to open the veil."

"Have you ever loved anyone?"

Nathan leaned forward, pinned Zoe's right arm against the wall, and placed the knife on Zoe's shoulder next to the hook sticking out of her body and whispered in her ear, "As I said, I loved your sister, and you took her away from me."

"You're a sick man," Zoe shot back, gritting her teeth and breathing hard. "She never loved you."

"Didn't she?" Nathan jammed the knife into Zoe's shoulder.

"Oooowwww," Zoe screamed, excruciating pain rippling through her body as the jagged steel blade was driven into her left shoulder while she fought back the tears.

"How does it feel, Zoe?" Nathan asked, moving the knife back and forth a couple of millimeters at a time.

Letting out another painful scream, Zoe's breathing became labored. She could feel the knife cutting up her shoulder. She winced in pain and bit her lower lip. "This isn't going to bring her back."

"Unfortunately, it won't," Nathan agreed while staring off into the distance for a moment. "I miss her."

"You're going to fail like last time," Zoe declared through the tears.

"Beg me," Nathan whispered in her ear, holding the knife firmly in his hand.

"Beg you for what?" Zoe was shivering in pain.

"Beg me for your life, Zoe." Nathan taunted her while continuing to wiggle the knife inside of her shoulder. "Beg me to spare your life."

"Do with me what you will," Zoe stated, fighting the pain. "You don't control this. If God decides this is my time, then this is my time. I'll never beg you for anything."

"I said, 'Beg!'" Nathan yelled, pushing the cold, hard blade of the knife to the right. Releasing a horrific scream, Zoe felt the knife shred another couple inches of her body.

David flew through the open portal of the veil, tucked his shoulder, rolled over, and came to a standing position in the middle of the barn floor. Standing there, he saw someone hurting Zoe. "Stop!"

Letting go of the knife in Zoe's shoulder, Nathan stood up, turned around, took a few steps toward David, and laughed, "Well, well, well, look what the cat dragged in… Glad you could join us, son."

"Dad?" David was stunned and angry.

"Welcome home," Nathan remarked, opening his arms wide.

"You?" David asked in confusion "Why?"

"No time to explain, son," Nathan responded. "It's started. It's not too late to join the winning side."

"Stop this, right now." David ordered, standing tall and sticking out his chest. "You don't have to do this."

"But, I do," Nathan laughed, walking toward David.

"I'll stop you," David said through gritted teeth.

"You ungrateful brat." Nathan yelled, taking a menacing step toward David and raising his fists. "I should've let Quyen kill you when he had the chance. That'll teach me to show mercy for my family ever again."

"Why are you doing this?"

"Why?" Nathan laughed. "The better question is 'Why not?' I have been promised things that far surpass the plebian life of a farmer. Things you can't even imagine. Why wouldn't I?"

"What could be worth what you are doing?"

"Immortality, world domination, power, money, women," Nathan yelled, laughing in celebration. "Take your pick, son. Join me and it's all yours, too."

"You can't have any of it."

"Why not?" Nathan asked, laughing in David's face. "Who's going to stop me? You?"

"Because this isn't what God has planned for the world."

"Well, I don't bow down to your God!"

"You will." David was scared, but stood resolute before taking a step toward Nathan. "So, you're right, I'm here to stop you."

Taking a couple more steps forward, David punched Nathan in the face. Laughing at David, Nathan looked at his son and raised his fists. "If that's the best you've got, I'm going to enjoy beating you to death."

"Bring it on," David yelled, raising his hands to defend himself.

David and Nathan started circling with their fists raised, looking for an opportunity to strike. Taking the first swing, Nathan landed a solid punch on David's jaw, but as he tried to connect with a second blow, David blocked the punch. Defending himself, David landed a body blow that stung Nathan's ribs.

"I taught you well," Nathan commented, rubbing his ribs, "but I didn't teach you everything."

Unloading a torrent of punches David was ill equipped to defend, Nathan connected on a one-two combination to David's face. While David protected his head, Nathan landed five or six body shots. Dodging a punch David had thrown, he continued to land another barrage of body shots before knocking David to the floor with a solid punch to the side of his head.

"No," Zoe yelled, watching David fall to his knees.

"You see, David," Nathan kicked David in the stomach, knocking him to the floor, "you're disappointing your dying aunt. What would your mother think of you?"

"Leave my mother out of this," David yelled, shooting up and landing a punch to Nathan's left eye. Nathan was stunned by the sucker punch, which allowed David to hit Nathan three more times in the face.

Regaining his composure and his footing, Nathan was taken aback by David's act of bravery to strike. Then, in a fit of rage, landing a violent barrage of body shots, Nathan landed one last punch to David's jaw that knocked David to the floor. Walking over to David and rolling him onto his back, Nathan sat on David's chest. Nathan placed his hands around David's neck while David tried to pull the hands off his neck so he could breathe.

"You've got your mother's eyes, David," Nathan commented, tightening his grip around David's neck. Realizing he couldn't get Nathan's hands off his neck, David let go. "That's right, son; let go. Stop fighting. It'll be easier that way."

Hitting Nathan as hard as he could with his right hand, David discharged a large blast of electricity from the Hellfire Device that launched Nathan three feet across the room and left Nathan writhing in pain on the floor. David rolled over and gasped for air. "I told you to leave my mother out of this."

Stumbling to his feet, forgetting to pick up the Hellfire Device, and walking over to Nathan, David stood over him. In a fit of rage, kicking Nathan in the ribs several times, David said one of the following sentences with every kick, "This is for my mother… This is for my daughter… This is for my family… This is for the year of my life you stole from me… This is for the people you have hurt… This is for Zoe… And this is for God who is so much more powerful than you."

"David," Zoe yelled, pulling the knife out of her shoulder and throwing it to him. "Finish him off."

Picking up the knife Zoe had thrown to him, David walked over to Nathan and sat on his chest. Pinning Nathan's arms under his knees, he held the knife to Nathan's neck. "Why did you have to do this to my daughter and my family?"

"Just kill me and get it over with," Nathan responded, laying in a weakened state from the electrical blast and the pummeling he had just taken from David.

"No, Nathan," David demanded. "I want to know why you disrupted my life. I want to know, before you die, if it was worth it?"

"You'd never understand."

"That's not good enough," David yelled, pressing the knife harder against Nathan's neck. "They're your grandchildren. How could you do this to them? Don't you care?"

"I care about what is good for me," Nathan yelled, thrusting his arms upward, grabbing David by the shoulders, and tossing him off his chest. When David hit the floor, the knife flew out of his hand and out of his reach. "I told you to kill me."

While trying to stand up, Nathan kicked David in the ribs and knocked him to the floor. David was trying to regain his footing when Nathan kicked him in the stomach and launched him into a barrel full of water that tipped over when David crashed into it.

Laying there in the water, Nathan walked over, sat on David's chest, and put both hands on his throat. "I do what I do because I want what is mine and only mine."

"You can't have it, Nathan," David pushed through his lips, fighting to remove Nathan's hands from his neck. But to no avail, he was out of options. He didn't have his Hellfire Device and he lost control of the knife. This was it. He was left to fight Nathan with nothing more than his will to live.

"Keep fighting, son, it's admirable." Nathan laughed, tightening the grip on David's neck. "You should have killed me when you had the chance."

Nathan's hands tightened around David's neck. He knew it was now or never. Struggling to grab a breath, he fought for his life. While fighting with Nathan, he heard something make a scratching noise across the concrete floor and hit the side of his hip.

Reaching down, David knew what it was. Zoe had taken her Hellfire Device and used all of her might to slide it across the floor to him. He didn't hesitate. Grabbing hold of the device, he delivered another electrical blast to Nathan. Releasing the grip on his neck, Nathan fell to the floor a couple of feet from David.

Rolling over, David saw the lid to the water barrel. It had a long rope attached to it. Grabbing the rope, David tied the Hellfire Device to it. Walking over to Nathan who was lying on the floor writhing in pain, he tied the rope around Nathan's arm.

"The difference between you and me, Nathan. I care about people." David said, locking down all five buttons of the Hellfire Device and dropping it into the puddle of water collecting on the floor. "Enjoy the swim."

Nathan disappeared with the device when it hit the puddle of water and activated. David stared at the spot where Nathan had just been before he ran over to Zoe. Kneeling down beside her, he could tell she had lost a lot of blood. Her breathing was growing weaker, so he gently put his hand on her shoulder.

"I am so sorry, Zoe. I couldn't kill him," David confessed, tears rolling down his cheek.

"It's okay, David," Zoe whispered, laboring to breathe and lifting her head to look at him. "We're not killers. He'll get what he deserves one day."

"But you sacrificed…"

"To save you," Zoe interrupted, whispering and smiling at him. "There's no greater love, David. You're still here, so it was worth it."

"I'm so sorry, Zoe."

"Don't be sorry, David," Zoe wheezed, closing her eyes. "I get to meet God face-to-face tonight. It's going to be amazing. I can't wait to see Him."

"But we have so much more to do," David muttered, wiping the tears from his eyes.

Using what little energy she had left in her body, Zoe raised her arm up and wrapped her hand on the back of his neck. Taking a couple of labored breaths, she continued, "I've done everything I'm supposed to do. It's time for me to go home to the Father. But you have more work to do. Peter, Sebastian, and Michael need you."

"Please don't go, Zoe," David pleaded, tears streaming down his cheek.

"I have to," Zoe replied, looking into his eyes. "It's my time. Please don't cry. I'll see you again. I love you."

"I love you, too," David responded. Zoe closed her eyes and lowered her chin to her chest. A few moments later, Zoe breathed her last breath, her right arm sliding off David's shoulder and falling into her lap.

"No," David yelled, sobbing while wiping away the tears. Giving Zoe a hug, he stood up and stumbled away with his head down and tears in his eyes.

"No," David yelled in anger. Grabbing an axe off the wall, he started slamming the axe into the control panel of the computer system. Sparks flew everywhere. The electrical charges at the top of each lamp stand subsiding, the opening in the veil above the altar closed.

Michael flew through the wall of the barn and landed with a thud. Staggering to his feet to go back out and fight the Fallen Angel, Michael took two steps and collapsed on the floor.

Walking over to the altar and looking down at Carissa who was sleeping, David kissed her on the cheek. "Sleep tight, baby girl. I'll be back soon. I've got work to do."

David crossed the barn, picked up his Hellfire Device, and walked over to Michael. He knelt down and felt for a pulse while watching

Sebastian dodge the winglike arms of the Fallen Angel through the hole in the barn that Michael's body had just made. The demon bellowed in pain while Sebastian delivered another surge of electricity before it reached down and knocked Sebastian across the barnyard. Sebastian's body slammed into the side of one of the sheds and when his feet touched the ground, his knees buckled under the weight of his body, and he collapsed.

Storming out of the barn, David screamed at the entity standing in his path, "I have had just about enough of you. I don't know who you think you are, but it's time for you to go back to whatever vile place you came from."

Rising to its menacing stature, the Fallen Angel faced David. Stretching its arms to a full eight feet wide to each side and locking its eyes on David, it hissed, "I accept your challenge."

Circling the Fallen Angel, David calculated the odds of defeating the creature on his own. Michael and Sebastian couldn't defeat the demonic entity as a pair. Considering they were better warriors, he knew the odds weren't in his favor. He was going to have to be smart about how he was going to attack the Fallen Angel, because every successful strike was going to end with him being knocked across the barnyard.

Increasing his speed, the Fallen Angel was unable to keep pace and an opening to attack presented itself. Charging the demon, he discharged an electrical blast on its back. Thrashing about in pain, David delivered as many electrical blasts as he could before he felt the arm of the entity slam into his body, launching him across the barnyard.

Landing on the ground with a heavy thud, he rolled over and brought himself to his knees. Watching the monster lower its head and bring its winglike arms up to its forehead to recover, he knew the constant barrage of electrical surges were weakening the Fallen Angel. He just didn't know if he would be able to outlast the creature before the strength of the Fallen Angel was just too much for his body to withstand. But, he also knew he had no other options.

He contemplated his next move while he stood up. Remembering what Sebastian told him about the abilities of the Fallen Angels on this side of the veil, he sprinted at the demon, delivered a blast of electricity, and kept on running.

The Fallen Angel screeched again. It saw David running across the barnyard and it started chasing him. The Fallen Angel was catching up and just as the demon took a swing at him, he activated the device. Disappearing, The Fallen Angel missed hitting David.

"Missed me." David taunted, reappearing on the other side of the barnyard. "What's wrong? Can't follow my vapor trail on this side of the veil?"

Filled with rage, the Fallen Angel charged at David. Standing in the doorway of the barn, he waited. His heart pounding against his chest, he had to time every move to perfection. Just as the Fallen Angel was upon him, it lifted its arm high above its head and swung. He disappeared as the Fallen Angel slammed into the side of the barn.

Stumbling backward after running into the side of the barn, the Fallen Angel watched David pop out of the shed. David started taunting the demonic spirit, "And here I thought you were so much smarter than the Zivlians. You demons are all just as dumb as can be, aren't you?"

David saw the fire in the eyes of the creature when it charged at him. He activated the device again and disappeared, but this time, the Fallen Angel reversed course, took two large steps in the other direction, and lifted its arm high above its head. When David reappeared, the arm of the demon slammed into his body.

Knowing he had made a grave miscalculation, David flew through the wall of the barn and crashed hard onto the floor inside. He wanted to quit. His body was beaten beyond any punishment he ever thought he could handle; he struggled to stand. He was weak, bruised, beaten, and broken. His energy level was flat lining, but he knew he couldn't quit. Too many people were counting on him. The world was counting on him. Believing in his heart there was a purpose for this battle, until the time came when he could no longer stand and fight, he was going to see the battle through to the end.

Taking a couple of deep breaths, rolling his throbbing head around his neck, and stretching his arms, David picked his Hellfire Device off the floor and limped through the hole in the barn his body had just made. He taunted the beast while it was walking away from the barn, "Where do you think you're going? I'm not done with you."

The Fallen Angel stopped walking away. It stared at David, waiting for him to make another attack. David needed a miracle. The odds were stacked against him and as he stood in the barnyard like an unarmed gunslinger in the Wild West, he knew God would provide.

Staggering toward the Fallen Angel, he saw something that changed his whole perspective on the battle he was waging. After trudging a few more steps toward the creature, he stopped and stared at the beast.

"You know you can never win." David tried to rationalize with the demonic entity. "You can try. You might even win this battle. Heck, you might even kill me. But you and I know the truth and the truth is simple, you will never win."

"Why not?" the demon hissed.

"Because I have the full armor of God. I'm wearing the buckle of truth. Truth is light. Your lies hide in the darkness. You know that."

"The truth is I will kill you," the demon uttered, lumbering toward David.

"The shield of faith will deflect everything you can throw at me." David walked with a renewed purpose toward the Fallen Angel. "I know the truth and so do you."

"Your faith will be your death," the Fallen Angel hissed.

Stopping in the middle of the barnyard and pointing at the Fallen Angel, David continued, "You're not supposed to be here. Evil never prevails. You can beat me, and maybe you're right. Maybe you will kill me, but the Word of God will never be defeated."

David put the Hellfire Device back on his belt while looking up at the Fallen Angel. Then, folding his hands in front of his body, David lowered his head to pray and stood there. The creature stared at him, anger engulfing its body. It made a vile noise, but David never moved.

David remained motionless while the Fallen Angel walked toward him. He looked peaceful while staring at the ground as the creature towered above him. They were standing only a few feet apart from each other, but David was steadfast in his resolve to remain immovable because as long as there were people to stand in the face of evil, he would not fear the forces of darkness.

Reaching down with both of its arms, the Fallen Angel lifted David high above the ground. It stared at him, but David did not fear the beast. He just stared back with a quiet resolve that confused the demonic entity. But the confusion didn't last long. The anger deep within the Fallen Angel welled up inside the creature. It made an evil sound and started to squeeze its hands together. Feeling the pressure of the Fallen Angels grasp on his rib cage, David cried out in pain.

Stepping out of the shadows of the barn, Peter jammed the Lightning Bolt into the lower back of the Fallen Angel and unleashed the full electrical blast of fifteen Hellfire Devices. The Fallen Angel threw David through the wall of the barn and tried to fend off the attack Peter was unleashing. The beast fought with every ounce it had, but Peter held the Lightning Bolt firmly in place while moving with the creature, but the strength of the creature was too much. Turning to face Peter, the Fallen Angel swung its winglike arm full strength into Peter. The force of the strike knocked Peter backward into a shed where he collapsed.

The Fallen Angel released a vile screech and looked around for any other members of The Network. Eric jumped up from behind a woodpile across the barnyard where he had hunkered down with Savannah to witness the battle between The Network and the Fallen Angel. He started discharging his weapon at the creature. When his clip was empty and he was reloading, the unharmed Fallen Angel started toward Eric with fire in its eyes.

Eric was afraid. He slid a new clip into his weapon and trained it on the Fallen Angel coming toward him when he heard the loudest clap of thunder he had ever heard. He was almost deafened by the sonic explosion above his head that sounded like the words, "Not your world" just before a blast of lightning flashed across the sky into the head of the Fallen Angel and it exploded into a million flickering shards of light before disappearing into the darkness.

"David," Savannah yelled, jumping up from behind the woodpile and running toward the barn to find her husband.

"Savannah, wait." Eric tried to stop Savannah but couldn't.

Fear gripped Savannah's heart like a vise while she ran toward the barn. She needed to know if David was alive, if Carissa was alive, and she needed an explanation for what she had just witnessed. Running toward the barn, her progress was halted by Nathan's sopping wet arm grabbing her and holding her tight in his grasp.

Inside the barn, dragging himself to his feet, David walked to the altar where Carissa was still strapped down and asleep. Taking off the restraints and removing the electrodes, he scooped her up in his arms and whispered, "Come on, baby girl. Time to go home."

"I love you, Daddy," Carissa whispered, wrapping her arms around his neck and resting her head on his shoulder.

"I love you, too." David kissed the top of her head.

Turning around with Carissa in his arms, David saw Nathan standing in the barn with a gun to Savannah's head. Nathan smiled. "I'm back."

"You don't have to do this, Nathan."

"Give me the girl, David."

"Don't you dare, David," Savannah yelled, struggling to break free of Nathan's grasp.

"You have a choice," Nathan offered, glaring at David with malice in his heart. "You can save your wife, or you can save your daughter."

"David, no," Savannah yelled again, still fighting for her freedom. "Don't you let him touch her."

"You can't save both of them," Nathan continued, holding Savannah tighter in his arm.

"Let her go, Nathan. It's over," David responded.

"A minor setback, David," Nathan responded, smiling and watching his every move. "Nothing that can't be rectified."

"I'm not giving you my daughter, Nathan."

"Then I'll take her from you."

"You'll have to kill me first," David said with conviction, staring down Nathan.

"That can be arranged," Nathan answered, pointing the gun at David.

"What if you miss and you hit Carissa?"

Nathan aimed at David's head. "I never miss."

Savannah bit Nathan's arm as hard as she could. Nathan yelled in pain and threw Savannah to the floor. As Savannah tried to escape, Nathan grabbed her arm. In the struggle that ensued, a solitary gunshot echoed throughout the barn.

The bullet ripped through Nathan's shoulder and he dropped the gun. A second gunshot rang out hitting Nathan above the knee. Falling to the floor, Nathan screamed in pain.

Savannah scurried away while Nathan tried to grab his gun; a final gun shot hit Nathan's outstretched hand. Racing across the barn, Eric secured Nathan while Savannah ran into the David's arms while he was still holding Carissa. Tears rolling down his face, David was overjoyed to hold his wife and daughter in his arms once again.

David mouthed the words, "Thank you" to Eric. After holstering his weapon, Eric tipped his head in silent acknowledgement to say, "You're welcome."

Burying his face into the embrace of his wife, David held his family in his arms for the first time in over a year.

<h1 style="text-align:center">Chapter 47</h1>

Within hours, Federal Agents, local law enforcement, and medical personnel swarmed the farm. Briefing law enforcement, Eric gave an abridged, altered version of the events that had transpired. They would never believe the truth. He didn't believe it, and he witnessed most of it.

Nathan was escorted to the hospital by a team of trusted agents. When fully recovered, he would be moved to a federal penitentiary before standing trial for his crimes.

Keeping his men and law enforcement away from the members of The Network, Eric walked over to the picnic table where David was sitting with Savannah and Carissa. He stood and waited for the medic to finish attending to David's cuts and bruises before asking, "Can I have a minute of your time?"

"Sure," David responded, standing up.

"Wait," Savannah warned, grabbing his arm. "Can you trust him?"

"We're good." David smiled at her. "I'd be in cuffs, if we weren't."

"I promise I'll have him back here in a few minutes," Eric added, nodding at Savannah.

Walking away from the table with Eric, David looked around at the activity of law enforcement in the barnyard. "Am I really good?"

"After what I've seen here tonight," Eric responded, "I wonder if any of us are?"

"For now," David chuckled, looking at Eric. "How do you resolve this case?"

"I haven't figured that out yet but leave it to me. You shouldn't be bothered by us, except to testify against your father."

"Nathan."

"Excuse me?" Eric was confused.

"After what I learned tonight, he's not my father. He's just Nathan."

"I can respect that."

"Thank you." David smiled. "And yes, I will testify against him."

"So, what happened here tonight?" Eric asked, letting out a sigh. "I've never seen anything like that creature."

"And God willing, you never will again."

"But what is it?"

"Remember how I told you I was part of a team that fought demons in order to protect the world?"

"That was one of them?"

"Yup."

"But what happened to it?" Eric questioned, trying to find answers for everything he had witnessed over the past few hours. "You and the other guy never touched it. Where did it go? Who won?"

"God won."

"Please forgive me, David," Eric said, running one hand through his hair while placing the other on his hip. "This is all new to me. I'm not sure I'm following your logic."

"The world is safe for now," David responded, pausing to collect his thoughts. "Or at least, it's the same as it was when the day began."

"But when does it end?" Eric was still trying to process everything he had seen. "When do those things stop attacking?"

"They don't," David responded, staring at him with a solemn expression. "There is always going to be a spiritual war until Jesus returns."

Eric looked around the barnyard. He was overwhelmed, confused, and scared about the revelations he witnessed firsthand. "So, this is what you have been doing for the last year?"

"Pretty much."

"Wow, and I thought my job was hard," Eric laughed, shaking his head. "Anyway, I just wanted to say, I'm sorry."

"Wait." David was dumfounded, staring at him with skepticism. "Come again?"

"I misjudged you," Eric admitted with humility. "I really got this whole thing wrong. I should have listened to you when you tried to warn me."

"You did mess things up," David chuckled, "but there's no way you could have known."

"Regardless, I put your family through hell." Eric was humble while holding out his hand. "I'm sorry. I hope you can forgive me."

"Nothing to apologize for, Special Agent," David responded while shaking his hand. "You were doing your job."

"Be that as it may…"

"Let me stop you right there, Special Agent," David interrupted, fighting back his emotions. "Thank you for saving my wife and daughter. I don't know what I would have done if Nathan had hurt either of them."

"That never would have happened."

"Thank you." David put his hand on Eric's shoulder and looked into his eyes. "I'm indebted to you."

"No thanks necessary, Mr. Zephyr…"

"David."

"Excuse me?"

"My friends call me David."

"No thanks necessary, David."

Seeing the medics wheel out the gurney with Zoe's body, David asked, "Do you mind?"

"No, not at all," Eric responded. "I'm sorry for your loss."

"Thank you for the sentiment, Agent Carmichael," David said, patting Eric's shoulder, "but stay close to your phone. I hear we may have a job opening soon."

"What?" Eric asked with a hint of confusion as David walked away. "What does that mean?"

Raising his hand and waving at Eric without turning around, David met up with the members of The Network standing around Zoe's gurney. Embracing in a group hug, they shared tears for a lost teammate. Holding each other tight, they celebrated the fact the mission was over, but their lives were irreparably changed. Sharing prayers for Zoe, they all shared a favorite memory of her with each other. Knowing she would be watching over them from Heaven, each member of The Network said their goodbyes to her and walked back to the barn.

Leaning over the gurney, David pulled back the sheet and stared into Zoe's face one last time. Tears streaming down his face, he said, "I love you, Aunt Zoe. I'll be seeing you."

Holding her hand and kissing her cheek, he pulled the sheet back over her head. Wiping the tears away, he walked back to the picnic table where his family was waiting for him. Picking up Carissa and taking Savannah's hand, David said, "Let's go home."

"You don't know how long I have waited to hear those words," Savannah responded, hugging him.

"You're going to hear them every night from now on," David responded before kissing her.

"Thank God," Savannah exclaimed, smiling at him. "Amen."

Thank you for reading *Behind the Veil*. I am honored and humbled. If you enjoyed reading this book, please leave a review online at Amazon, Goodreads, or anywhere books are sold so other people can experience this novel as well.

Thank you,
Doug

Acknowledgments

There are so many people I need to thank for helping with this book. There were many eyes and hearts encouraging and inspiring me to get this story from my head to the bookstore. Thank you!

Thank you, Nicole Hampton, for your invaluable guidance and insights on my writing journey. You were truly sent from God when I needed it most. You continue to offer valuable lessons into the profession, and I hope you see those seeds of wisdom come to life in *Behind the Veil.* Thank you, Nicole, for always challenging me to take my stories to a higher level.

Thank you, Kathi Welch, for reading through *Behind the Veil* many times to make sure I stayed on track, grammatically and with the story line. Your comments and suggestions made the writing so much stronger. Thank you. Now we just need tickets to watch "7" play some college ball.

Thank you, Jessica Tilles, for just being a rock star on both *Intercepted* and *Behind the Veil.* Your sage advice is quintessential and your willingness to always problem solve is critical. In a world where so many things can go wrong, thank you for making sure everything stays on track. Thank you for all your attention to detail and the small touches that you accentuate throughout the book make a world of difference. It is a testament to your professionalism and character.

Thank you to my son, Josh, who had the difficult task of the final read to scrub the book of as many missed details as possible. It is a thankless task, and you do it with grace and precision. Please know it means the world to me that you are as excited about the projects as I am.

Thank you, Mark, Sue, Aunt Renate, Uncle David, Josh, Chloe, Steve, Tom and Stephanie, for reading the book at the various stages of editing. Your honest insights, opinions, and engagement with the characters helped me to hone the direction of the story and fix what you, the readers, saw in this story as I wrote the next iterations of the book. Thank you for your help.

I will never be able to properly thank my beautiful wife, Stephanie. Between teaching, coaching football, helping in the community, and raising our two awesome kids, you have been my biggest fan as this book took on life. You have been my rock, supported me through the long days and nights of writing and editing, and then writing and editing some more, and in the frustrating times when I was overcome with writer's block. You kept reminding me that all good things will happen in His time and that made all the difference. You were the answer to my prayers so many years ago, and you continue to be the answer to my prayers every day. Thank you for your patience as Behind the Veil slowly came to fruition. I hope it was worth the wait and most of all, I hope you love the final version.

And finally, thank you God for bringing all of these people into my life and for being a part of this project. You knew I would need them to complete this project. Thank you for your vision, your love, and your grace. Amen.

About the Author

Born in New York City, Doug grew up in Connecticut while still exploring the city he called home. He spent a lot of his youth exploring his imagination. He dabbled in plays, screen plays, poetry, lyricism, essays, and writing stories.

After graduating from Roger Williams College, Doug went on to work for educational non-profits and school systems. He never lost his enthusiasm for writing, creating, and performing, though. Over the years, Doug has been a writer, an actor, a lead singer, a comedian, a DJ, a fantasy football commissioner, a poet, a lyricist, and a really bad guitarist. He finally honed all of those skills so he could teach middle school students and bring education to life for the next generation.

Doug lives in North Carolina. He is a teacher, a football coach, a loving husband, and a proud father who spends his free time creating stories to share with the world. His goal is to bring characters you love to life and to share their stories as they relate to the world around us all, and most of all, honor God.